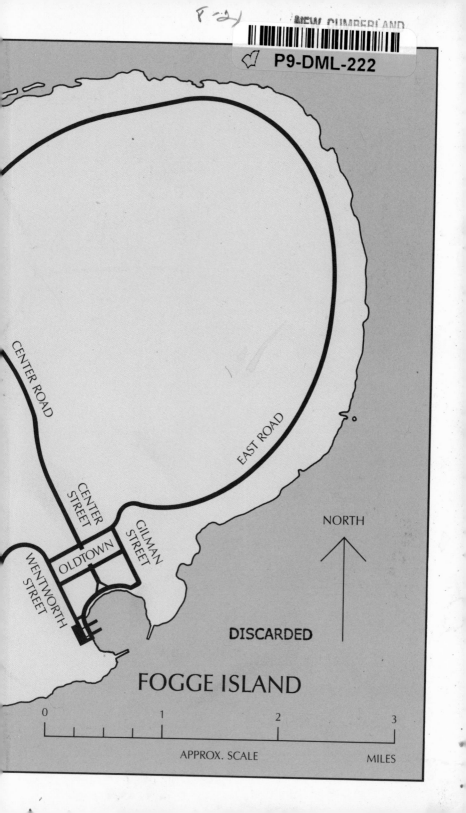

NEW CUMBERLAND

CENTER ROAD

EAST ROAD

CENTER STREET

GILMAN STREET

OLDTOWN

WENTWORTH STREET

NORTH

DISCARDED

FOGGE ISLAND

0			1		2		3

APPROX. SCALE

MILES

KILLING
COUSINS

KILLING COUSINS

BY GENE STRATTON

Ancestry
Publishing
P.O. Box 476
Salt Lake City, UT 84110

Library of Congress Cataloging in Publication Data

Stratton, Gene.
  Killing cousins.

  I. Title.
PS3569.T691335K55 1988 813'.54 88-34316
ISBN Number 0-916489-38-8

Design and Production: Robert J. Welsh and Robb Barr
Typesetting: Scott Mulvay, Type Connection

First Printing 1989
10 9 8 7 6 5 4 3 2 1

Printed in the United States of America.

To my love, my life, my all;
to one who is always there–
my wife, Ginger.

Cast of Characters

Alice (nee Delano) BEETON, cook at the Gorges mansion on Fogge Island, and distant cousin to Martha Gorges.

Belinda BEETON, maid at the Gorges mansion and daughter to Mrs. Beeton, the cook; born with a club foot.

Sergeant Priscilla BOOTH, police detective in charge of case, true blue.

Lieutenant Nathaniel BUMPUS, head of Bay City homicide. He was willing to take a chance on a woman.

Mason CROSBY, owner of the island's pharmacy. His wife assisted him in the store, and he needed a replacement for her.

Richard (Old Richie) CROSBY, at 93 the island's oldest resident. He took pleasure in reading obituaries.

Delano DELANO, owner of the Admiral's Arms pub. He was stopped from telling on his cousin.

Dr. Thomas DELANO, the island's physician, accused of murder. He had a secret.

Corporal John DINGLEY, assistant to Sergeant Priscilla Booth.

Ken FUSETTI, newspaper reporter, a nice guy, but you better level with him, or else.

Arthur GIFFARD, butler at the Gorges mansion. He didn't do it.

Senator Atherton GORGES, richest person on Fogge Island. Not a typically rich, altruistic, avuncular type.

Dudley GORGES, Atherton and Martha's nephew. He bit the hand that fed him.

Esther GORGES, Atherton and Martha's niece; third victim. She searched high and low for thrills. She found the ultimate.

Ferdinand GORGES, Atherton and Martha's son; first victim. The happy stage of his life was a short one.

Lettice GORGES, Atherton and Martha's daughter. She knew what she wanted and was willing to pay for it.

Martha (nee Mann) GORGES, Atherton's wife, very quiet. She did not care for genealogists, or other muckrakers.

Constable Nehemiah GORGES, cousin to Atherton Gorges. The island's only police officer, he was relieved to be relieved.

Maria de la Concepcion HERNANDEZ, Ferdinand's fiancee, she never got the wedding ring.

Benjamin MANN, owner of the Mann Hotel, nephew of Martha Gorges, in love with Priscilla Booth.

Margaret (nee Samson) MANN, second cousin and assistant to Deborah Samson; sister-in-law to Ben Mann. Did she have a secret, too?

Sylvester MANN, a lawyer, cousin to Benjamin Mann. He had a conflict of interest.

Sylvia (nee Crosby) MANN, a former nurse, second wife of Sylvester Mann, and cousin to Mason Crosby. Some of her interests conflicted, too.

Jacob (Cobber) PALGRAVE, a beach bum; second victim. He knew the value of a good wife.

Lucy (nee Samson) PALGRAVE, Cobber Palgrave's second wife, a waitress at the Admiral's Arms pub.

Deborah SAMSON, FIGS executive officer and librarian, a well known genealogist. How did she get that scar?

Tina SAMSON, divorced from Delano Delano, she continued working at his pub as a waitress.

Mortimer SINCLAIR, genealogist, police consultant.

The countless cousins . . . as multi-
tudinous as are the spheres.
                    –Samuel Hoffenstein

Yet each man kills the thing he loves,
By each let this be heard,
Some do it with a bitter look,
Some with a flattering word,
The coward does it with a kiss,
The brave man with a sword.
                    –Oscar Wilde

One murder made a villain,
Millions a hero. Princes were
priviledged
To kill, and numbers sanctified the
crime.
                    –Beilby Porteus

One

MORTIMER SINCLAIR FORCED HIMSELF TO SIT patiently on an ancient and very uncomfortable wooden armchair in the busy outer office of Lieutenant Nathaniel Bumpus. A female police officer of indeterminate age, wearing a light blue blouse and dark blue slacks, manned a small, equally ancient desk in front of him. She hunted and pecked on a manual Royal typewriter, the rhythmic click made by her two operational fingers suggesting the march from *Aida*. She held a cigarette tightly between hot pink lips; occasionally, as she answered the phone or yelled a terse reply to some new person sticking a questioning head in the door, she placed the cigarette on a pile of smoldering butts in a large glass ashtray. The smoke drifted throughout the room, and it was impossible for Mort to stay clear of it. A reformed two-pack-a-day man, he now loathed the smell of tobacco and made quixotic attempts to wave the smoke away.

He glanced again at yesterday's *Bay City Gazette*. The headlines were the usual provincial ones: "County Auditor Commits Suicide." "B.C. Man Hits Tri-State Lottery." "Governor Pardons Former Aide." "Storm Watch Over." For the umpteenth time, in spite of himself, Mort read the small item in the bottom right corner: "Fogge I. Ferry Hike." He knew it by heart. The one-way fare was going up from $4.50 to $6.00 on the fifteenth of February, and monthly commuter tickets would go from $61.00 to $75.00. Having already calculated the break commuters were getting over the tourists, who were probably subsidizing the ferry operation, he wondered how often he would be going back and forth, and if it would pay him to buy a commuter ticket. There was nothing else to make of the story.

How long would he be on the island anyway? A week? Could it take a month to finish his assignment? Presumably Lieutenant Bumpus would give him some idea. And of course Bumpus would fill him in on the murders. Three of them. Cyanide. What else did he know about them? At this point, he had to admit, not much.

Through the high window Mort could see an anvil-shaped cumulonimbus cloud threatening snow. Inside, three other nondescript chairs were occupied by nondescript people. The man closest to Mort was smoking a cigar. I don't really need this fee, thought Mort. The hallway door opened, and a man with an unshaven face yelled to the typist, "Natty see me yet?" The typist elevated her eyes to the ceiling. The face disappeared from the door.

Now the door to the inner office opened, and a raspy voice called out, "Gotcha, Natty! It won't happen again. Y'can bet on it." A uniformed policeman rushed past the typist and out of the room. The inner office door closed automatically, and a few seconds later a buzzer sounded on the typist's desk.

"Lieutenant Bumpus will see you now, Dr. Sinclair." The typist pointed a finger at the inner office door behind her, the one with the name of the occupant in large black letters:

Lt. Nathaniel Bumpus, J.D.

Homicide

Mort picked up his shiny oft-repaired brown leather briefcase, nodded perfunctorily to the receptionist, and entered the door. Tact, he told himself, tact.

The lieutenant, in mufti, was a big man, obviously younger than Mort, handsome in an athletic sort of way, as if he used to participate in hammer throws at field meets. But the pictures and certificates on the wall told a somewhat different story. Bumpus was, it seemed, a prize-winning sailboat enthusiast, and the center display framed a newspaper headline: "Bumpus Wins Gorges Cup." That must be the tall silver cup on top of the chipped green metal bookcase. Bumpus offered Mort instant coffee but took hot chocolate for himself.

The lieutenant sipped his drink in a leisurely fashion, all the while staring intently at his visitor. Mort stared back, wondering if this was to be a contest.

Finally, glancing at a sheet of paper in his hand, Bumpus said, "You've got a lot of initials after your name."

"Including the J.D. I share with you."

"A law degree helps in police work. Where'd you get yours?"

"Georgetown."

"Mine's Harvard," said Bumpus in reply to Mort's unspoken question. "What's the Ph.D. in?"

"History. Cambridge." He half expected Bumpus to say that he had been a Rhodes Scholar.

The lieutenant nodded to show due respect, but merely said, "Oh." Then, "What's a C.G.?"

"Certified Genealogist." It's all there in my brochure, you lout, Mort thought.

"And an F.A.S.G.?"

"As you can see in the brochure you have there, it stands for Fellow of the American Society of Genealogists."

"Impressive. Lawyer. Historian. Genealogist. Anything else?"

"I am mainly a genealogical consultant and writer. But I've also been closely involved with investigative work in the past: I have been a security officer with the U.S. Foreign Service, I've lectured on the use of genealogy in medicine and forensics, and I served on the President's Commission for Standardized Police Educational Guidelines."

"Writer? Anything published?"

"Nothing worth mentioning." The list of publications was in the brochure if Bumpus cared to look.

"Well," said Bumpus, "police work can use consultants of all types. I've used psychiatrists and psychics, pimps and prostitutes, quacks and queers. Why not a genealogist?"

"Why not, indeed?" Why, Mort wondered, was this obviously

busy police officer wasting so much time on chit-chat. Did he realize that his department was being charged for this time, as well as for the hour Mort had spent in the outer office?

As if sensing Mort's thoughts, Lieutenant Bumpus started talking business.

"Actually, Sergeant Booth's the one who insisted we hire you. I put her in charge of the case."

"Her?" Not that it mattered. A woman could head a murder investigation just as well as a man, couldn't she? She could not be any worse to work with than Bumpus.

"Yes, I said 'her.' If I had my way, they'd all stay in the kitchen and bedroom, where they belong. But I didn't make this world, Mr. Sinclair. Or do you prefer Dr. Sinclair?"

"I have no preference." Actually, he preferred to be called Mort.

"Give her a chance to put her ass in a sling," Bumpus said, "and then maybe they'll get off my back and let me run my section as I see fit. Or maybe she'll succeed, and I'll have a feather in my cap for taking a chance on a woman. These days you have to move with the times."

He suddenly stood up, offered his hand, and said, "See Booth and she'll give you the details. You're her consultant, Dr. Sinclair, and if she's satisfied with your work, I'm satisfied."

He was being dismissed! Bumpus had never intended to discuss the case with him. All he wanted was to size him up. And put him firmly in his place. Mort was working for Sergeant Booth, and Lieutenant Bumpus would be out of the picture. That is, unless Mort had some complaint against Booth. He sensed that this was the message Bumpus was sending—that Mort was more than welcome to visit the lieutenant again if there were any indications of incompetence on Booth's part. Cretin! He already felt somewhat sympathetic toward the otherwise unknown Sergeant Booth. Mort knew few details about this multiple murder case, but one thing was certain—if Booth were halfway decent, he would want her to be the one solving it.

There were half a dozen people in the outer office now. The typist was still smoking and pecking. Mort figured he had waited fifty minutes for a five minute interview in which he had learned nothing, except that he was going to like Sergeant Booth and was not going to skimp on expenses. Although he had traveled to Bay City economy class as a matter of habit, it would be first class from now on. As he walked past the receptionist, everyone seemed to be trying to get into the lieutenant's office all at once. "Hey, Natty, I only need a minute," said one. "Gimme a break," said another. Mort asked a few questions of the receptionist and left.

Relieved to get out of that office and the smoke, he took a deep breath. The cold damp air went straight through his lined Burberry trench coat and chilled him to the marrow. He wore no hat, even though he would have liked to, but that was one concession he would not make to age. He shivered and hunched his shoulders. Maybe he should buy a hat after all, just to wear while he was up here. Winter on the New England seacoast could be damned unpleasant.

◆　　　　◆　　　　◆

The police station was situated on a central square with one side open to the harbor. Mort looked out at the moored fishing boats rolling in unison with the pitch of the sea, their empty masts and spars against the sky looking like a Mondrian study in gray. Beyond the harbor the sea itself was choppy. In the distance was a blurry outline of something more than sea, probably Fogge Island. He had been there once before, but that was years ago. There had been so many other islands since then: Friday Harbor on San Juan; the luxurious hideaways on Martha's Vineyard; the phoniness of Capri; Murder Mile; and keeping his back to the wall on Cyprus, Spetsai, and Spetsopoula; Ypsos and cold lobster slices with lemon butter on Corfu; a girl he met once during an interlude on Rhodes. . . . Islamania, Lawrence Durrell had called it.

He searched his memory for anything at all about Fogge Island. There was the Genealogical Society, commonly called FIGS. It had a good library, he remembered, though he could not recall what it looked like or even its size—it must be small. And wasn't there a woman in charge who was fairly well known in the genealogical community? What was her name?—he would not have forgotten it. And was she still alive? Or still working there? It was one of the old names.

Samson. Miss Samson, in fact. An authority on the old island families. He had met her once some years back while doing research at FIGS during a genealogical conference on the island; she had, he remembered, been of great help to him. He was getting a picture of a sweet older lady with gracious old-fashioned ways, and yet he also remembered an outspoken, sharp-tongued woman. Was he thinking of two different people?

Sergeant Booth, the police typist had told Mort, was virtually living on Fogge Island now. The luxury summer resorts on the far side of the island were all closed in winter, but the Mann Hotel in Oldtown was open, and that was where Booth was staying. There would be no need for a reservation in winter, but Mort telephoned anyway before boarding the Fogge Island ferry for the thirty-minute trip across the sound. He must have stayed at the Mann Hotel. The typist had said it was the only hotel in the town, and there was only the one town on the island. Oh, yes, now he remembered it—he could never forget a place with superb cuisine. Though he did not like to spend money needlessly, Mort never complained about paying the price for really good food.

He looked at his watch. He had been on the deck of the ferry for more than twenty minutes, and they were still at the landing. The ferry should have left ten minutes ago, yet he had been told that it was quite punctual. "Why are we late in leaving?" he asked a deck hand lounging near the gangplank.

The deck hand smiled. "The Senator's taking this trip. We're waiting for him."

"What Senator?"

"You new here?"

"Yes."

Another smile. "Senator Gorges, sir. He owns the line. And just about everything else. We don't move until he comes aboard."

A vague recollection came to mind: a prominent man on Fogge Island who had been a state senator briefly during his younger years, and then forever wore the title as if it were a part of his name.

"Tell me something about the Senator," he said.

"Wha'dya wanna know?"

"Does he live on the island?"

"Live on it? He owns it!" the sailor said. And then, "Hey, you ain't a reporter, are ya?"

Mort started to say he was a police consultant, but thought better of it. "I'm visiting the Genealogical Society. Just curious."

"Curiosity don't go over big here." The sailor turned his back, and Mort knew he was not going to learn anything more from him.

♦   ♦   ♦

The dampness continued making inroads on his body, and Mort proceeded to the passenger cabin, half hoping to find some kind of bar where he could buy a brandy. He was disappointed, for there wasn't even a coffee machine—only a water cooler. There were some ten tables in the ship's one great passenger cabin, each capable of seating up to six people. The room held only a dozen or so passengers, spread out in singles and twos, so that they occupied all the tables but one. Mort sat at the vacant table and wondered how long it would be before departure. He seemed to have spent most of his day wasting time.

His thoughts drifted back to the Samson woman. Deborah—that was her name—but of course he should be familiar with it, for she contributed sporadically to the genealogical journals. A good genealogist, she did not just accept something because it appeared in print somewhere. She questioned how the writer could have come into possession of the facts, and she relied considerably on primary sources to document her statements, thus letting readers judge for themselves the merits of her work.

The size of FIGS was coming back to him, too. It had an amazing collection of books and other sources for a non-profit organization on an island whose year-round population could not be more than a thousand. Important manuscript files supplied information unavailable elsewhere on local families; during his previous visit he had made some significant discoveries using the Moriarty notes on New England island families. He also recalled that Deborah Samson had an assistant. Was this why he'd thought he was remembering two women? Was one graciously charming and the other argumentative and biting? In that case, which was which?

No, it was Deborah Samson herself who had impressed him both ways. She could turn on the charm when she wanted, but she could also be tough. The assistant had made no lasting impression, as if she lacked a personality of her own. He remembered a rather noisy incident that took place when he was at FIGS, but it was Deborah Samson doing all the yelling, the same Deborah Samson who had sweetly offered him tea and finger sandwiches earlier that day.

Only now someone else was yelling.

"You gotta get up. This table's reserved." It was the sailor from the gangplank. "I said this table's reserved for the Senator."

"Nothing said it was reserved."

"People up here know this table's always for the Senator when he's on board." With a loud bang, the sailor slammed a metal-bottomed "Reserved" sign on the table about two inches away from Mort's hand.

Approaching the table was a tall, thin man wearing a black Greek sailor's cap and a navy blue pea jacket that fit as if it had been tailor-made. He was an older man, with sharp features and a dark moustache clipped at the corners, very British, a man who knew his place and expected all others to know theirs. The man—he had to be Senator Gorges—paused in his step, eyes staring blankly ahead as if he were seeing no one but obviously aware that someone was at his table, for he slowed his approach waiting for its occupant to leave. No doubt, he took it for granted that the deck hand would have explained the situation.

Mort made him wait. It wasn't that he wanted to make a scene over the table. He could easily move; he did not mind rules, nor did he mind privilege. He did not even mind the deck hand's rudeness. It was only Gorges's silence that irritated him. After all, Gorges could have spoken for himself and said, "Excuse me, but I own this line, this is my table, and I choose to sit alone." So Mort waited. Now there was no way for Gorges to avoid some awkwardness.

The deck hand spoke again. "Do I gotta get some help?"

"That's all right," said Mort. "I'll move. *Noblesse oblige.*"

The Senator stiffened slightly, then slid into his seat as Mort was rising from his. Their eyes met just briefly, as if each were saying to the other, I want to remember your face.

Mort chose a nearby table where a well-dressed young man was sitting by himself. His new companion smiled and said, "They could have been nicer about it. I take it you're a stranger to the island."

"More or less," Mort said good-naturedly. "I was here once before."

"I don't belong here either, but I recognize Senator Atherton Gorges when I see him, the head of the clan himself. I'm a reporter for the *Boston Times*." He spoke with a broad prep-school twang, and he introduced himself as Ken Fusetti.

Out of the corner of his eye, Mort noticed his sailor acquaintance come back into the cabin with a large mug of steaming liquid which he respectfully placed in front of the Senator.

"You must be covering the murder case," said Mort.

"Just assigned to it. Read anything about it?"

"Not a thing," Mort said truthfully, since he had flown to Boston from Salt Lake City and then rented a car to get to Bay City without so much as seeing a single newspaper story on the latest murder. He knew only what he had been told over the phone by some assistant to Lieutenant Bumpus, and that wasn't much. There had been another unsolved murder on Fogge Island, the third in about a year. He vaguely recalled reading about the first murder but could not remember any details.

"It's a small island," the reporter said. "Everyone knows everyone, everyone's related to everyone. But it hits close to home when you're sitting next to the table of the father of one of the victims."

"Senator Gorges?"

"His son Ferdinand was the first one murdered, and his niece is the latest victim." Fusetti pulled a pocket flask from inside his coat. "Medicine for the dampness. Care for a nip?" He went over to the water cooler and reached for the paper cups.

"Don't mind if I do," Mort said. "This dampness goes right to the bones."

They drank in silence until the reporter spoke again. "Mike, the guy who had the assignment before me, they took him off the story. Fell in love with the female police officer in charge and couldn't give it the kind of coverage the paper wanted."

"Interesting," said Mort. "She good-looking?"

"Haven't seen her yet. But Mike swears she's a raving beauty."

"Did she return his love?"

"Naw, that's the trouble. She always kept him at arm's length, and he got so frustrated he couldn't work. Said she's got a heart of ice."

A raving beauty with a heart of ice, now that was even more interesting. Mort just hoped she would keep on being icy and businesslike. After that affair with Penny in Greece, he was definitely not ready for another romantic entanglement.

Two

PRISCILLA BOOTH LOVED THE COLOR BLUE. Her parents, who enjoyed teasing her, liked to say that she only joined the police force because the uniform was blue. Even though the move had cost her the uniform, Priscilla had not quit when her superiors reassigned her to the detective bureau. But she always made sure that some part of her outfit was blue: she chose lingerie in delicate shades of blue, and her personal car was a powder blue Ford Thunderbird. Surrounding herself with her favorite color was, however, Priscilla's only indulgence. In all other matters she was restrained if not refreshingly subdued.

It was, in fact, because of her old-fashioned orthodox feelings that she was Priscilla Booth instead of Mrs. George Downing. Of course, the historical reason she was not Mrs. George Downing was that when the judge unexpectedly asked her if she wanted to reassume her maiden name, she said, "Er, yes." But the reason for the "yes" went right to the depths of Priscilla's soul.

A handsome man, George was a rising star in the district attorney's office, blessed with the charm and family connections for a brilliant political career. Had she kept him, Priscilla someday might well have become first lady of the state, and who knew from there? But Priscilla was blessed, or cursed, with a persona ruled by the dictum of Polonius, and she would have found it easier to flap her arms and fly like a bird than to be untrue to herself. She loved music, Brahms, Beethoven, Mozart, Wagner, Vivaldi, Bartok, and dozens of others. She loved the open air; she loved the sea; she loved travel, especially European travel; she loved history and genealogy; she loved poetry and novels; she loved small animals and large plants; she loved watching public TV, especially *Masterpiece Theater* and *Mystery;* and she loved conversation with interesting people. George had only two loves: hunting and women, and with him the latter was just a specialized form of the former.

When they were first married, Priscilla was on the night shift and thus slow to read the telltale signs, from lipstick smudges on glasses she hadn't used to unfamiliar perfume on the sofa cushions. When she was transferred to day work, she saw George off on hunting weekends with his buddies and, at night, took telephone calls for him from "Marge, from his office," or "Susan, from the gun club," or "Darlene, an old friend," or, in one case, "his aunt."

George gave her all the equity in the condo as part of the divorce settlement, and Priscilla's department gave her—much to her surprise—a promotion to sergeant. She had heard that the Bay City Police would have to promote one woman to that rank, but she assumed she would be the last to have a chance. She had made the highest score on the written examination, but in the department they used the word "brainy" like an expletive. After the promotion she learned it had been due to her being considered the least offensive—that is, the least pushy—of the qualified women officers, but though this might not be the most personally satisfying reason for career advancement, she was not going to turn it down on that account. Priscilla also understood that the promotion was the limit of Bumpus's largess. Lilly, Bumpus's receptionist, told her that the lieutenant had roared loudly enough to be heard on the other side of the closed door: "Damn it, I might have to promote her, but I'll be damned if I ever put her in charge of anything important. As far as I'm concerned, she's just window dressing."

Following her promotion, Priscilla was able to keep up the monthly condo payments and still do a little traveling during her vacation leave, even attending at least one national genealogical conference yearly. Two years after her divorce, she looked younger than her twenty-seven years and about as far removed from any stereotyped concept of a policewoman as could be imagined. On men in general her attitude was: This time shame on George, next time shame on me. Somewhere out there, there had to be a Mr. Right.

◆   ◆   ◆

It had been almost a year since the murder of Ferdinand Gorges. Priscilla had gone out with Ferdinand once, long before she met George, and though Ferdie never asked for a second date—nor would she have accepted one—she was as shocked at the thought of his being no longer among the living as if she were a schoolteacher rather than a homicide detective. Constable Nehemiah Gorges, a first cousin of the victim's father, had been assigned the case under the anomalous arrangement whereby Fogge Island kept its one all-purpose policeman after being annexed to Bay City. The constable reported his progress, or lack thereof, to Lieutenant Bumpus.

Ferdinand had been twenty-six years old, handsome, an arrogant playboy and foul-mouthed snob admired by few and liked by virtually no one. He had once been charged with murder himself, but got off with a plea of self-defense when the victim's wife testified that her husband had gone berserk upon finding her in bed with Ferdinand. But shortly before his death Ferdinand had undergone a metamorphosis. He became polite—if not actually considerate—even-tempered, and given to clean speech. Ferdinand had fallen in love.

The family approved of Ferdinand's transformed personality as much as they disapproved of his romantic choice. Surely he would not go so far as to marry the maid of a New York socialite! Senator Atherton Gorges said softly, "I'll cut him off without a cent." His wife reminded him that Ferdinand had already inherited a small fortune from his Aunt Mabel. "Besides, dear, it happens in the best of families. And it might just keep him out of trouble, even out of the newspapers." Those were more words than Martha Gorges usually spoke in an entire day.

The Senator accepted defeat graciously. Ferdinand had, at least, well demonstrated his heterosexuality, and Atherton's segment of the Gorges line would be carried on. He and Martha invited the happy couple to their mansion, where, not waiting for Ferdinand to introduce her, his fiancee curtsied proudly and said, "Maria de la Concepcion Hernandez *a su servicio.*" They drank tea together and talked about the weather, and Concha, as she was called, in her broken English complimented the Senator and Martha on their good taste in furniture and paintings. Gradually the conversation wound down, and after a few awkward silences, Concha took Ferdinand's hand and dismissed herself with another curtsey and a polite *"Con permiso."* Martha, to be equally polite, said, *"Con permiso* to you, too."

Two days later Atherton and Martha gave a farewell reception for their son and Concha before their departure for Guadalajara, where the wedding was to take place. The year-round population of Fogge Island, acceptable contingent, showed up at the reception. Giffard, the butler, served champagne and cocktails; while the cook, Mrs. Beeton, passed around cleverly assembled canapés of caviar, king crab, truffled pâté de foie gras, Smithfield ham, and smoked Scottish salmon. Mrs. Beeton's daughter, Belinda, the household maid, alternated with Lucy Palgrave, who had been hired just for the night, in carrying other delights to the buffet table and taking dirty dishes back to the kitchen for immediate recycling.

Sylvester Mann and his wife Sylvia were congratulating Ferdinand when Sylvester noticed that Ferdinand did not seem to have heard him. "Something wrong, Ferdie? You all right?"

Ferdinand turned to face him, carefully set his glass down on the tray Giffard was carrying by at the moment, opened his mouth as if to say something, and sank to the floor. Following a few gasps and murmurs, Dr. Thomas Delano crossed the room, knelt, examined the body, and then looked up to announce to no one in particular, "Christ, he's dead!"

Concha, beautifully dressed in a bare-shoulder gown, yelled *"Ay, chingada!"* and fainted. Several guests screamed, and even the cook was so shaken by the horrible event that she had to be taken to Dr. Delano's clinic, which served as the closest thing to a hospital on the island.

Laboratory analysis showed that Ferdinand had been poisoned.

His stomach was full of champagne, scotch, caviar, butter, onion, crab meat, truffles, pâté, ham, salmon, various spices and condiments, and bread; his urine showed traces of marijuana and cocaine. The coroner's report attributed the poisoning to cyanide "ingested with some as yet unknown substance, probably food or drink." Presumably, anyone at the Gorges house that night, guest or servant, would have had an opportunity to administer the poison.

As time dragged on without an arrest in the highly publicized case, the police department earned a black eye. Lieutenant Bumpus made several trips to the island without advancing the investigation so much as a step. The poison had not been traced. The exact means of administering it was still unknown, though it was suspected that it might have been in the glass that Ferdinand conveniently deposited on Giffard's tray just before he expired—Giffard had certainly been quick in having the glasses washed. In one sense everyone was a suspect; in another, no one was since there was not a scrap of evidence against a single guest or servant. The lugubrious bride-to-have-been, having lost the most by the murder, was beyond suspicion, and she soon returned to whence she had come. The possibility that Ferdinand had committed suicide was considered and rejected, there being no reason whatsoever why he might do such a thing.

The whole affair took on renewed significance six months later when "Cobber" Palgrave died of cyanide poisoning while drinking gin at what was quaintly called his "beach house." Having been a beach bum, a man of no visible means of support, Jacob Bradstreet Palgrave (his infrequently used full name) had of course not been invited to Ferdinand's reception, though his wife, Lucy, had worked at the Gorges mansion that night as a temporary maid. Lucy took her husband's death calmly, catastrophe—as she told everyone who would listen—being her lot in life.

Cobber's movements that day, as related by Lucy, were uncomplicated. He got out of bed around 1:00 p.m., found a quarter-full bottle of vodka that he had somehow misplaced the night before, drained the bottle, swore at Lucy for not having more liquor on the premises, got her promise to bring home another bottle, staggered back to bed again, and fell asleep. Lucy tidied up the shanty and left for her job at the Admiral's Arms around four o'clock.

Lucy discovered Cobber's corpse slumped over the cabin's solitary table when she returned around midnight. In front of him on the table were an empty juice glass and a pint-size bottle of gin with perhaps a third of the contents gone; laboratory analysis showed nothing added to the gin in the bottle, but traces of cyanide in the glass. Lucy was able to give evidence that Cobber had been drinking with some other person, for she found a clean juice glass in the wrong place in the cupboard. Lucy, who had a good memory and a habit of neatness, swore that she had washed the dishes just before leaving and returned the glass to its usual place.

The conclusion was that some as yet unidentified person had brought Cobber a bottle of gin and drunk it sitting with him at the table. Having put cyanide in Cobber's glass, it was surmised, the murderer washed and put away his or her own glass, making the mistake only of putting it in the wrong place. This had occurred, according to the forensics report, around six o'clock in the evening.

The bottle of gin had been wiped clean of fingerprints, but at least the bottle was easily tracked down. Fogge Island had just two sources of hard liquor, the Talleyrand Room and Bar of the Mann Hotel and the Admiral's Arms pub. Both bought liquor wholesale from Bay City and sold it on the island, by the drink for on-premise consumption and by the bottle for off-premise use. The two outlets used different distributors and thus had different brands. The brand of gin found at Cobber's place had come from the Admiral's Arms. Delano Delano, the pub's owner, readily identified it but said it was not in heavy demand, adding that he had not sold any for off-site use in a long time. He admitted that he was not careful with his inventory, and someone conceivably could have stolen a bottle.

Constable Gorges was technically assigned the case, though Lieutenant Bumpus had a number of his people looking over the constable's shoulder. Cobber Palgrave's beach house was on the opposite side of the island from Oldtown, at the back of Meerstead Cove, and it had somehow been grandfathered into continued existence when the rest of that shore was zoned into five-acre or larger estates. The other buildings in the area were either resort hotels or luxury summer homes owned by leisured rich people of non-island origin. Cobber had arrived on Fogge Island about five years earlier just barely solvent enough to buy the dilapidated cabin from its previous absentee owner. The summer estate people, never dreaming that anyone would actually live in such a hut, could do nothing but wring their hands when Cobber the Beachcomber and his two successive wives became the only year-round residents of Meerstead Cove. His first wife having left him after a few years on Fogge Island, he married Lucy some seven months before his death.

The pressure on Constable Gorges and Lieutenant Bumpus and all their superiors up the line was still to find the murderer of Ferdinand Gorges. If that person or persons happened to be the same who had murdered Cobber Palgrave, well and good, but it was understood that the defunct Cobber was just a statistic, while the defunct Ferdinand was a potentially powerful political factor. Other than the fact that both had died by cyanide, there was nothing to connect the two deaths and no reason for thinking that the murderer was necessarily the same in each case. On the one hand, Cobber's death could have been a copycat murder. On the other, and this was the theory officialdom leaned to, Cobber could conceivably have murdered Ferdinand and then committed suicide. This, the perfect solution, was undermined by Lucy's testimony about the glass, by the absence of fingerprints on the bottle, and by any evidence in favor of suicide.

Lucy, when interrogated, answered all questions with a frankness and naivete that made it impossible for anyone to suppose she was holding anything back. Six months earlier, questioned about the first murder, she had said she reported to the Gorges mansion at 5:00 p.m. on the day in question. Giffard let her in the back door and led her immediately to Mrs. Beeton, who had watched Lucy's every move in the kitchen as she helped prepare food, and at the reception as she brought trays in and out. Lucy, dismissed shortly after the murder, had gone home, as was her custom, by foot, covering the three miles or so in about an hour.

As time passed, so did the urgency of the two cases. The newspapers were given to understand, quite unofficially, that the police still held to their belief in murder followed by the suicide of the murderer. If the murderer had indeed taken his own life, justice had been served as well as could be expected, and what more was there to be done?

Six months after the second murder came the third, blasting this comfortable but totally unsubstantiated theory right out of the water. The phrases "mass murderer" and "serial homicidal maniac" began to be heard all over the island. People bought more secure locks for their doors and windows, though none of the murders had involved breaking and entering. The few places of evening entertainment in Oldtown—Meg's Muffin Shoppe, the Mann Hotel Talleyrand Room and Bar, and even the Admiral's Arms—began closing earlier. No one wanted to be out late, even though all the crimes had taken place indoors.

The third victim was Esther Gorges, "Mad Estie," the wild niece who lived with Atherton and Martha Gorges. Esther, in her mid-twenties, had looked years older—still attractive but considerably dissipated. She had had, she once claimed, more intimate encounters with life than the combined experiences of all the rest of the island folk put together. She had traveled further, drunk more, experimented with more drugs, engaged in more different types of sexual congress than most people knew existed, seen more depravity, joined more cults, and spent more money than all the others. It was the spending of money that had led her to continued dependence on her uncle and aunt for sustenance. She and her brother, Dudley Gorges, had gone to live with Atherton and Martha Gorges after losing their parents in an airplane crash many years earlier. They inherited small fortunes on their respective eighteenth birthdays, Esther first, being the older. Esther was also the first of the two to run through the capital, though Dudley soon followed, after which the Senator provided them with board and room and a modest allowance.

Esther was found dead one morning by the maid, Belinda, who brought in her morning coffee. She was in bed nude and had been watching video cassettes—pornographic movies, in fact. Her glass had fallen to the floor unbroken; a half-empty bottle of liquor labeled absinthe was on the table beside the canopied bed. Upon analysis the liquor turned out to be absinthe laced with cyanide. The autopsy not only showed cyanide to be the cause of death but also revealed the unmarried Esther to be between two and three months pregnant. The police entertained just briefly the wishful thought that Esther had murdered both her cousin Ferdinand and Cobber Palgrave, had found herself pregnant, and had then in fear committed suicide—but where was the evidence for such a theory? Esther's death also terminated the assignment of the murder cases to Constable Nehemiah Gorges, much to the relief of Nehemiah.

Priscilla wondered who would now be put in charge of the three murder investigations, which had been combined to make one case. There had been talk of sending a team over, and she suspected that she would be part of the team. Lieutenant Bumpus might exercise close supervision, but he would never take the assignment himself. There were two other sergeants in homicide, Zwiebel and Gamotos, either one of whom would be the obvious choice to put in charge. Having worked with both of them, Priscilla had no preference. She did not like Zwiebel, who wore polyester suits and smelled of rotten onions, but he was happily married and left her alone. Gamotos, who smelled of a nice cologne and wore upscale casual clothing, was always trying to get into her light blue panties.

When Bumpus put her in charge of the case, Priscilla was even more astonished than she had been the day she was promoted to sergeant—too shocked, in fact, to relish Bumpus's eating his words.

"Sergeant," he said solemnly, as he clasped her shoulder, "you've been patient in assisting your peers on past cases, but the time has come for you to be on your own. This is your golden opportunity. Understand? Just don't besmirch it, sweetheart!" He assigned Corporal Dingley to be her assistant, told Constable Gorges on the island to put his one-man office at her disposal, and authorized her to stay at the island hotel at department expense whenever she had to work late. "This is your baby," he said paternally, as she backed out of his office.

Although Priscilla was experienced in murder cases, the same could not be said about murder mysteries. The average Bay City murder case was one of two styles. Either the murderer telephoned and said, "I've just killed my wife, so you better come and arrest me," or he fled after being observed doing the deed by twenty competent witnesses. Most of the energy on such a case went to making sure that the murderer's rights were not violated. The salient points about the Fogge Island case amounted to a murderer, or murderers, still completely unknown—along with a lack of clues, evidence, believable motives, and plausible suspects. *Corragio*, Priscilla steeled herself, *corragio!*

Lieutenant Bumpus had taken initial charge of the investigation of Esther's murder himself, and he left Priscilla a series of reports made by himself and others. She studied and restudied them, then went over the same ground by requestioning all those who might have any light to shed on the event. In the beginning she was unable to improve upon the thoroughness of the work of her predecessors, though she did obtain a somewhat different view of Esther. Esther, Priscilla decided, was more to be pitied than condemned. The first-born child, she had disappointed her parents by coming out female and from the beginning had been treated as an outsider in the family. With her parents both dead, she and her brother Dudley went to live with their Uncle Atherton, where she again found herself not really wanted.

Esther, a bright girl who showed signs of being a good student, had, after the death of her parents, become interested in history and genealogy. The island had one grammar school, but the older students, including Esther, took the ferry each day to attend high school in Bay City. On her return from school, she would normally spend her afternoons at the FIGS library, where she immersed herself in the past. She showed the attention to detail characteristic of a good genealogist, and for a while she spoke of wanting to research and write family histories. It was Martha Gorges who dissuaded her niece from such idle pastimes and encouraged her to see more of the world. Before Esther was old enough to inherit her own money, Martha paid for summers in Europe. During the school year, Martha tried to ensure popularity for her niece by giving her frequent parties, making sure she had the most expensive and trendiest wardrobe, and providing her with a generous allowance, supplementing the one her uncle still gave her, to encourage more after-school activities in Bay City.

By the time Esther came into her inheritance, she had upgraded beer to champagne, pot to snow, and heavy petting to group sex. By means of an open pocketbook she was able to gratify her every desire, and had gone miles beyond the popularity her aunt had craved for her. The end of the money curtailed some of her extravaganzas, but her character had been conditioned for life, which, as it turned out, wasn't that long.

When Priscilla found herself at a standstill on the investigation of Esther's murder, she started re-examining all the facts collected thus far in the other two murders. She found being in charge a lonely affair. There was no one to talk to as an equal, no one to confide in, no one to chew theories over with.

As she started making highly significant discoveries involving family relationships, the idea occurred to her that the use of a contract, consulting genealogist might be justified. From her attendance at conferences, she knew the names and faces of nationally prominent genealogists; more and more, one name and face fixed itself in her mind. When Bumpus conceded her permission to hire a consultant, she knew just the man she wanted.

Three

THE INTERIOR OF THE MANN HOTEL HAD that intimate, well-run personality of an owner-managed lodging house. Everything seemed to be in its place, and cleanliness was an everyday condition. The entrance led to the main lobby with a reception desk of reddish brown solid mahogany to the left, a passageway to ground floor rooms plus a stairway leading to an upper level in the center, and an enormous mahogany arch on the right opening to a huge room divided by a verdant center wall of plants. Carved wood lettering on the arch proclaimed it to be the Talleyrand Room. Behind the clerk at the reception desk was a room with an open door, and inside the room Mort could see two men and a woman sitting around a rectangular table engaged in casual conversation interrupted frequently by laughter.

Mort gave his name to the clerk, registered, and was asked if he had a preference as to first, second, or third floor. There seemed to be no elevator and the stairs were fairly steep, for the ornate plastered ceiling was high, but he chose a third-floor front room for the view. The room was comfortable, clean, and of ample size, and the front view was not disappointing. When Mort returned to the lobby, the clerk was no longer at the desk. After waiting a minute or so, Mort made his inquiry of the three people in the back room. "Can you tell me how to get to Constable Gorges's office?"

"I can do better than that," said the older of the two men, a grizzled tall person with crew-cut hair. As the man stood up, Mort could see he was wearing some kind of uniform with dark blue shirt and tie and a star pinned over his left shirt pocket. "You're talking to Constable Gorges," he said.

Mort identified himself and said he understood that he could get in touch with Sergeant Booth through the constable.

The police officer took Mort's measure with a deep look and evidently decided there was nothing wrong with him. "She told me about you. But she's not here now. Coming in on a later ferry."

Mort thanked him and both stood in awkward silence.

After a moment, the constable said, "We're sure having a mild winter."

"You're lucky. You should see the snow and ice storms we've been having in Salt Lake City."

The younger man inside the room now came out and with his eyes gave Mort a lengthy, relentless examination. Of pale complexion and softly handsome features, he was perspiring and seemed to move with effort. Well dressed, he must have been in his late twenties. Just minutes earlier he had been engaged in joking conversation with the others, but now there was not the slightest crack of a smile on his whitened face. The policeman's scrutiny of Mort had been part of the makeup of every law enforcement officer the world over, but this young man's silent scowling glare was far more intense. Mort knew that the residents on Fogge Island were not xenophobic; they were too used to visitors and too dependent on tourist income to resent new faces. But there seemed to be something personal in the man's staring, as if it were Mort himself who displeased him.

Time passed slowly until the scrutiny abruptly ended, and the man hesitantly stretched his hand toward Mort and introduced himself as Benjamin Mann, owner of the hotel. The woman who came to the doorway behind him looked friendlier, and Benjamin Mann introduced her as Margaret Mann, his sister-in-law. Ben Mann had a disconcertingly firm way of speaking, nor did he seem to lack for self-assurance. But having made the introductions, he became hesitant again. Finally the muscles in his face relaxed a bit, and he said, "Come in and have a cup of coffee with us, or tea if you prefer."

Mort said coffee would be welcome and took the fourth chair around the table.

"Is your room satisfactory?" Ben Mann asked. "Anything we can do to make you more comfortable?"

"Nothing I can think of. You seem to have a pleasant place here."

Mann told him that there would be a newspaper outside his door as soon as the first ferry arrived in the morning. The Talleyrand Room opened for breakfast at seven thirty and stayed open continuously until eleven at night, and there was room service during the same hours, "though sometimes in the winter if it's quiet, I let the staff go after nine o'clock. The bar's open in winter from noon to eleven, and you can buy liquor by the bottle for your room much cheaper than the per-drink price if you please."

"Not a bad idea," agreed Mort, who liked a nightcap. "Do you have any all-malt scotch?"

Mann, now more relaxed, laughed. "The islanders don't drink expensive liquor. The only demand for pure malt scotch is during the tourist season. But let me go out to the bar and see what I can find." In a minute or two he was back, proudly displaying a bottle in each hand. "All we've got, two full bottles of Glenfiddich," he said, "left over from last summer. Think these will do you?"

"I guess it depends on how long I'll be staying. Can you send one to my room and put it on my bill?" Mort did not ask how much it cost, but he mentally figured that he would be lucky if the price for a bottle was no more than thirty dollars.

"Sure," said Ben. "How about laundry? I have a woman come in every day at nine to pick it up."

Mort was fine for laundry, but thanked the hotel owner for his thoughtfulness. It was obvious that Mann's instincts as the hotel's host had overcome his initial aversion to his guest, but the question lingered in Mort's mind as to why the antagonism in the first place.

Mort had apparently not interrupted a conversation of any importance. Constable Gorges was doing some legwork for Sergeant Booth, who wanted him to check over the hotel register. Margaret Mann had just dropped in to invite Ben Mann to dinner Saturday night. She was considerably older than her brother-in-law but younger than

Constable Gorges, perhaps between forty and forty-five. She was tallish, thin, and pale, once attractive, now a bit severe in her looks, as if she had known her share of anguish. She had an air of studied friendliness, as if she were making demands on herself to try to like people.

"Do you get many visitors in winter?" Mort asked the hotel owner.

"A few salesmen," said Ben, "and an occasional tourist, usually the older type that likes to avoid the rush season. But since these senseless murders, we've been putting up more police officers and newspeople than anything else. They come and go. We just got a reporter from Boston today."

"Ken Fusetti. I came over on the ferry with him. Nice guy."

"They're all nice guys," said Ben, "until they write their stories. I can't forget the girl who started her news item with, 'Imagine a pretentious hotel from yesteryear with a yuppie owner . . . .'" He laughed.

Mort said, "I guess I ought to mention that I'm working with the police as a consultant."

"Yes, I know."

The coffee was good—strong, the way Mort liked it—the conversation had become interesting, and before Mort had a chance to digest what he was learning about Fogge Island, Constable Gorges was saying, "Ferry's in. Priscilla's probably at the office now if you want to see her."

Mort telephoned, and Sergeant Booth answered. She pronounced herself delighted that he had arrived and gave him directions on how to find her.

◆   ◆   ◆

As he walked down Sea Drive, Mort thought about the small island which was his temporary residence. Most of Fogge Island's population lived in Oldtown, the seaport and only business area. A few fishermen and farmers lived in isolated coves or in the middle of the island; the wealthy summer residents lived on the remote north side facing the open sea, as far from Oldtown as they could get. The luxurious resort hotels, also on the north side, provided accommodations for guests between Memorial Day and Labor Day, but for all other purposes Fogge Island and Oldtown were almost synonymous.

Oldtown was stretched in a crescent between two points of scrub-pine-covered high rocks. The crescent was formed by a fairly deep and well-sheltered harbor with a breakwater and pier at the higher west promontory and a rather large house with outbuildings at the lower east point. In the harbor below the house was another breakwater. That large house, Mort remembered, was the mansion of Senator Atherton Gorges. Things were coming back to him now. The main street, Sea Drive, ran along the shore from the pier at one end to the gateway of the Gorges mansion at the other, open to the sea on one side and lined with tightly packed houses, stores, and other buildings on the land side. The continuity of Sea Drive was broken only in the middle where a triangle containing a steepled, white wooden church, originally Congregational and now Unitarian, was isolated by two small streets that met behind the triangle and continued as a single street perpendicular to the crescent. Each end of Sea Drive terminated in another perpendicular street running back in the direction of the center of the island.

The Mann Hotel stood at the west end where Sea Drive turned inland to join Wentworth Street, and the hotel's entrance faced the gray-patinated wooden pier, where the ferry was starting to whistle for its return journey. Beyond the pier, brightly painted lobster buoys were bouncing haphazardly on the swells, and little whitecaps crested the blackish green waves. The sky was overcast and the weather still damp. Since Constable Gorges's office was at the opposite end of town, where Sea Drive met Gilman Street kitty-corner from the cast iron, filigreed gateway of Senator Gorges's driveway, Mort had to walk the entire length of the main thoroughfare. This was fortunate since he would be seeing almost the whole town. The three streets pointing inland, he remembered, just continued for a block or two before the houses became more and more sparsely laid out, and then the macadam streets turned into dirt roads with an occasional house every quarter mile or so. If Oldtown was Fogge Island, so was Sea Drive Oldtown.

He strolled past a variety store, a bar called the "Admiral's Arms," a drugstore, a grocery store, and several other small buildings until he came to the west tine of the Center Street fork. He crossed the street and continued walking past the church until he had crossed the east tine. Then he hesitated. The story-and-a-half, grayish clapboard building in front of him had a plaque of tarnished brass nailed at eye level beside the center double door; on it were engraved the words "Fogge Island Genealogical Society." In smaller letters at the bottom he read, "This building donated by Captain Bildad Gorges, 1911." Another less impressive painted sign gave the open days and hours, Tuesday through Saturday, 8:00 a.m. to 5:00 p.m. Yes, he remembered it now, and he was tempted to go and ask if Deborah Samson was still there, and if so, to say hello. But he did not want to keep Sergeant Booth waiting.

An occasional car cruised slowly past Mort as he continued walking. Overhead, greedy gulls made gurgling noises as they hungrily searched the sea. Sea Drive was a wide, one-way street with traffic from west to east and diagonal parking for cars on the store side. Both sides had sidewalks, and the sea side was buttressed from the waves by a low wall. Mort could imagine how busy with people the street would be in summer. He walked past more small buildings, including an electrical appliance store, a small book and greeting card shop, and a part-time branch office of the Bay City Bank. The next-to-last building on Sea Drive was Meg's Muffin Shoppe, and beyond it, with its entrance around the corner, was the feed store, which rented out one of its back rooms, with a window on Sea Drive, to the police as an office for Constable Nehemiah Gorges. Sergeant Booth caught sight of Mort from inside as he walked by and she rushed out to meet him.

As she neared him with outstretched hand, his first impression was: Maybe not a raving beauty, but damned attractive!

"I'm Priscilla Booth," she said with a smile. "And you're Mortimer Sinclair. I'd recognize you anywhere. I've read almost all your articles and books, and I attended your lectures on medieval genealogy at the San Francisco conference. In fact, you won't remember it, but you autographed a book for me in San Francisco. Care for some coffee? Let's go in here." She paused; and then, as if he were not responding fast enough, she put her arm through his and led him in the direction of Meg's Muffin Shoppe.

The cafe was long and narrow and filled with tray-size tables for two that actually had four chairs around them. Since this was not the tourist season, Mort was surprised to find most of the tables were occupied. The cafe must have had the standing of a local institution, the kind of place to Oldtown that Florian's was to Venice, Zonar's to Athens, or Sanborn's to Mexico City. Three waitresses were scurrying back and forth, almost running, to keep up with all the orders, and it appeared that almost everyone was having the same thing, some kind of muffin or scone.

"You must try their crumpets dripping with melted butter, real butter," Priscilla advised. A waitress appeared and Priscilla ordered, "Two crumpets and two coffees." Turning to Mort, she apologized, "You didn't mind? Am I talking too fast? I've always wanted to have the chance to sit and talk with you. I don't mean to be forward, but do you know you have the most beautiful blue eyes?"

To which Mort said, "You're a genealogist?"

"Amateur. As who isn't around here? Especially on the island. Not that I'm from the island. My family is in Fallway, north of Bay City." She hesitated, then said, "I don't usually talk so much or so fast. I don't mean any harm. I guess I just feel as if I know you."

"I am delighted at such a propitious beginning," Mort said. He thought of what the reporter Ken Fusetti had said about her coldness. If that's what they call a heart of ice, it would be awesome to run into someone they call passionate. "I understand you are responsible for me being here. How can I help?"

Priscilla sipped her coffee, keeping her eyes on his. She lifted a forefinger to her chin, as if thinking of where to start the story. After ascertaining that he knew almost no details about the case, she went back and related them from the beginning.

"After I was assigned to the case, I made a couple of lucky discoveries," she said. "At least, Lieutenant Bumpus thought they were important. I sensed a genealogical angle, and that's where you come in. Frankly, I wanted to get the best genealogical consultant in the country, and for once Lieutenant Bumpus paid attention to me.

"The biggest puzzle was the fact that victims one and three were so closely related, first cousins living under the same roof—and victim two seemed to have no significant connection at all with them. How did Cobber Palgrave fit into the picture? It didn't seem realistic to think of the three murders as having no pattern. So I began concentrating more on the seemingly meaningless murder of Cobber Palgrave six months earlier.

"I got the clue one day when I was talking to Deborah Samson at FIGS. I said, 'This island seems to be full of secrets,' and Deborah said, 'This island has more secrets than people.' I asked her, what Cobber Palgrave's secret was. Deborah always seems reluctant to answer direct questions like that, but in fact she's a regular one-woman gossip exchange. People from the island and many of the regular mainland visitors come to the library as much to talk to her as to do research. They give her some tit of information, and she repays them with some tat which she heard from an earlier visitor. So I just encouraged her to talk, and she just rambled on covering a number of topics. But whenever I could get her to talk about Cobber, she seemed to be implying that he might not have been as much a stranger to the island when he arrived as he'd made out. She didn't say anything more at the time, but that was enough of a clue for a start."

"So you started doing some genealogical research," said Mort.

"I started with a hypothesis: Cobber Palgrave was not a stranger but belonged to some island family. I then made a few rough charts to see which family he might fit into. It was a lot of work. For the more recent decades, I could use the transcribed Bay City vital records registers, but all the older Fogge Island records before the incorporation in 1946 are stored in boxes in the basement of the city hall in Bay City. I sifted through every birth, death, and marriage record for Fogge Island going back to 1920. There was nothing there directly relating to Cobber, but some of the people born on the island naturally left, either going over to live on the mainland or moving to faraway parts. With some help from Deborah Samson and Margaret Mann, I was able to piece together my charts so that I had what I thought was a reasonably complete record of any family that Cobber might belong to. I wanted to identify especially those female family members who had left the island and perhaps married a Palgrave. The interesting one was Penelope Gorges, the daughter of Marmaduke Gorges."

"Excuse me," Mort said. "Without having your charts in front of me, it is difficult to keep track of all these Gorgeses."

Priscilla took a napkin and began writing names and drawing lines. "You know Atherton Gorges?—he's sort of the patriarch of the island."

Mort nodded agreement.

"Well, he's the son of Ferdinand Gorges, who in turn was the oldest son of the senior Bildad Gorges. Bildad, incidentally, was the one who established FIGS and set up the trust fund which keeps it going. Well, anyway, Marmaduke Gorges was the second son of Bildad Gorges, just as Charles Gorges was the third son. Now, the oldest brother Ferdinand had—among other children—Atherton; the middle brother Marmaduke had Penelope Gorges; and the youngest brother Charles had Nehemiah Gorges, the constable. Thus Atherton, Penelope, and Nehemiah were all first cousins to each other. Nehemiah is a bachelor, and Atherton had two children—Ferdinand, who was murdered, and Lettice. Am I getting you confused?"

"Just a bit. It's all very interesting, but I take it the most important thing right now is what happened to Penelope Gorges, Atherton's cousin." Mort knew he was not being dense. Anyone, no matter how experienced, would find it difficult to keep track of genealogical relationships when exposed the first time to discussion of a large family. A written guide was virtually a necessity, and he resolved to start preparing some charts as soon as possible.

"Penelope left the island when she was young and just disappeared," Priscilla said. "After I zeroed in on her, I went back to Deborah and asked her specifically if she knew what happened to Penelope. Deborah did not know for sure, but she told me that she had heard Penelope moved to the Connecticut River Valley and was living in one of the big cities there. And Deborah thought she had heard something about Penelope marrying a man named Palgrave. That was why she was suspicious about Cobber when he arrived. Well, of course, the Connecticut River Valley means somewhere in Vermont, New Hampshire, Massachusetts, or Connecticut, and there aren't many big cities in the valley. I started with Springfield, Massachusetts, and checked various records for Springfield and Hampden

County. Sure enough, there was a marriage record in Longmeadow for Penelope Gorges and Jacob Palgrave.

"Then I checked the birth records and learned that three months after they were married they had a son, but unfortunately they hadn't named him yet and he was just listed as "baby boy" in the records. Then I checked death records and learned that Penelope Palgrave died shortly after she had the baby boy. Jacob Palgrave must have raised his son by himself. At least, there was no record of a remarriage. Jacob died six years ago. So I checked the Hampden County probate records, and there it was. Jacob Palgrave in his will left everything he had— perhaps several thousand dollars—to his son Jacob Bradstreet Palgrave, Jr. *Quod erat demonstrandum.*"

"Very good. Very good, indeed! So this Cobber Palgrave, rather than being a stranger to the island and unconnected to the other victims, was actually a member of the Gorges family himself. The first and third victims were first cousins to each other, and the second victim, Cobber, was a second cousin to them. I suppose Lieutenant Bumpus was pleased."

"I thought he was going to kiss me," Priscilla said with a smile. "I was convinced then that there was some genealogical motive behind the murders, and after a few days I suggested to him that we retain a good genealogical consultant. Having you in mind, of course."

"And he went along with the idea."

"Not at first. But let me tell you my next discovery. I was curious about how Cobber managed to buy his so-called beach house. As dilapidated as the shack is, the land alone is worth much more than he must have received from his father's will. So I went to the Registry of Deeds and checked land records. Cobber paid five thousand dollars cash and took out a balloon mortgage for another ten thousand. That mortgage was due in full just a few months before Cobber was murdered. Cobber would not have had the money himself, but someone paid off the mortgage for him."

"I wouldn't dare to guess, but I imagine it turned out to be someone no one would think of, someone strange."

"Strange? Weird!" she said. "Esther Gorges paid off the mortgage, or rather she bought the house from Cobber and paid off the mortgage as part of the deal. And the weirdest thing is that she took out the new deed as a joint tenancy with right of survivorship for herself and Cobber's wife, Lucy. Now doesn't that open up a can of questions?"

"You mean that the third murder victim paid the mortgage for the second murder victim and put the house in the joint names of herself and the second victim's wife?"

"Exactly. Of course, there had only been one victim up to the time the mortgage was paid off. It was when I reported this additional information to Lieutenant Bumpus that he agreed to my request for a genealogical consultant. But you see what this means?—now we have both genealogical and business connections between all the victims. And we also have someone gaining from Esther's death. Lucy Palgrave gained a house."

"You must have questioned Lucy."

"Oh, yes, I've questioned Lucy. I couldn't count all the times I questioned Lucy." Priscilla turned her hands palms up. "Lucy claims she didn't even know the house was in her name. She thought at the time she was signing some papers to help Cobber keep the house. Lucy looks for all the world like a girl who couldn't possibly hide information from anybody, but I'm convinced she was lying about something—just as I'm convinced that she was afraid of something. It was a second marriage for both her and Cobber, you know. His first wife left him and ran off with some other man. They fled from the island and have not been seen since. Lucy's first husband was sent to the state penitentiary for drug pushing and was knifed to death there. Lucy was probably relieved, since word has it that he used to beat up on her horribly. Lucy was thus legally capable of marrying Cobber, though it's not certain that Cobber's first wife took the trouble to get a divorce. So possibly Cobber was a bigamist. Lucy appears to be the innocent in this, but she's not telling all she knows."

"And Lucy was a temporary maid at the reception when Ferdinand was killed. Any connection there?"

"Nothing apparent."

"Tell me, is Lucy related to the Gorges family?"

"Perhaps very distantly," Priscilla said. "Scratch deeply enough and you'll find that everyone on this island is related to everyone else. But I don't know of any close connection. Lucy was a Samson before she married and thus much more closely related to Deborah Samson and Margaret Mann, whose maiden name was Samson."

"But you suspect some inheritance motivation for the crime?"

"Did you ever see the Alex Guinness movie *Kind Hearts and Coronets?* The one where the eighth or tenth heir down the line to a title killed off all the heirs with higher precedence until only he was left to inherit?"

"I saw it on late re-runs. Just for the record, whose inheritance are we talking about?"

"Well, the richest man on the island by far is Senator Atherton Gorges. The important point to my mind is that each of the three murder victims was a potential heir to Senator Gorges—depending, of course, on his will if he made one, or on the state laws of inheritance if he did not, or possibly on some combination of the two, such as if the heir in his will predeceased him."

"And if Atherton Gorges should die now?"

"Since his son Ferdinand is already dead, Atherton's daughter Lettice would be his main heir."

The waitress refilled their coffee cups, and they were quiet for a while. Time passed idly. Mort found himself intrigued not only with the case but also with the detective/amateur genealogist sitting across from him who was so vivacious and charming. After the death of his wife he had resolved never to get seriously involved again. And although there had been a number of entanglements over the years—a very sad one recently—he certainly was not going to allow himself to get involved with a pretty policewoman who was almost young enough to be his daughter, no matter how interesting and obviously intelligent. Still it was pleasant being with her, and Mort was glad the assignment was turning out the way it was. He was not superstitious, but he thoroughly believed that enterprises that start out in the right key almost always come to the happiest conclusions.

"The name Booth . . . ," he said. "Is that one of the old-time names in this area?"

Priscilla laughed, "You'd never guess that it was originally Brewster, but one of my ancestors lisped, and a court clerk couldn't spell, and it's been Booth ever since."

"Sounds reasonable. Sort of like De La Noye becoming Delano."

"Sort of."

"And if anything happens to Lettice Gorges, who would be Atherton's heir?"

"His nephew, Dudley Gorges. And if anything happened to Dudley? I'm not sure. Constable Nehemiah Gorges might figure into it, but inheritance usually goes down, not up. I don't think Nehemiah is a likely suspect. I guess the really intriguing thing is that there are so many contingencies as long as the person holding the fortune is still alive. By selectively killing off other potential heirs in the right sequence, the killer could direct the heirship almost any way he or she wanted. Suppose, for example, both of Atherton's main heirs predeceased him and he left his entire estate to his wife, Martha. Then, if Martha died, her heirs would be one set of people. On the other hand, if Martha predeceased Atherton, and if Atherton left the bulk of his estate to his nephew Dudley Gorges, and then Dudley died, his heirs would be a completely different set."

"And what is my role? What do you want me to do?"

"For starters," she said, "I'd like you to come to a party with me tonight." Seeing his expression, she explained, "Well, it's really a reception. At FIGS. A lot of the people whose names have been mentioned in connection with the case will be there, and I think you ought to meet them. You see, FIGS could not possibly exist on members' dues alone, even though they have some members all over the country. Basically it's supported by the income from a trust fund supplemented by generous contributions from a few rich island families, especially Atherton Gorges. The sponsoring families like to get a social occasion out of it, and so several times a year there is a large reception at FIGS. Seven o'clock. Will you be there?"

"Of course. I certainly have nothing better to do. But I assume you expect more work from me than just attending a reception."

"Certainly. You know my views on the case. I want to follow up on this inheritance angle as much as possible. But it's tricky. Not only because there are so many people with varying degrees of relationship but also because state law gets awfully complicated after the most obvious relatives are no longer available. You have a law degree. I'd appreciate it if you could both research the laws of inheritance and compile some detailed charts of all the family relationships of the people involved. In fact, I can start you off with the rough charts I made, and you can do some research at FIGS to make them more complete."

"Excellent. Let me study the family genealogies first. You're right about how tricky inheritance can be. Are you acquainted with Berkeley Castle in England?"

"I visited it during a tour to England two years ago, but can't say I know much about it."

"When one owner died without issue in 1916, the castle went to a second cousin once removed. But when that owner died in 1942 without issue, the castle went to Robert John Grantley Berkeley, who was about a fourteenth cousin to the last owner."

"Fourteenth cousin! You can't get much more remote than that."

He smiled, and finished drinking his coffee. "How sure are you that the motivation for the murders involves genealogy?"

Priscilla was pensive. "I'm not really sure of anything, Mort. Do you mind if I call you Mort? Please call me Priscilla. I'm just following a hunch on the one hand, and, on the other, I've nothing else to go on. But I'm glad to have you on the case with me. It's been lonely." She paused. "At the department, they're saying that if the case doesn't get solved soon, public opinion will demand a scapegoat, and you can guess who that's going to be."

Four

"**I** SUPPOSE YOU HAVE HEARD, MARgaret, that *the* Mortimer Sinclair is on the island." Deborah Samson sat at the desk in the FIGS library, while her assistant used a feather brush to dust the furniture lightly. "Did you hear me, Margaret? I was speaking to you."

"I'm sorry, dear," Margaret Mann said. "What were you saying?"

"I was saying that Mort Sinclair is on the island. I heard the police have hired him as a consultant in the murder case. I must say I cannot imagine why. It is like carrying coals to Newcastle, if you ask me." Deborah's nose sniffled into a slight wrinkle. She sat regally upright, her face in her sixty-first year full of large features depicting character more than beauty. A long, curved, hard, white scar began on her forehead, jumped past the opening of her left eye to run down the pouch of her cheek, and continued across the corner of her lip.

"Oh, yes," said Margaret, "I met him over at the hotel. He seemed nice enough."

"Oh, you did, did you?" Deborah said through her nose.

"I also was wondering why they need to import a genealogist," continued Margaret, quick to catch the implication of her companion's changed tone. "Dr. Sinclair might be one of the foremost genealogists in the country, but if the police need a genealogist to help them, I would think they'd look at home. Certainly no one has your knowledge of island families, Deborah, dear."

"Are you implying, Margaret, dear, that I am not one of the foremost genealogists in the country?" Deborah's voice rose a few decibels, her nose poked up in the air, and her lower lip jutted out like a ship's prow.

"Nothing of the kind, Deborah. It's just his reputation, well, you know, I . . . ." She searched for the right words, but they were not forthcoming. "Now, don't take me wrong. You know very well what I meant. Of course you're one of the foremost genealogists in the country. Everyone knows that. The police were . . . insulting."

"Well, it is all thanks to that Booth girl. She travels all over the country going to genealogical conferences and gets her head full of fancy ideas. It is this younger generation. They have no respect for the talent right next door. As for Mr. Sinclair, or Dr. Sinclair, or whatever he calls himself, he is highly overrated in the genealogical community." Deborah opened a book and closed the conversation.

Margaret went on with her dusting. She had removed the rope barrier and was out of sight in the wraparound rear section when she heard Deborah calling. "Yes, Deborah?" she called back from around the corner.

"I have an appointment at the hairdresser, and then I think I will go home for a little rest before tonight's activities. Will you keep your eye on the library in case of visitors? I know in winter it is all local folk, but even they have had horse thieves in their backgrounds. And Lucy Palgrave is due before five to help the caterer. Do instruct her to put the less expensive food out first so as to conserve the other— I mean, with the price of crabmeat! Benjamin Mann will be supplying the wine from the hotel, but we will use our own glasses. You might set them out." By this time Deborah, having reached the hallway door, stuck her head back in the library one more time to see that Margaret was coming. Satisfied, she got her coat and left.

◆   ◆   ◆

Mort passed her as he approached the building. She paid him scant attention, but he paused and glanced at her to confirm his feeling that he knew the face. Deborah walked briskly by, oblivious to him or anyone else on the street. The sun was already sinking, and it was getting colder. He went in and hung his coat on a hallway hook. At first there seemed to be no one there. Then he heard footsteps from the rear, and suddenly a woman appeared from around the corner. Still thinking of Deborah, Mort paid little attention to the features of the thin, middle-aged woman who approached him.

"Well, Dr. Sinclair . . . ," the woman said, "I'm afraid Deborah, Miss Samson, isn't here. She just left. I'm so sorry. Might I help you?"

He was a little surprised at being so readily recognized. The woman looked vaguely familiar. Had she been here during his earlier visit?

"I thought I might do a little browsing," he said hesitatingly.

Margaret laughed and said, "You don't recognize me, do you? We met just a short while ago in the hotel. I'm Margaret Mann, Ben's sister-in-law." She offered her hand again.

"I'm sorry," he said, chagrined. Known to be absent-minded, he often had occasion to say, "I never forget a name, but sometimes have difficulty in remembering faces." He apologized again, realized he was just making matters worse, took the proffered hand and shook it warmly. Again he said, "I thought I might browse a bit."

"Well, of course," said Margaret. "Let me orient you. The family histories are on that side in alphabetical order. Published vital records and other original sources are on those two walls in order of locality. Bound journals, censuses, and other sources are in this middle section. We also have some excellent probate and land records on microfilm in the hall."

Mort had turned to the first wall she had indicated. He did not have much time and really just wanted to reacquaint himself with the library's contents. "I'll just browse here with the family histories," he said.

"Of course. I'll try not to disturb you. But don't hesitate to ask me anything. We close at five." She went into the hallway and returned shortly with a tray full of wine glasses, which she carefully set down on the table near the center stacks.

It would be useful, Mort knew, to start with an overview of the genealogies of the island's main families, the Gorgeses, Delanos, Manns, Samsons, and perhaps a few others. He quickly located individual books on several of the families, together with some typescripts covering branches not found in the printed volumes, and took these to the closest table. They were all basically alike, either undocumented or sparsely documented; he would not expect them to be either complete or substantially free of error. They were typical secondary sources. Apparently no skilled genealogist had yet taken the trouble to compile a really definitive book on any of the principal families. With one exception, none of the printed volumes covered anything more recent than the nineteenth century, and of the typescripts only two of them, on the Gorges and Samson families, touched upon people that might be living now. Surely, there must be something more up to date on these families.

"I see you're interested in local families." Margaret Mann's voice came from behind his back. "Do you have ancestry on Fogge Island?"

"No, none of these is mine," Mort said. "Tell me, is there anything here more up to date on, say, the Gorges family, or the Mann family, or anything on the Crosbys, or some of the other island families? I would think that the main families on the island would have wanted more done on their own genealogies."

"Well, I'd be happy to tell you anything I can. I mean, I'm not the genealogist Deborah is, but, well, I'm not sure what to say. We don't meet such a distinguished genealogist everyday."

Mort hated to have people make a fuss over him. A total nonentity outside the genealogical and historical world, he was, among those who knew genealogical authorities, like a movie star or prominent politician. Just riding the elevator of a library, he might become aware of someone staring at him, and finally be asked if he wasn't Mortimer Sinclair; other times someone might stare and say, "Gee, you look familiar," and then, just as he prepared himself to be recognized, the person would say, "Are you the weatherman on Channel 5?" On the whole, Mort preferred not being recognized.

Somehow his question about up-to-date family histories never got answered to his full satisfaction. Margaret started to explain something about there being a tradition at the library not to make available information on recent generations of island families. The trustees, who from the beginning had considered such research a private matter, did not encourage what they called "prying." Then, sitting down across the table from him, Margaret led him from one subject to another. What was he doing here? Was it true that the police had hired him to solve the Gorges murder case? Hadn't he solved other murder cases in the past? Wasn't he just as much a detective as a genealogist? Had he ever been to Fogge Island before?

By a comparison of notes, they determined that his one previous visit had taken place before Margaret began working at FIGS. That was before her husband died. Mort learned all about her husband and her family. Margaret was of the Samson family, her parents having been Jonathan Samson and Mary Dingley. Yes, she was distantly related to Corporal Dingley, who was working with Sergeant Booth. Deborah Samson was also her distant cousin, being the daughter of Samuel Samson and Deborah Whitney. Lucy Palgrave was her second cousin.

Margaret had married Percival Mann, the brother of Benjamin Mann, who owned the Mann Hotel and was the president of FIGS. Percival had caught some form of flu during one of the epidemics and died some ten years ago. Later Margaret started working for FIGS as one of its two salaried employees. She had never really been interested in genealogy before, but after working closely with Deborah Samson for a number of years, she became addicted to it. She was even hoping to get an article published in the acme of genealogical journals, *The American Genealogist.*

Deborah was such a dear. She had been an ardent genealogist from early girlhood. She had never married, though Margaret had heard that Deborah was once engaged to Atherton Gorges. Margaret had spent many years off the island, first getting a university education and then working until she returned and married Percival. Deborah, whose father had been a well-known author, had never left the island in her entire life. Though she had not attended college, Deborah had received an outstanding education from her mother, who was reputed to be one of the most intelligent and well-read people on the island, and Deborah knew everything about everything. Everyone on the island sought her advice, and largely thanks to her presence FIGS was the social center of the island.

Deborah had just gone to the hairdresser because there was to be a reception in the library tonight. Was Mort coming? He was certainly welcome to come. Everyone would want to meet him. And Deborah spoke so highly of him. He was coming? How nice! He had made such an impression on Ben Mann at the hotel. Oh, he should know that the Talleyrand Room served excellent food. Good food was a long tradition at the hotel, a tradition that Ben Mann faithfully continued. In fact, during summer the guests at the fancy resort hotels frequently ate at the Mann Hotel because the cuisine was known to be the best on the island. Ben would be at the reception tonight. If Dr. Sinclair had any preference for food, he should mention it to Ben, for Ben would consider it an honor to see that such a distinguished genealogist was well taken care of.

Through the window behind the corner desk, Mort could see the approach of darkness. A street lamp highlighted dancing flakes of snow; a lone car trudged slowly past. The clock above the door read ten minutes past five. The front door opened, and an attractive blonde woman in a dark gray cloak rushed in, shook the snow off her shoulders and murmured, "Cold out there." She looked to be in her mid to late twenties, her face was pale and creamy smooth but with a permanent wrinkle in the center of her forehead.

"This is Dr. Sinclair, Lucy," Margaret said. "Dr. Sinclair, this is my cousin, Lucy Palgrave. She's helping with the reception tonight."

Lucy held her eyes down as she offered her hand and quietly said, "Pleased to meet you." When Mort gripped her hand she responded for a brief moment with an added surge of firmness in her own light grip, then quickly drew her hand back. "I better get started," she said.

Mort said goodbye to both women and returned to the hotel.

◆   ◆   ◆

When he returned to FIGS that evening, Priscilla Booth seemed to be waiting for him. She had positioned herself just in front of the double doors and could observe everyone who entered. At the moment Mort came in, she was in conversation with Benjamin Mann, who was dressed in dinner jacket and black tie. Mort had but two suits with him, brown and blue, and he wore the blue that night. A quick look at the other guests assured him that no male guest was wearing a tuxedo except Ben Mann and one other, whom he spotted inside the library with his back turned. Priscilla started to introduce Mort to Ben, but both men simultaneously informed her that they had already met.

Remembering that Ben was Margaret Mann's brother-in-law, Mort tried to understand the relationship. Margaret Mann was at least forty, and her husband, Percival Mann, had died at least ten years earlier, so Benjamin must still have been in his teens when Percival died. There must have been a big difference in age between Ben and his brother. Ben again seemed to be antagonistic toward Mort, or, at best, was being stiffly formal. Again he asked if Mort was comfortable at the hotel, and, as president of FIGS, informed Mort that the society was pleased to have him as a guest. He was aware that Mort had done a good bit of writing but seemed not to have read any of his articles or books. After a few minutes, Ben excused himself, leaving Mort alone with Priscilla.

"Fill me in," Mort asked her. "How does Benjamin Mann relate to the murder victims?"

Priscilla smiled. "You could have at least started out by saying how nice it was to see me again." She was wearing a royal blue and white pleated cocktail dress with a baby blue silk scarf around her neck. She had on a bit more makeup than he'd noticed earlier in the day.

She was, in any case, a lovely woman. "I'm sorry," he said. "It is a sheer delight to see you again." Though the tone of his voice was comically exaggerated, inwardly he found himself agreeing with his words.

"Good," she said. "Now that you've sung for your supper, I'll answer your question." She told him that Benjamin Mann was the nephew of Martha, the wife of Senator Atherton Gorges. Martha's maiden name was Mann, and she was the sister of Benjamin's late mother, Myra Mann. Thus Benjamin was a first cousin to Ferdinand Gorges but related only by marriage to Esther Gorges and of course even more distantly by marriage to Cobber Palgrave. When Ensign Mann died, the bulk of his estate consisted of the Mann Shipyard on the mainland and the Mann Hotel on the island. His two sons were minors at the time, though Percival was much older than Benjamin. The estate was put in trust until they reached their majority, with Percival getting the shipyard and Benjamin getting the hotel.

"Unfortunately for Percival," said Priscilla, "the shipyard was heavily in debt, and he obtained it just at the time when American shipyards were losing business to the Europeans and Japanese. About seven or eight years after he received his inheritance, he had to declare bankruptcy. Shortly after that he died, and the stress of the business losses may have contributed to his death. Benjamin, on the other hand, made a considerable success out of the hotel." She added, "I attended college with Ben, incidentally."

Mort found himself studying her face as she said the last words, wondering if there might be anything more than friendship between Priscilla and Benjamin.

"Is he married?"

"No," Priscilla said, dragging out the word. "No, he's not married yet. Well, I suppose I should be frank with you. He wants to marry me."

"Have you accepted him?" Mort asked, mentally pinching himself the moment the words were out. "I apologize. That's not exactly any of my business, is it?"

"Not exactly," said Priscilla, still smiling. "But I'll answer the question anyway. He's asked me twice, and I've refused twice."

"They say the third time is a charm," Mort commented dryly, precipitating another pinch. What inspired him to make that stupid remark? Why was he trying to draw her out more on her relationship with Benjamin Mann?

Priscilla reached to take him by the arm and turn him toward the door into the library room. "Let's go in and have you meet some people."

Though a few guests remained in the hallway, the library room was crowded with people, mostly on their feet in groups of two, three, or four, except for the corner opposite the doorway, where Deborah Samson sat at her desk and held court with eight or ten men and women standing in attendance. Mort recognized only Margaret Mann, who stood behind Deborah.

"Deborah," Priscilla called, as she made her way to the desk with Mort in tow, "I want you to meet my guest, Dr. Mortimer Sinclair."

All eyes turned toward Mort, who heard at least two or three under-the-breath murmurs indicating that his identity was known and his attendance anticipated.

"Oh, yes, thank you for bringing him, Priscilla, dear." Deborah Samson put forth her hand toward Mort palm down, as if expecting him to press it to his lips.

Mort reached to shake her hand gently.

"How very nice to see you again, Dr. Sinclair. You have not aged a day since we last met—when was that, ten, perhaps twelve years ago? I was telling Margaret just this afternoon that there is not a more experienced or accomplished genealogist in the country, and I, of course, am one of your most devoted fans. I still treasure the book you autographed for me during your previous visit."

Deborah's bluish-white hair was swept up and coiffured in a high Victorian mound, soft and silky but not a hair out of place. A cameo on a tight-fitting black silk band encircled her neck. Mort now remembered seeing the scar before, but Deborah wore it well, as if she were saying, "If I do not let it bother me, why should it bother you?" Someone had told Mort that the scar resulted from an accidental fall many years ago.

Her words cut through the air with bell-like pronunciation "We were just talking about the origin of families, Dr. Sinclair. Perhaps you can come to my assistance if I fail in one." Deborah turned her head to one side, "Get Dr. Sinclair a glass of wine, Margaret, and tell Lucy to bring over a tray of sandwiches." And, as an afterthought, "Including the crab canapés."

Deborah addressed herself to the group again. "Now, as I was saying, the first Crapo in this country—and it is always pronounced with a long *a*—was Peter Crapo, who came from France to New England in the late 1600s. The DeMaranvilles appear about a generation later. Louis DeMaranville was the progenitor. In fact, Louis DeMaranville married a daughter of Peter Crapo and Penelope White—Penelope, incidentally, was a *Mayflower* descendant. Of course, it was not until the nineteenth century that the first Crapo came to Fogge Island, and the only DeMaranville coming to live here was Marie DeMaranville, Lucy Palgrave's grandmother."

"How do you keep all these facts in your head, Miss Samson?" said an admirer from the circle around her.

She smiled and lowered her eyes for a moment before continuing. "Thus all Crapos and all DeMaranvilles are *Mayflower* descendants, for even though Peter Crapo had a second wife, Ann Luce, he had no children by her."

"As of course all Delanos are *Mayflower* descendants." A hoarse voice belonging to a man to Deborah's left broke into the conversation.

"There, there, Dr. Delano," Deborah said, "we like to think so, but unfortunately there has been no definitive study of all the early Delanos, and so we cannot say for sure. Of course, your own *Mayflower* credentials are indisputably authentic."

Mort turned to look at Dr. Thomas Delano—the man who, Priscilla had told him, pronounced Ferdinand Gorges dead. The doctor was short and husky, built like a wrestler with the face of a bulldog. He must have been near the end of middle age, but it was difficult to estimate his years with certainty; he had few wrinkles and his hair was still a dark reddish brown, yet his eyes looked older than the rest of his features. His suit was rumpled, his hair had tufts going in all directions, and his shoes looked as though they had not encountered polish for years. Clearly he was not the sort of man who subscribed to *Gentlemen's Quarterly.*

"There's the *Delano Genealogy*," the doctor said with a snort.

"And there are fairy tales by Hans Christian Anderson," Deborah Samson said. "But I said definitive study."

"Are you calling the *Delano Genealogy* by Major Joel Delano a fairy tale?"

"No, no, Dr. Delano. No need to get so belligerent." Deborah patted the air with her hand in a slow downward motion. "The *Delano Genealogy* is invaluable for clues, just like Savage, Pope,

Davis, and so many others, but they are not adequately documented and can be taken for no more than starting points. There is significant error in all these books, as you should very well know."

"Why should I know? I'm a doctor, not a genealogist."

"Now, now, what is Dr. Sinclair going to think of us? All this distasteful bickering."

Delano turned to Mort. "Is that doctor as in M.D. or doctor as in Ph.D.?" His breath smelled of alcohol.

Skipping over his Ph.D., Mort said, "That is doctor as in Juris Doctor."

"I thought you were a Ph.D.," said Deborah.

"Well," Mort said, "I am that, too, but I thought I would keep it quiet, since Dr. Delano evidently thinks it is a dirty word."

"No, no," said Dr. Delano, waving his hand in the air. "I don't mean to be rude. I was just talking through my hat. I'd better go home and get some sleep."

Priscilla took advantage of the lull to introduce Mort to the others around the circle. With one exception, the names meant little to him. But the slender woman standing quietly beside him, he learned, was Martha Gorges, wife of the Senator. She was rather pale, and her features were small and delicate. She smiled when they were introduced, but before and after she looked sad and distant. But then, thought Mort, her son was murdered a year ago, followed by her niece now. How could she be expected to act?

Martha did not seem interested in participating in a conversation, but with an effort she said, "We speak of definitive books. I suppose your investigation of these horrible murders will be definitive, too. I suppose you'll have to rake up all kinds of muck."

"Genealogists are not muckrakers."

"Aren't they?" Her expression clearly said that she knew better.

Mort began explaining his role with the police, but Martha had stopped listening, as if neither he nor she were there any longer.

Though Priscilla tried to introduce him to as many people as she could, it was impossible to cover the whole room. One person he particularly wanted to meet was fortunately standing by himself across the room. Senator Atherton Gorges, the other man wearing a tuxedo, had his back to the bookcases and was paging through a thin volume. Mort told Priscilla he would like to meet the Senator. She took his arm again and led him to the other side of the room. After introducing them, Priscilla tactfully excused herself and walked away.

"A pity there was no one on the ferry to introduce us," the Senator said. "A bit of awkwardness, no?"

They shook hands, Senator Gorges exerting a very precise amount of pressure. He seemed older up close; Mort could see that at a distance the man's tanned lean face would take years off his appearance.

Mort looked at the clock above the door and noted that it was a few minutes after nine. Priscilla was at the far end of the room now in deep conversation with two people Mort did not recognize. Lucy came by with a tray of *pâté de choux* canapés stuffed with shrimp salad. Mort took two, but Gorges just waved her away.

The Senator seemed interested in genealogy, and he commented on some of the books in the shelves, pointing out one as good, another as fair, and another as riddled with error. Mort found that he generally agreed with Gorges's opinions, and when he disagreed he kept it to himself. Atherton Gorges seemed to have something on his mind but to be awaiting some other moment to bring it up.

The room was rapidly emptying. Priscilla came by and said, "Since we're staying at the same hotel, I'll let you walk me home." Again she took his arm. Turning to Senator Gorges, she said, "It's late, Senator. I hope you don't mind our leaving."

"I have to go myself," he said. Gorges followed them into the hallway and stood behind Mort as he reclaimed his coat from the wall hook.

Mort helped Priscilla with her coat and walked her to the outer doors. Just as he was opening the door on the right, Senator Gorges called from behind them. "By the way, Sinclair, I'd like to have a talk with you. Could you be at my house tomorrow morning, say around ten?"

Mort looked to Priscilla to see if she had anything planned for him at that time. She nodded her approval. "Right," he called back over his shoulder. "I'll be there at ten sharp."

Five

THE AIR WAS BRACINGLY COLD BUT NO longer damp, and the snow had stopped, leaving just a few traces in patches here and there. Streetlights illuminated the fronts of stores and houses so that their lines looked like artistically contrived stripes of gold. Mort and Priscilla crossed in front of the church and continued toward the hotel. Low in the sky, a full moon illuminated the breakwater behind the ferry landing; beyond the breakwater they could make out the dark shapes of huge rocks lurking over shining cascades of moonlit, rippling sea surface.

"It's funny," said Mort. "I never noticed those rocks during the day."

"They've seen many a shipwreck." Priscilla responded. "There's an entire line of them both above water and just below the surface all the way from here to a point north of Bay City. Nowadays there's a well-marked channel, but in the old days a considerable number of ships thought they could find a safe passage only to crash violently on the rocks."

"Sunken treasure?"

"There's supposed to be," Priscilla said, "but I think most of the wrecks that have been found yielded nothing of value except for souvenirs and a few museum curiosities. In colonial times, a ship carrying gold coins sunk somewhere in this general area, possibly on those rocks, possibly not. It's never been found, but one of the favorite summer sports on the island is to go scuba diving and look for any sign of shipwrecks. I've done it myself, not that I've ever had any luck. But Ben Mann once found a heavily encrusted sword right beyond that huge rock over there. The museum told him it was from the seventeenth century, so you can imagine how that spurred people on."

"No results?"

"No. And that was five years ago. The area's been pretty well scoured by divers by now."

They took their time as they continued walking. "We'll be going past the Admiral's Arms—it's the only place likely to be open at this late hour of nine twenty-five, since Ben said the Talleyrand Room would close early tonight. If you don't have anything better to do, I'll take you in and buy you a beer."

"When I was a young man, it was the boy who bought the girl a drink."

"You're not a young man anymore."

"Yes," he said softly, "I guess I'm not."

"I didn't mean it like that. I only meant that times change. Would you prefer to buy me a beer?"

"Hell, no," he said. "I might as well get something out of these changing times."

The pub was identified by a brightly lit neon sign. Its interior was long and narrow, lined with booths on the left, tables in the middle, and a bar further down on the right. The walls were covered with various nautical trappings, some obviously genuine and others more like instant-atmosphere accouterments. Looking around, Mort recognized a few faces from the reception, but most of them he had never seen before. The pub was less than a quarter full.

A barrel-chested young man standing inside the entrance in front of a large, glowing fireplace greeted Priscilla warmly. "Well, if it ain't the prettiest detective on Fogge Island."

Priscilla introduced Mort to Delano Delano, the owner of the Admiral's Arms.

"Pleased to meet you," said Delano in a loud jovial voice. "You a detective too?"

"No. I'm a genealogist."

"You don't say," he said, shrugging his shoulders. "Since this is your first visit, you be sure to tell the waitress that Del Delano said the first drink is on the house. You remember that, now."

They chose a table near the fireplace and sat down. "Seems to be a shortage of names in this place," Mort said.

"Delano Delano is a second cousin to Dr. Thomas Delano," Priscilla said, "though I understand they're not exactly on good terms."

Mort wondered if he was using his imagination too freely, for he thought he could see not only a family resemblance in the huge faces of the two Delano second cousins but perhaps a feature or two in common with Franklin Delano Roosevelt. They would all be descendants of the original seventeenth-century immigrant Philip Delano, but it seemed fantastic that the resemblance should be so strong in cousins as distant as the Fogge Island Delanos must have been to the family of President Roosevelt's mother, Sara Delano.

The waitress who came to take their order greeted Priscilla with polite familiarity, and Priscilla called her "Tina." Tina, an attractive woman of about thirty, hummed a happy little tune as she waited patiently.

"Sam Adams," ordered Priscilla, and Mort decided he'd have a Sam Adams, too. "It's nice to have an alternative to the . . . , what shall I call it?" she asked. "I know what my father calls it, but I don't use that kind of language. I'll just say to the insipidly foul liquid that the big breweries try to foist on us."

"Your father is a man after my own heart," said Mort. "If it is not made with one hundred percent barley malt, it is not beer as far as I am concerned. None of their 'adjuncts' for me."

"That's why they have to serve big brewery beer icy cold, so it will freeze your taste buds and you won't know how disgusting it tastes. The beer for people who can't stand beer."

"Agreed, but I am surprised we have the same taste. I thought your generation went in for lightness. I thought you people were afraid of flavor."

"I'm not a slave to my generation, but I take from it whatever I think is good," Priscilla said. The flame from the fire highlighted the dark red of her hair, and the dimples in her cheeks flashed as she laughed. "And I'm not concerned about gaining weight. A policewoman's job is not light work." Tapping her fingers on the table, she said, "Do you like classical music? I do hope you like classical music."

"As a matter of fact, I do. But why?"

"You seem to be the type. I would have been disappointed if you didn't." She straightened up in her chair, looked at him intently, then said, "Speak to me in classical music!"

"Speak to you in classical music?" He paused to wonder how, then began slowly. "Your eyes are dancing, like the first movement of Mendelssohn's *Italian Symphony.* Your hair is many-hued and exotic, like something out of Rimsky-Korsakov or Khatchaturian. You are as fresh, charming, and sparkling as a serenade by Mozart, as catchy as, say, *Eine kleine Nachtmusik.* But you also have deep strength of character, along the lines of Brahms's *Violin Concerto* or Beethoven's *Seventh Symphony.* You are as pure as Turandot, as celestial as Aida, and as schoolgirlish as Yum Yum. And best of all . . . . " He hesitated, and the seconds went by.

"Yes," she said, leaning her elbow on the table and her chin on her open palm. "Yes, yes, go on."

Mort grinned. "You are as tenacious as Katesha, as demanding as the mistress of Venusberg, and as evil-intentioned as the black swan from *Swan Lake.*"

"You spiteful thing—you didn't mean any of it!"

"My turn," Mort said. "I'll bet you like BBC television."

"As a matter of fact, I do. But why?"

"Because it just seems to fit you. I would have been disappointed if you didn't. Speak to me in BBC television!"

"I thought I was in control of this conversation," she said. "As Mr. Reagan said in New Hampshire, 'I'm paying for this beer.'"

"I thought it was a microphone. Anyway, do as you are told or I'll pay for the beer after all."

"All right, I'll play. You're as arrogant as Ross Poldark, as tactless as Basil Fawlty, as vacillating as Phineas Finn, and as merciless as Caligula, and as you get older you will probably get as fat as Hercule Poirot and as wrinkled as the porter on The *Duchess of Duke Street.*

There!"

They laughed, ordered another beer, and ate the roasted pumpkin seeds served gratis with the drinks. It had been a long day, and they were both tired.

"You seem to know a lot of these people," Mort said.

"If you'd been using the FIGS library as many years as I have, you'd know quite a few of them too. Of course, most of the ones I know are people into genealogy or who otherwise have something to do with the library."

"Plus a few others such as Ferdinand Gorges and Benjamin Mann."

"Yes. I knew some of the people on the island before I got interested in genealogy. I went to college with both Ferdie and Ben. I owe Ben a great favor." She was silent, and since it was apparent to Mort that she was not going to say anything more, he changed the subject again.

"Tell me, do you have any suspects at all in this case?"

"If you turn your head a little to the left," Priscilla said, "you'll see a couple sitting at the table directly in line with the end of the bar. The man is about forty-five, slim, with a moustache, and the woman is somewhat older, has dirty blond hair, and is still attractive."

Mort eased his head casually to his left and immediately recognized the couple Priscilla had described. They had also been at the FIGS reception, though Mort had not met them. They were talking in hushed tones, and neither looked very happy.

"They are Sylvester and Sylvia Mann," Priscilla said, "and they've got quite an interesting history. He's a lawyer with offices both on the island and in Bay City. Incidentally, he's one of several lawyers retained by Atherton Gorges. Sylvester and Sylvia have only been married for a year or so, though both are Fogge Island natives. Sylvester's first wife divorced him about three years ago, and it looked for a while as if he were going to marry Esther Gorges. They were engaged, even though he was considerably older than she, but all of a sudden Esther called it off.

"Sylvia was Dr. Thomas Delano's nurse when she was very young. She was ambitious and left the island years and years ago to take a job at Boston General Hospital, where I understand she became a nursing supervisor and married a wealthy doctor. Her husband died four years ago, and she returned to the island as a rich widow . . . . It's funny how cruel island people can be. When you leave the island for a long period, they seem to feel that you've turned your back on them, and they never fully accept you again. When Sylvia came back, it was as if she were a perfect stranger. Most people were stiffly polite to her but not really friendly. This was around the time that Sylvester Mann's wife divorced him and he became engaged to Esther.

"Island gossip has it that Cobber Palgrave had something to do with Esther breaking off the engagement. Cobber, as you may have gathered, had no visible means of support, yet he somehow managed always to have enough money to keep himself in alcohol. He'd beg wherever he could, and I suspect he may have stolen some things, too. He also engaged in a little blackmail here and there. Apparently Sylvester sent a letter to his ex-wife, who was living on the west coast, telling her that he still loved her but he was going to marry Esther in the hopes that Atherton Gorges would leave at least some of his industrial complex to him—as both his lawyer and nephew-in-law—instead of leaving everything to Ferdinand, who had shown himself to be completely incompetent. The ex-wife had been chummy with Cobber and for some reason or other sent him the letter she received from Sylvester. Island gossip has it that Cobber first tried to get money from Sylvester in return for not showing the letter to Esther, but Sylvester refused to let himself be blackmailed. Then Cobber must have turned over the letter to Esther, because it was around this time that she broke off her engagement to Sylvester. Needless to say, there was no love lost between Sylvester and Cobber.

"In the meantime, Sylvia was feeling quite lonely, and she started dating several men, at least two. One of them was Delano Delano, the pub owner, even though he was many years younger than she."

Mort turned to look at the burly young man now standing behind the bar.

"Something happened there. Then she decided she wanted to marry Sylvester Mann. I understand her former boss, Dr. Delano, aided her in her plans, for he invited both Sylvia and Sylvester to spend an evening with him at his vacation cabin on the other side of the island and then conveniently left to attend a patient, taking his wife with him and leaving Sylvester and Sylvia alone for the night. Human nature being what it is, and Sylvia having a considerable fortune, it's not surprising that she and Sylvester got married. Sylvester is greedy and has expensive tastes, but it was only after he married Sylvia that he was able to live on a scale that he considered suitable for himself.

"Can you think of any reason why Sylvester might have wanted to murder Ferdinand Gorges?" Mort said.

"No," Priscilla said, "but he is the person Ferdinand was talking to at the reception when he was poisoned. Sylvester hated Cobber Palgrave, the next victim, for ruining his chances to marry Esther, and of course he wasn't too happy about being rejected by the most recent victim, Esther. That is not the kind of evidence I'd want to present to the district attorney, but at the moment Sylvester is the next best thing we have to a suspect."

"How do they fit into the island's families?"

"Silvester Mann is a cousin to Benjamin Mann and distantly related to Martha Gorges. Surprisingly, though, Sylvester shares little blood with most families here. I guess his line of Manns mostly went to the mainland to find wives, and so he doesn't have the intermarriage in his background that so many others have. Sylvia was born a Crosby, and she's a first cousin to Mason Crosby, who owns the pharmacy. I don't think Sylvia is closely related to any of the other living people here—except, of course, she's a granddaughter of Old Richie Crosby."

"How do you keep track of all these relationships?"

"I can't claim one hundred percent accuracy, and I may have misled you on one or more of the connections. That's why you're going to do research and come up with definitive charts on all these families. Then you'll be the expert, and I'll be asking you the questions." Catching a movement out of the corner of her eye, Priscilla turned toward the bar. "Here are two more people coming who I want you to take in—at least you should become familiar with their faces."

She nodded her head toward a tall, blond man in his very early twenties and a girl perhaps a few years older, of average height and attractive, but severe, looks. The girl had dark blazing eyes, as if intense thoughts were going on behind them, and her lips were full and bright crimson red. Next to her the young man seemed rather vapid, his face expressionless, his body limp. They came up to Mort and Priscilla's table.

"We've only met once, Sergeant Booth," said the girl. "I'm Lettice Gorges, and you probably already know my cousin, Dudley Gorges. May we join you for a minute?"

There were so many people named Gorges on the island that Mort had to push his memory to sort these two out. Slowly it came to him. Lettice Gorges would be the younger sister of the unfortunate Ferdinand Gorges, hence the daughter of Atherton and Martha; while Dudley Gorges would be Atherton's nephew who was staying with him, the younger brother of the most recent murder victim, Esther Gorges.

"I'm glad you dropped by," said Priscilla. "Of course, I've talked to Dudley, but you've been away for a while, Ms. Gorges." She introduced Mort to them, and they sat down.

"We were just leaving," said Dudley, "but now you've given us the excuse for one more drink." He called the waitress and ordered a Rob Roy and an Old Fashioned with Southern Comfort.

Ignoring Mort, Lettice said to Priscilla, "My friends call me Letty, and I wish you would, too. D'you mind if I call you Priscilla? We just stopped by to let you know I'm back on the island and more than happy to make myself available for questioning whenever you please." She spoke with just a hint of affectation, lingering over certain words. "D'you *mind* if I call you Priscilla? We just stopped by to let you know I'm back on the island, and *more* than happy to make myself available for questioning *whenever* you please."

"Letty was off to Northampton on one of her escapades," added Dudley. His sneer was the first sign of animation Mort had noticed on his face.

"Oh, do be *still,* you ass," Lettice said to her cousin. "I'm only with him," she explained, "because there is absolutely no one *else* available."

"Oh, for God's sake, Letty, don't get your knickers in a twitch."

"Isn't he *cute?*" said Lettice. "Well, I've just got to powder my *nose.* Will you come *with* me, Priscilla?"

Priscilla said, "Well, it's certainly an idea whose time has come." She got to her feet, and the two women left.

Alone with Dudley, whose expression had become very morose, Mort tried to make polite conversation but did not get far. Dudley seemed to think he was a police detective from L.A., New York, or some other big city.

"I don't understand," said Mort, "why everyone here has the idea that I'm a detective. I'm a genealogist, that's all."

"Oh, get off it," said Dudley. "We're not klutzes up here. Sorry your cover's blown, but it's not my goddamned fault."

After a couple of minutes of silence, Dudley said, "Do you have any idea who did it to my sister?"

"All I know is what I have heard from Priscilla. She certainly didn't act as if they knew who the killer was."

"I don't mean the killer," Dudley said with another sneer. "I mean the guy who knocked her up, not that they necessarily have to be mutually exclusive."

Mort just shook his head.

"Well, I'll give you a clue. Don't overlook my uncle. He was acting pretty sweet on Esther, and I don't mean in a normal avuncular way. And she could twist more money out of that old goat in a week than I could in a year."

"I gather you have had a lot to drink." Mort said.

"Your outdated morals would like to make you think so. Go ahead, ask him, and watch his face when you do." After another few moments of silence, he perked up. "Well, here comes my cousin, Miss Bitch."

Lettice, followed at a distance by Priscilla, approached the table simultaneously with Tina, who was bringing the drinks. Tossing a ten-dollar bill on Tina's tray, Lettice said, "Donate the *drinks* to your favorite charity." She turned to walk away.

Dudley stood and held out his arm in mock politeness for Lettice, who put her arm in his and headed toward the door without so much as a word to Mort nor a goodbye to Priscilla.

Mort rose to help Priscilla to her seat, "That's quite a couple."

"You don't know the half of it!" Priscilla said. "Why, that

woman, that woman, I don't know what to say . . . !" Her face was
red and she was waving her hands, all flustered. She took a long swig
of beer, grimaced, and turned to face Mort with an odd look on her
face. He was not sure if it was more bewilderment or indignation.

"What on earth happened?"

"Do you know what happened? Do you have any idea what she
did? That woman just propositioned me! In the ladies' room! She just
calmly and casually suggested that . . . well, I won't use her words.
But she wanted—she expected, suggested—that we have a sexual experience together. And me a policewoman! Can you imagine?"

"I could see that I obviously wasn't her type."

Priscilla broke into a burst of laughter. Well, of course, I'd heard
all about her. Only, I'd thought . . . or I guess I had not thought that
she'd actually proposition a policewoman."

"I take it you rejected her."

"I almost hit her. I think in the end she was afraid of me."

"Is she a suspect?"

"But definitely." Finishing her beer, she said, "Mort, we should
go. I have to catch the first ferry to the mainland tomorrow morning."

They called for the check, and Mort filled Priscilla in on his conversation with Dudley.

It was no surprise to Priscilla. "Dudley made the same accusation to me about the Senator and Esther, but he could offer no
evidence. I haven't mentioned it to the Senator yet, for various
reasons. I intend to, but I want to do a little more digging first. I think
you'll find, Mort, that the more you get to know about the Senator,
the less you'll like him."

"I don't think I need much more," he said, as Tina arrived with
their check. "Oh, if you are going to insist on paying, don't forget
that the first drinks were on the house."

Priscilla looked startled.

"It's the Scots in me," he said. "I am allergic to paying more than
I have to."

"I guess we're just paying for the second two beers," Priscilla
said to Tina. "Make sure you keep the rest as your tip, which shouldn't
be on the house."

Once they were outside, Mort said, "You'd rather I had not reminded you."

"No, that's all right. I respect your right to be prudent with money. It's just not me."

"I should have let you do it your way."

"Yes. But it's not important. We're not expected to be alike. Anyway, I'm glad we dropped in." She turned to smile at him. "I want you to meet as many of the people involved as possible."

They turned into the hotel. Priscilla was on the second floor, and so they said goodnight outside her door, with Mort continuing on to the next floor.

He stayed awake in bed for a long time, incongruous thoughts passing through his mind. Sylvester and Sylvia Mann . . . the cousins Dudley and Lettice . . . Delano Delano, why did his parents have to name him that? . . . drinks on the house . . . he wasn't being cheap, miserly. It just went against his grain to overpay but he didn't mind paying for value . . . he was not ungenerous. He had enjoyed the evening—up to a point.

Six

IN THE MORNING MORT COULD NOT RESIST
checking to see if Priscilla might still be in the hotel after all. But as
expected, her telephone didn't answer, and later the woman at the
desk said she had left at dawn. Mort had breakfast in the Talleyrand
Room, and when he finished it was time to start walking over to the
Senator's house.

The skies were overcast but clear; the ubiquitous sea gulls were
crisscrossing each other overhead, endlessly scrounging for one more
bite. There were a few cars driving by on Sea Drive going in the same
direction as Mort. He passed the Admiral's Arms and noticed Delano
Delano cleaning the outside window. They nodded to each other,
and Mort continued along his way. When he got to the FIGS building, he hesitated. His watch told him he was a bit early for his appointment, and on an impulse he went inside.

Deborah Samson was at the library desk. She smiled sweetly as
he entered the room.

He explained that he had just a few minutes. "But I wondered if
you had the International Genealogical Index."

"I am afraid not, Dr. Sinclair. I've ordered the newest fiche, but
they have not arrived yet. Now tell me, how do you find our little
place on your second visit?"

Deborah could be gracious when she wanted, and Mort found it difficult to extricate himself from his impromptu visit. She talked on. When the hands on the wall clock above the door reached one minute to ten, he interrupted her, apologized, said he had an appointment with Atherton Gorges, and left.

He crossed the street, hurriedly entered through the open gateway to Gorges's estate, and walked up the rather steep drive to the clearing on top. He was five minutes late.

Giffard—tall, stiff, and monotonal—admitted him to the mansion. "You are expected, sir. There will be a slight delay. Would you mind waiting in the library?"

If he had to wait, there was no place Mort would prefer to pass the time than in a good library, and Senator Gorges possessed a private library that would fill the hearts of lesser bibliophiles than Mort with guilty envy. There were a desk and a table, several padded side chairs, plus two large, overstuffed chairs in comfortably soft persimmon leather. The bookcases reached to the ceiling, and a small ladder with retractable wheels gave access to the higher shelves. Just on convenient eye level alone Mort could see that the library was compartmentalized with sections housing fiction, history, genealogy, biography, art and music, geography and travel, science and astronomy, business and finance, general reference, law, architecture and landscaping, sailing, photography, computers, and electronics. A veritable renaissance man, thought Mort, pleased to see two of his own books in the genealogy section and one with the histories. Many of the books had been rebound, and the library gave off the musty but pleasantly evocative scent of bookbinding leather and polish.

"I beg your pardon, sir, I didn't know the room was occupied."

Mort, hearing a female voice behind him, whirled around. He saw at the entrance a woman of twenty-five or so years wearing an apron and holding a book in her hand. She was attractive, with a turned up nose, high cheekbones, and deep-set hazel eyes. She also had a pretty figure, Mort noted, but as he lowered his glance he saw that she was crippled with a clubfoot.

"I was just going to return this book," she said, "but I can do that later."

"No," Mort said, "please don't let me disturb you. I am just waiting here."

She looked at Mort for a long moment, then slowly crossed the floor in front of him, almost dragging her left foot.

As she came within arm's reach, Mort offered a hand toward the book and said, "What are you returning?"

She clutched the thick book to her bosom; then, suddenly changing her mind, thrust it forward for Mort to see.

Glancing at the title, he said, "Thomas Mann, *The Magic Mountain.* You have good taste. You've been reading this yourself?"

"Of course," the girl said. Then after a pause, she added cautiously, "I sometimes think of myself as Hans Castorp. I would not want to come down either." She noticed that Mort was looking down at her feet and drew herself up to her full height. "You needn't feel sorry for me. I don't want anyone to feel sorry for me."

"I didn't mean to stare."

"It's going to be fixed," she said. "And then I'll be like normal people."

"I'm sure you will. Are you going to have an operation?"

"Dr. Delano's arranging it. Do you know him? He's been checking, and he says it's possible."

"That's good of him," Mort said, glad to learn that the rough-natured, unkempt man he had met last night had hidden reserves of goodness. To the girl he said, "Do you read a lot? I guess you live here."

"My mother is the cook, and at this time I'm employed here as a maid." She seemed to emphasize the words *at this time.* "My name's Belinda," she said. "Yes, I read a lot. I like to read. Have you read *Of Human Bondage*? Philip Carey had a clubfoot too."

Mort nodded, then introduced himself. "I'm Mort Sinclair."

"It's a sad book, but I like it," Belinda said. "There are so many wonderful books here, and Mrs. Gorges is so nice to let me read whatever I want." She walked to a bookcase, replaced her book on the shelf where it belonged, then turned to go.

"Isn't there some other book you want now?" Mort said. "Please don't let me interfere with your making a selection."

"I've others in my room, thank you." Belinda made her way to the door and was gone.

What an interesting young woman, Mort thought. He began walking around the library, absorbing more details.

On one wall the bookcases did not reach the ceiling but stopped short so that their tops could serve as a display shelf for a dozen or so pieces of ancient Greek pottery, all of museum quality. He recognized on one case a Mycenaean stirrup cup; two geometric bowls, probably also Mycenaean; a proto-Corinthian kylix; an exquisite archaic black-figure Attic kylix; and an archaic solid black Attic kantharos. Another case top held a stately red-figure krater painted in the style of Douros and of perfect classical proportions, followed by two more red-figure pieces of the classical period, a lekynthos, and a beautifully shaped delicate red-figure kylix. The remaining pieces were also red-figure but overly ornate, with handles curved in on themselves, needless fluting of the bowls, and effete painted figures, characteristic of the decadent style that occurred almost simultaneously with the defeat of Athens by Sparta.

He stopped in front of a large glass bookcase standing by itself away from the wall full of first and other rare editions: Norman Douglas's *South Wind,* Anthony Trollope's *The Warden,* Benjamin Disraeli's *Vivian Grey,* J. Horace Round's *Geoffrey de Mandeville,* Hawthorne's *The Marble Faun,* Cooper's *The Deerslayer,* Melville's *Moby Dick,* Charles Reade's *The Cloister and the Hearth,* Fielding's *Joseph Andrews* . . . . Whatever else Senator Atherton Gorges was, he was a man of good taste.

He was also, when he finally arrived with an apology, fifteen minutes late. "I cannot tolerate being tardy," he said.

Gorges, Mort realized, was apologizing for a personal dereliction rather than for any inconvenience he had caused his visitor. Mort knew that no man was harsher with others than the man who was intolerant even of himself.

Martha Gorges walked into the room on the heels of her husband's apology.

"Ah, Martha," the Senator said. "Are you planning to join us?"

"If you don't mind," she said quietly. Was there a touch of resignation in her voice? She sat down at the Senator's desk.

"No, no, not at all," Gorges said.

Mort felt certain that he was not quite telling the truth.

"Now to the point," said Gorges. "Oh, but first, would you care for coffee?" When Mort said no, Gorges said, "I think I would like something hot to drink. Would you get me a cup of malted milk, Martha?"

She obediently rose from behind the desk, left the room, and within seconds returned. "Belinda's getting it," she said, again taking her seat at the desk.

"Well, now," the Senator said, "the thing of it is that I understand you're a private detective."

"That seems to be a popular misconception on this island. I'm a professional genealogist, not a detective."

"Oh, well, I must have misunderstood," he said. "But you do carry out investigations into people's backgrounds?"

"Well, yes, in a sense. I research family connections—usually for past, not living, generations." Mort thought of the Senator's books on genealogy and his conversation of the previous night. Gorges was no stranger to the subject. Why, then, was he acting so unbelievably naive?

"Yes, I see," said the Senator, though his tone was doubtful. He glanced at his wife and then back to Mort. "But the techniques would be the same. I guess the important thing is confidentiality. I take it you are discreet with your findings?"

"Discretion is part of a professional genealogist's stock in trade."

"Of course. Very well. I want you to conduct an investigation for me. I'll pay any reasonable fee."

Mort straightened up, not at all sure he liked the turn the conversation was taking. "You know I'm working for the police. I could not take on any project that might involve a conflict of interest."

"Will you hear me out, sir, before you say no?" Gorges said, raising his voice. "All I want you to do is research my own background. There's no conflict there, is there?"

Martha Gorges stood up and faced her husband. "You're determined," she said with quiet dignity, "to go ahead with this notion of yours?"

"You would probably feel more comfortable, Martha," Gorges said, carefully but softly enunciating his words, "if you left the room." Martha rose from her chair and departed.

"What I'm asking has nothing at all to do with the horrible criminal matters that have taken place here," Gorges told Mort. "But life must go on. And I have a need to have my own background investigated. If the police agree that there is no conflict of interest, will you take the assignment?"

"What do you mean, investigate your background?"

The Senator explained that he wanted Mort to go back to his teenage years and work forward, checking anything he could find for any information on him.

"You are obviously looking for something specific," Mort said. "Yet you should know what that is yourself. Why use me? I'm sorry, but even if the police have no objection I couldn't work for anyone without knowing what is going on."

"All right, all right." Gorges said. "It must be understood that this is strictly confidential."

"Provided that in my judgment, it has no bearing on this case. And that still does not mean I accept, only that I will listen to you."

"Fair enough." He went on somewhat haltingly to explain that he had been asked by one of the political parties to run for state governor. His election should be almost a certainty. However, there had been an unfortunate incident in his past—and he was not going into details on that—which, if discovered and given exposure and media interpretation, might easily scuttle his campaign and put him in the embarrassing position of having to let down his party. He wanted to run, but would do so only if he felt that this episode from his past would not surface.

Somehow it made just a bit of sense to Mort. "Even if the police don't object," he said, "you realize that I would still be working primarily for them. But why don't you just hire some private detective not connected with the island?"

"I understand you would still be reporting to the police. As far as unknown private detectives are concerned, I'm informed they can be an unscrupulous lot. I do not want to take any chances of opening myself up to future blackmail, as might happen if I became governor and then found some detective ready to sell me information on my past at an exorbitant fee. I have made checks on you with Sergeant Booth and Lieutenant Bumpus, and you are a known factor.

With your permission, I will ask Lieutenant Bumpus specifically about any possible conflict of interest, but I can assure you there will be no objection."

"With some misgivings," said Mort, "I'll take the case if the police agree there is no conflict."

At this point Belinda lumbered in with a tray holding a cup of steaming white liquid. "Are you sure you will not have coffee, or something else?" Gorges asked. Mort again declined. Belinda showed him to the front door, and he thanked her with a smile. The entire visit, including all the waiting time, had taken half an hour.

♦   ♦   ♦

After lunch, Mort decided to spend the rest of the day at FIGS. Deborah Samson, still sitting at the desk in the library section when Mort entered, seemed pleased to see him again. An older man was perched at the far table with a pile of books heaped up in front of him, but otherwise the library was devoid of visitors. Deborah explained that Margaret, who had worked late on cleaning up after the reception, had the day off.

"The telephone keeps ringing," she said, "the mail has to be answered, visitors coming in and out—they really should have some consideration for me. It makes me almost forget what I wanted to say to you. Oh, yes, I have a question. I had always thought that the royal line of Elder William Wentworth of New Hampshire was a perfectly valid one, but I heard recently that it was cut. Do you know anything about this?"

Mort, always delighted to be asked a question he could easily answer, said, "There is an article in the current issue of *The Genealogist* with proof that the line as claimed is false. What you heard is correct." After a moment, he said, "Now let me ask you a question. Yesterday Margaret said something about a policy against keeping documentation on recent generations of local families."

"That Margaret—she's always getting things mixed up. There is no policy as such, it is just that in the past some of the island families have felt it uncouth to set down detailed information that might affect living people."

"Affect people? How?"

"Well," said Deborah, with some distaste, "you know how it is genealogically on a small island. An illegitimate child here, a babbling idiot in the family there, someone dying of what used to be considered unspeakable diseases . . . . Well, with everyone related to everyone else, it was just considered uncouth to hang out dirty laundry, so to speak, and so more a custom than a policy developed that the library would not encourage research into recent generations."

Mort laughed. "Well, this could be a bit embarrassing. I have been commissioned by the police to do precisely that."

Deborah waved her hand across her face as if she were swishing away a fly. "Oh, don't worry about that. Obviously, no one is going to tell the police that they have to restrict their investigation. You will have to go to Bay City too, of course, but if I can be of any assistance to you here—either to help you get started or to double-check your results for any errors or omissions—I would be delighted to help. And, oh, by the way, Dr. Sinclair, the table in the rear section is usually reserved for meetings and for the trustees' personal use. But do feel free to use it any time you want, for you will find it much easier to concentrate there."

Mort thanked her and said he would start by familiarizing himself with the origins of the old families. Deborah told him which shelves would be of most value.

◆　　　　◆　　　　◆

The next morning Mort checked for Priscilla again, but she was still in Bay City. He had a late breakfast by himself and left a message at the reception desk telling Priscilla that he would be at the FIGS library all day.

In the privacy of the rear section again, he took up where he had left off the previous day, soon completely absorbed in reading and taking notes. He was surprised to learn that the "old" families of the island were not really that old from a genealogical point of view. The island had been settled in the mid-seventeenth century by Caleb

Fogge, an immigrant from county Suffolk, England. Since the island was small and rocky—and, given the agricultural practices of the time, not large enough to sustain many families—Fogge was granted exclusive ownership for £75. He lived all his remaining life there with his family and a few servants.

Caleb Fogge had ten or more children of which two survived him to adulthood. The older, Ezra Fogge, inherited his mother's estate in Suffolk and returned to England to claim it. Ezra sold his rights in the island to his brother, Micajah Fogge, who then, like his father before him, spent the rest of his life eking out a living from the land, cultivating the soil, and putting cattle and goats out to graze. Two of Micajah's sons became fishermen and were lost at sea in a storm, a common occurrence among families living near the sea in colonial New England. Two daughters were given their portions during the father's lifetime, and at his death the only surviving son, Caleb II, became the proprietor of Fogge Island.

Servants came and went, some with families but most without. There was little to tempt them to stay once they saved enough to buy a little land on the mainland, especially as new lands were continually being opened up further west. Thus, for six generations, the only permanent inhabitants of Fogge Island were the succession of Fogge heirs, the last one being Thomas Fogge, who died in 1799. Since Thomas had but two sons, both killed in the Revolution, his daughter, Susanna—who had married one of the hired men, Elkanah Gorges—inherited, and thus the island passed into the hands of the Gorges family.

Though Elkanah Gorges continued the agricultural pursuit of the land, he came from a seafaring family and gradually acquired a small fleet of fishing and trading vessels. The harbor in the southeast corner of the island was well sheltered, and Elkanah Gorges prospered. He provided his sailors and other employees with small lots for houses in what was coming to be called Oldtown, and he subdivided some interior land to sell as small farms, attracting still other new inhabitants from the mainland. Charles Mann, one of his sailors who had lost a leg and was confined to shore, started an inn at one end of the harbor, and Obadiah Delano retired from the sea to found a general store. The sea made the Gorges family wealthy, and their wealth in turn helped keep the island prosperous. A cousin of Obadiah Delano, Elisha Samson, came from the mainland to help Delano in his store; and Elisha's son, Elijah, built a small shipyard, which complemented Gorges's sailing fleet.

Thus by the early 1800s there was no longer a Fogge family on Fogge Island, and the island's richest citizens—the Gorgeses, the Manns, the Delanos, and the Samsons—had been there only one or two generations. In the early years people had little choice but to find spouses from the mainland. But from the second generation on, the "new" families found an occasional mate from no further than a hundred feet away. A daughter of Charles Mann married a son of Obadiah Delano, and Elias Samson, the son of Elijah, married a great-granddaughter of Thomas Fogge. Though new generations continued to select mates from outside the island, endogamous marriage was sufficiently frequent so that by the late twentieth century virtually every member of any given family was related to one or more of the other families that had been on the island for more than a generation or two. In fact, the state legislature had to pass a special exception for Fogge Island from the anti-nepotism law, which made it illegal for town councils to award contracts to anyone related to anyone on the council. On Fogge Island that would have caused unreasonable hardship since any prospective contractor was virtually certain to be related to one or more of the island council members.

As an experienced genealogist, Mort Sinclair knew that any search far enough back in any family would inevitably find the marriage of cousins, hence some inbreeding in everyone. On small islands such inbreeding would be even more common. But Mort also knew that the popular notion of family degeneracy through inbreeding was based on a misconception. True, when both marriage partners came from the same genetic stock, family traits were likely to become more pronounced in subsequent generations than would be true in less inbred families. But that included desirable and neutral traits as well as undesirable ones, and inbreeding did not ordinarily result in degeneracy unless degenerate traits existed in a given family in the first place. Still, as Mort had had occasion to note in the past, why take chances? The Gorges family should not have been so distressed when their son Ferdinand wanted to marry Maria de la Concepcion

Hernandez. Even the bluest of blood might benefit from an occasional transfusion.

It was also clear to Mort that not all people on Fogge Island had the same degree of inbreeding. Some people might go back to a given immigrant family ancestor in three or more distinct lines, while others might not go back to that particular person at all. Individual A might share Samson blood with individual B, but not Gorges blood; while individual C might share Gorges blood with individual A, but not Samson blood. The possible combinations of relationships seemed almost limitless.

When absorbed in his work, Mort was usually oblivious to happenings around him, but this morning he was dimly aware that something was going on. During the hour or so that he had been in the library, whenever he used the bookshelves in the main section he could sense an air of apprehension. There had been little whispered conferences between Deborah and Margaret, and once or twice he had the impression that Deborah was just bursting to speak to him.

From the corner of his eye he caught a movement in the passageway. Looking up, he saw Deborah determinedly bearing down on him, alarm stamped all over her normally composed features. Something was assuredly wrong!

Seven

PRISCILLA MISSED THE FIRST FERRY BACK TO the island and had to wait for its second trip. She had spent all of the previous day in Bay City working on various aspects of the murder case. Lieutenant Bumpus had not been especially happy about developments in the case. At one point he seemed to want to arrest Sylvester Mann, if only for the sake of showing some kind of progress, but he knew that he lacked sufficient evidence to bring Mann to trial. He gave Priscilla thirty minutes of his valuable time, more than she had ever had by herself before. She still had some currency with Bumpus for her initial discoveries on Cobber Palgrave, but she had the feeling she was spending it fast.

It was a clear day, not at all cold, but as Priscilla stood by the cabin window gazing on the verdant cover of pine trees that rose above Oldtown, she began to shiver. It was, she realized, a premonition; the kind of shiver she'd had many years ago just before learning that one of her cats had been run over. She wanted to wake up and look back on it—whatever "it" was—as a dream, as something that had never really happened. But she knew she was awake, not dreaming; she knew without the smallest doubt that she would arrive back on the island to find something most definitely wrong.

She was, accordingly, not surprised when she saw Corporal

Dingley waiting with an impatient look on his face at the ferry landing; and his impatience immediately communicated itself to her. Why was the captain taking so much time to pull into the rubber-tire-lined slip? Why were people on the ferry moving in slow motion? Why were they blocking her from being the first one off?

Corporal Dingley confirmed her fears. "It's bad, Priscilla. Delano Delano has been murdered."

Her reaction was to ask herself if the whole thing could have been prevented had she stayed on the island. That was nonsense, she knew, but since childhood it was the way her thoughts customarily dictated to her. They began walking rapidly toward the Admiral's Arms. "Word hasn't gotten around yet," Dingley said. "Margaret Mann reported it to Constable Gorges, who telephoned me at the hotel immediately. I sent Margaret to her work at the FIGS office and cautioned her not to tell anyone. Nehemiah's with the body at the pub."

"Did you get Dr. Thomas Delano to examine the body?"

The corporal's face reddened. "I didn't think I should contact him until you arrived," he said. "See, Priscilla, Dr. Delano and Del Delano had a fight late last night. There was a witness, Tina Samson, and she left while they were still fighting. Later Del was found with his head bashed in."

"He wasn't killed by poison?" asked Priscilla, disturbed at the thought of some unexpected new element entering her case uninvited.

"Of course, there's been no medical examination, but it's obvious that he was killed by blows to the head, probably from the blood-stained stool found near the body."

Corporal Nehemiah Gorges let them in when they rang the front doorbell, relocked the door and led them to the room behind the kitchen that served as storeroom, pantry, and office. Propped against a table leg, the body of Delano Delano lay sprawled out on the floor, resting partly on its back and partly on its side. One arm was raised a bit stiffly, and the face was half obscured by dried blood. The mouth was open in a twisted expression of agony.

"Have you called the mainland?" Priscilla asked Dingley.

"I called," said Constable Gorges. "I wanted everything done

just right. I called Lieutenant Bumpus, and he's sending some technicians on the next ferry."

That would be about two more hours, which meant Priscilla
would have to wait. Murder on a remote island did not fall within
her previous experience of sirens, flashing red lights, and instant ex-
pertise stepping out of a car. At the minimum there would be a photog-
rapher and a fingerprint expert accompanying the medical examiner.
Perhaps even Bumpus himself. She was not even sure if this was her
case. Was it related to the three poisonings? Had the murder been
committed by the same person? Or was this a completely separate,
coincidental event?

Leaving the corpse, Priscilla, Corporal Dingley, and Constable
Gorges went into the public room and took a table. She removed her
notepad and a pen from her handbag and began taking notes as Gorges
and Dingley alternately told her what they knew. The known facts
were simple enough: Dr. Thomas Delano had come into the pub last
night just before closing time. He ordered a Scotch and soda at the
bar and refused to leave with the other few remaining customers,
staying behind with Del Delano and the one waitress who was still
there, Tina Samson. The two second cousins had an argument; Del
ordered the doctor to leave, turned his back, and walked to the rear
room. Dr. Delano followed Del and confronted him in the storeroom.
Tina cautiously followed and looked on through the doorway as the
doctor swung and hit the pub owner, knocking him to the floor. Del
rose on one elbow, told Tina he would be all right, and ordered her
to go home. Afraid to disobey, she did as he said, leaving the two
men there with Del still lying on the floor.

Tina Samson, Nehemiah Gorges explained, had once been married to Delano Delano. She had a miscarriage and blamed Del for it,
since he apparently had roughed her up several times during her pregnancy. She divorced him and resumed her maiden name but kept on
working for him as a waitress, renting a room at the house of Margaret Mann, who was a first cousin. After she left the pub, she went
directly home and told Margaret what had happened. They discussed
getting in touch with Constable Gorges about the fight, but decided
against it. Doctor Thomas Delano was not known to be a violent man.
He had already had the satisfaction of winning the fight. Probably he

would have left right after Tina, and Delano Delano would have gotten up and gone to bed in his room over the pub. The two women agreed that they would feel silly sending Constable Gorges over to the pub only to find Del Delano peacefully asleep.

In the morning they again discussed what had happened, and Margaret said she would look in on the pub on her way to open up the FIGS building. She left earlier than usual with the intention of not only looking in but also perhaps having a cup of coffee with Del and leading him into a discussion of last night's events. Tina, who was a little afraid of her ex-husband, agreed that Margaret might be able to elicit explanations from Del.

Margaret, after trying unsuccessfully to get Del to answer the doorbell in front, went to the rear, it being common knowledge that the door there was never locked. The rear door entered directly on the storeroom, and even in the dim light of the dawn she could see that Del was stretched out on the floor. She touched nothing except the light switch, turning it on to see better. The moment she saw the blood all over his face and the nearby floor, she shrieked to high heaven, slammed the door, and ran immediately to Nehemiah Gorges's house. All this happened a few minutes after seven o'clock.

Priscilla had had occasion before to reflect that island facilities for a murder investigation were somewhat primitive, but in mapping out her immediate course of action she realized just how primitive. She telephoned Lieutenant Bumpus, who told her he would not be coming over. The news inspired mixed feelings; she felt she was capable of handling the matter, yet it would have been comforting to have the more experienced officer take charge. Eager to demonstrate the knowledge and experience she had already acquired, she nonetheless recognized that she could stand to acquire more. Bumpus told her he had a crew of four on their way, but they were taking the ferry, not the police boat, which was being repaired. Priscilla was in charge until further notice. Her job now was to get all the facts as soon as possible, then telephone him again.

As soon as the police crew arrived, Priscilla started on her preplanned course. She would not, she decided, bring Mort to the pub. There was no need for him to get involved with the thousands of technical details presented by a cadaver so clearly the victim of foul play. She assumed he would be at the FIGS library, and she was going there anyway to see Margaret Mann.

Priscilla sent Corporal Dingley to find Dr. Thomas Delano. "Stay with him," she said. "Keep him isolated until I'm ready to question him. Don't arrest him if he cooperates, but if he won't stay still, tell him he's under arrest as a suspect in the murder."

Next she sent Constable Gorges to get Tina Samson and hold her anywhere, perhaps in Meg's Muffin Shoppe, until Priscilla needed her. She would use the constable's office for questioning, and Dingley and Gorges should telephone her there when they had accomplished their tasks. Leaving the pub in the care of the police technical crew, Priscilla circled around to the front of the building via the side alleyway and began her short journey.

She should not have been surprised to find eager, animated faces bobbing up and down outside the pub window. Some of the onlookers had undoubtedly become curious when they sighted the police technical crew getting off the ferry and had just followed them. Others, though, probably knew as many details about the murder as she herself did. Small islands might have primitive physical facilities, but they had wondrously fast communication systems.

Priscilla and Mort spotted each other the moment she entered the rear section of the library where he was working. He came right over to her. "Deborah told me about it earlier," he said, "but I didn't go to the pub for fear of getting in the way. I was not even sure you were back yet."

"I'm going to get some facts from people at the constable's office," Priscilla said. "It might be a good idea for you to join me." She was in charge and would have to take the lead, but Mort could fill her need for support in a way that Corporal Dingley or Constable Gorges could not.

There was one man sitting at the front table in the main room, and a young couple were conferring over books at the rear table. Deborah Samson and Margaret Mann, huddled in whispered conversation at the desk when Priscilla entered, now sat expectantly silent. As she approached Deborah's desk, Priscilla felt all eyes turning upon her.

"Is it murder?" Deborah asked in a hoarse whisper.

Priscilla, exasperated as all police officers are on finding they cannot control human nature, said nothing, but stared at Margaret as a schoolteacher might stare at a little girl who had wet her pants again.

Margaret bit at her lower lip and said, "Well, I had to tell Deborah. I don't keep any secrets from her. And besides, I had to explain why I was late in opening up, didn't I?"

Priscilla told Margaret she would have to ask her some questions and preferred to do so at the constable's office. Deborah looked disappointed, but said nothing. Mort, feeling a bit like a fifth wheel, dutifully followed Priscilla and Margaret out of the building. A few passersby gawked at their procession as the three of them marched to the feed store in silence.

◆   ◆   ◆

Since the window of the constable's single-room office in the feed store looked out on Sea Drive, the only way to block people from staring was to lower the shade and turn on the light. Fortunately there was one more chair than needed.

"Let's get your facts, Margaret," said Priscilla in her most businesslike tone. Then as the older woman began to cry, she said, "I know how horrible this is for you, Margaret, but it isn't easy on any of us."

Margaret wiped her eyes with a tissue from her purse and sat up straight. She repeated the story more or less as Priscilla had heard it from Corporal Dingley. Having stayed up late last night watching TV, she saw Tina arrive about eleven o'clock. The news had just started, and she had resented the interruption until she realized that Tina had something important to say. In the morning she went over to the pub and was surprised when Del Delano failed to answer the doorbell—he was a creature of habit who almost invariably rose early to prepare for the new day's business. When she went in the back way, she didn't touch anything except the light switch. Though she screamed loudly at first, hearing her own voice had a calming effect on her and she immediately ran over to Constable Gorges's house. When Gorges dismissed her, she went directly to the FIGS building, arriving there about eight-thirty. Deborah had already opened up the building and was wondering where Margaret was. Margaret, feeling that she had to offer some kind of explanation, told Deborah the whole story. There were two people sitting at the front table in the library at the time, and apparently they overheard her and left to tell others. She was surprised, though, at how fast word had traveled: only a few minutes later, she received a telephone call from Senator Atherton Gorges asking her all about the murder.

Things began happening to Priscilla all at once. Mort was asking her a question, and she still had questions she wanted to ask Margaret, and the telephone was ringing, and suddenly a reporter came bursting through the office door.

"Remember me?" the reporter said, "I'm Ken Fusetti from the *Boston Times.* Can I get the details from you?"

"Later!" Priscilla said, half shouting, half begging. She got up to steer Fusetti out of the office. Returning to her chair, she said to Mort, "The reporters will be coming like flies now."

Margaret fidgeted in her chair, and Priscilla paused to gather her thoughts. The phone rang, and she signaled Mort to answer it. "It's Constable Gorges for you," Mort said. Gorges informed her that as soon as he told Tina Samson the news she became hysterical. He could no sooner get her calmed down than she would start again. Might he bring her to the office now? Priscilla agreed, then turned back to Margaret.

"Did you know of any bad blood between Dr. Delano and Delano Delano?"

"Everybody knew," said Margaret. "I think it was something that was connected with Sylvia Mann. Delano Delano had been dating Sylvia, then they broke up and she married Sylvester Mann. Apparently Del blamed his cousin for the break-up. At least, the two Delanos haven't been friends since Sylvia and Sylvester married." Margaret lowered her voice. "But I think something else must have happened between the doctor and Del more recently, because in the past week their dislike seemed to change to hatred. I have no idea why."

Again the telephone rang, and Corporal Dingley said he was at the clinic with Dr. Delano, who was fully cooperative. What should he do now? Priscilla told him to stay there with Delano until she telephoned for them.

Priscilla told Margaret that she would probably want to ask her some more questions later, and Margaret left.

The telephone rang again, and this time it was the medical examiner. "We're taking the body to the mainland on the next ferry," he said, "and tomorrow I can give you something more specific on time of death—but for now I'd estimate that he died sometime around midnight, give or take an hour. Death was apparently caused by a hard blow to the right temple with a blunt instrument, probably the stool."

"Can you tell from the wound if the blow was inflicted while he was lying down, or could he have been standing or sitting?"

"Right now it's hard to say," the examiner said. "None of the above would have been impossible."

Priscilla thanked him. Between 11:00 p.m. and 1:00 a.m., she mused, that's helpful. To Mort she said, "You see how confusing a murder case can get. Everything happens all at once."

Mort nodded in agreement. "I have had some experience with murder cases before, but not quite on this level. How do you ever get anything done with all the interruptions?"

Senator Atherton Gorges telephoned for Priscilla, who tried to be patient, but cut him off abruptly as Constable Nehemiah Gorges escorted Tina Samson into the office. Tina sat in one chair and Nehemiah, after looking at Priscilla to see if she wanted him to stay, took the other. Tina looked as if she had been dicing onions, eyes red and cheeks tear-stained. Priscilla had just started to question her when the telephone rang again, Lieutenant Bumpus wanting a progress report. Priscilla told him no new significant facts had emerged and promised to call him back later.

It took her twice as long to get information out of Tina as it had out of Margaret. Everything had to be repeated, questions rephrased, answers restated. Tina said the other waitress, Lucy, went home early, leaving her and Del Delano to close up the pub at eleven o'clock. All the customers had left except Dr. Thomas Delano, who had come in just a few minutes earlier and ordered a drink at the bar. Tina had served him, even though it was obvious to her that he had already had quite a bit to drink. She was cleaning table tops; she knew Del and the doctor were talking but didn't know what about. She noticed that their voices were getting louder, and suddenly she heard Del tell the doctor in a loud voice to get out, it was past closing time.

"Was this a routine request for the doctor to leave because it was past closing time?" Priscilla asked, "or did Del make an issue over the time because he wanted to get rid of the doctor?"

Tina seemed confused, and Priscilla rephrased the question. The rephrasing did not help: Tina simply did not know the answer. All she knew was that Del stopped cleaning up the bar and walked out of the bar area, going through the kitchen to the storeroom. The doctor followed him and said in a loud voice, "If you say anything, I'll kill you, I'll kill you."

"Were those his exact words?"

Tina repeated the words and assured Priscilla that they had come out of the doctor's mouth exactly that way. Both men were very angry now, and when the doctor followed Del to the storeroom, Tina went quietly to the doorway between the kitchen and the storeroom. She got there just in time to see Dr. Delano lash out with a fist and hit Del on the cheek, or maybe his chin. Del fell to the floor. Tina wanted to rush in to help him, but he got halfway up, resting himself on an elbow, and just glared at the doctor for a minute. Then, seeing Tina, he said, "It's all right, Tina. The fight's over. There won't be any more trouble. You go home now. I mean it."

She was reluctant to leave him, but Dr. Delano turned and said to her, "I'm sorry I lost my temper, Tina. There'll be no more trouble. Why don't you go home as he said?" Tina was not unacquainted with bar fights. She knew their way of building up to a point where neither participant had control over himself, where something had to happen. She also knew that once each man had regained control, a fight was unlikely to continue. She assumed from the calmness shown by both men that this one really was over, and so she went home. She saw no one on her way home, and she told no one about the fight except Margaret Mann, who was still up when she reached the house. She and Margaret discussed the matter briefly, and then she took a cup of hot chocolate and went to bed. She got up earlier than usual and discussed the matter again with Margaret, who offered to look in on Del on her way to work.

"Do you know what Dr. Delano meant when he said 'If you say anything?'" Priscilla asked. Tina had no idea. Did Tina think that Dr. Delano meant it when he said he would kill Del, or was it just an expression said in anger? After rephrasing the question, Priscilla got a clear answer from Tina: it had been, she thought, just an overheated expression—she'd been worried that they might come to blows but had not thought Dr. Delano really meant he wanted to kill the other man. Besides, Del was much younger and stronger than the man who had hit him and, if he wanted to, he could easily have fought back and won.

Priscilla was through for the moment with Tina, and at this point she would normally have suggested that a person under such strain see a doctor, but the only doctor on the island was Dr. Delano. She merely told Tina not to go back to the pub, which would be closed for an indefinite period of time. Tina started sobbing and was still leaking tears when she left the office.

"Tina was holding something back," Priscilla told Mort. "I don't think she was deliberately lying, but she kept something secret all the same. It reminds me of what Deborah Samson said about this island having more secrets than people. Tina has her secret, too, and I can't help wondering if it has anything to do with her relations with Del Delano."

"You mean you wonder about the possibility of post-divorce hanky-panky between her and her ex-husband?"

"Something like that," Priscilla said, then turned to Constable Gorges. "Go over to the pub and see if the technicians have left," she told him. "If so, make sure that everything has been locked up. And if that reporter is still around, tell him to come in and I'll talk to him now."

Ken Fusetti came in fifteen minutes later and nodded to acknowledge his slight acquaintance with Mort. Priscilla gave the reporter an edited version of what had happened; she would have preferred greater candor, but she knew that was Lieutenant Bumpus's prerogative, not hers. At least the details she gave out seemed to satisfy Fusetti for the moment, and he left.

Priscilla then telephoned the clinic and asked Corporal Dingley to bring Dr. Delano to the office. "It looks bad for him," she told

Mort. "A man has a fight with another man, says he's going to kill him, and within two hours—maybe within minutes—the other man is murdered. District attorneys love evidence like that."

"You don't think it was Dr. Delano?"

"I don't know. I guess I hope it wasn't. He's a bit gruff in his manner, but he's a kind man and one of the most liked people on this island."

Dr. Delano's manner was more than a bit gruff when Corporal Dingley brought him into the office. He became more cooperative as Priscilla demonstrated that she was not going to subject him to hostile questioning. Under her friendly, let's-reason-this-out-together approach, the doctor admitted that he had threatened to kill Delano Delano but of course hadn't meant it—he'd just been hot under the collar. Yes, he had hit Del, but the moment he realized what he had done, he was horrified.

"I knew I'd been drinking too much," he told Priscilla. "The fact is, I was ashamed."

"What happened after Tina left?"

"I apologized to Del, then left. By then Del had picked himself up and was sitting up at a table."

Dr. Delano did not even recall what the fight had been about. They got into some kind of discussion and disagreed on something. There was some name-calling, and other insults passed between them, and one thing led to another. Dr. Delano did not remember uttering the words "If you say anything . . . ." In fact, he was sure he hadn't, for there would have been no reason to use such a phrase. Tina must have misunderstood the words.

"I understand you and your cousin have not been on the best of terms," Priscilla said. "In fact, I've heard that there was bad blood between you."

Dr. Delano managed a weak smile. "Not all cousins get along, you know. We didn't particularly like each other, but we didn't particularly dislike each other either. We just were not close."

He was hiding something, Priscilla was sure. Another islander, another secret. She was also sure that she was not going to get anything more out of him. She asked him to wait outside with Corporal Dingley while she telephoned her superior. The telephone call was one-sided, with Lieutenant Bumpus doing most of the talking and Priscilla replying in one- and two-word answers.

When Dingley and Delano reentered the office, Priscilla stood up and said to the doctor, "I have to arrest you on the charge of murder. I'll read you your rights, and then Corporal Dingley will escort you to the Bay City police department."

After Priscilla informed him of his rights, Dr. Delano said, "I don't think I should answer any more questions until I speak with my lawyer. May I make a call?"

Priscilla offered him the telephone. He telephoned Sylvester Mann, learned that he was out on business, and left a message for Sylvester to see him at the police department.

Corporal Dingley looked apologetically at both Priscilla and Dr. Delano. "I'm sorry, Doctor," he said, "but I'll have to use the cuffs. It's regulation, and if I didn't and anything happened, it'd be my ass."

"No handcuffs," Priscilla said. "I'll assume responsibility."

After they left, Mort said, "According to my research, Delano Delano was a nephew, via his mother, of Martha Gorges. So if your theory of inheritance is right, and if these murders are connected as part of a scheme to eliminate heirs first of the Senator and then of Martha, we could say that another heir has been eliminated."

Priscilla nodded.

"But it must have occurred to you," he said, "that on this island it would be all but impossible to murder any four people who are not related."

"That's certainly occurred to me."

"What do we do now?"

"How about going to the hotel bar and having a drink?" Priscilla said. "I think at this point I could use one."

Eight

As PRISCILLA AND MORT SAT DOWN FOR DIN-
ner in the Talleyrand Room, she said, "Sorry, I forgot to mention
what Lieutenant Bumpus said to tell you." Mort, she guessed, was not
going to like this. "It's okay if you want to accept that assignment
from Senator Gorges. Bumpus sees no possible conflict of interest."

Priscilla suspected that Benjamin Mann had told his maître d' to
give her the most favored treatment at all times; at any rate, they certainly had the best table in the restaurant, being seated in a little bower
blocked off on three sides by potted palms, large ferns, and a variety
of plants.

Mort ordered a filet mignon with Bearnaise sauce, and Priscilla
followed suit. "My father taught me to love good food," she said,
"and that sounds good to me."

"Then may I suggest soufflé Grand Marnier for two for dessert?"

"Why not wait to see how hungry we might be?"

"If it's to be good, it has to be ordered in advance."

"Anything we order here will be good. Ben Mann's chef has an
excellent reputation. My father says so, and he's a gourmet chef himself. In our house my father does all the fancy cooking." She took
another look at her table-dwarfing menu, said, "Okay, soufflé it will
be," and handed her menu back to Mort.

Mort ordered a bottle of Premiat 1982 Pinot Noir. "It is Rumanian, unbelievably inexpensive, but superb for the price, better than anything else costing five times as much." He let the menus protrude over the edge of the table. "I mean, I've got to be true to my ancestors. As a Scotsman, I expect to get value for my money."

A candle in a lantern chimney flickered in the center of the table. Mort gazed into the flame as he spoke. "It's not very flattering, you know."

"What? My father doing the fancy cooking, or you ordering a bottle of what Horace Rumpole would call plonk?

"Would ye hae a Scotsman throw money away, lassie?"

Priscilla laughed and reached across the table to touch his hand lightly.

"I meant Bumpus not feeling that there could be any possible conflict of interest," he said.

Priscilla knew she was going to have to be very tactful with her explanation. Mort was a paradox, so cosmopolitan on the one hand and yet at times almost childlike on the other. "Well, you see," she said, "Bumpus doesn't really think of you as a full participant in this case. Now, don't misunderstand. I'm not agreeing, I'm just trying to explain how he thinks. To him you're an outside technician. Like a librarian if he needed someone to recommend a book or a pharmacist explaining what kind of medicine was meant by a particular prescription. You're a specialist."

"He doesn't think it's possible," Mort replied, " that a consulting genealogist's interpretations might be biased if he is also being paid by one of the suspects?"

"It's outside Bumpus's realm of possibility that genealogical evidence could be misinterpreted," Priscilla said. "The information's all there for anyone to see. If you made a mistake either deliberately or unintentionally, someone else would quickly spot it."

"Oh, brother!" Mort said. "He knows even less about my work than I do about his. Suppression of evidence alone could conceivably change an inheritance picture. And that is all the more true when you are dealing with multiple relationships. Someone could be known as a third cousin on one side of the family who conceivably might also be an unknown second cousin on another side. Tell him to read about the Howard Hughes case."

"Bumpus isn't a genealogist. And does it matter that much?"

"Well, I'll take the Senator's job, but more to satisfy my curiosity about his background than for his money. Conceivably there could be something that might tie in with the assignment I am doing for you."

"Would that be within your professional ethics?"

"There! You see there could be a conflict. In any event, Gorges knows that if I take his job, the police will have full access to anything I learn. I made sure that he understood that. And here you are admitting that there could be a conceivable conflict without that understanding."

"Certainly," Priscilla said, happy to bolster up his image of himself. She was not just flattering him, for, knowing much more about genealogy than Bumpus did, she was certain that there could at times be significant differences in the results depending on how skillful and honest one was in interpreting genealogical evidence.

"Telephone for Sergeant Booth," a waiter announced, as they were finishing their meal. Priscilla excused herself and went out to the lobby.

"It was Lieutenant Bumpus—again," she said when she returned. "I've got to go to the mainland tomorrow. He wants me to be present when he interrogates Dr. Delano."

"I thought you already interrogated him this afternoon."

"I doubt that Lieutenant Bumpus would call what I did an interrogation. Bumpus has come up with a beautiful solution to all the murders. Del Delano poisoned the other three, and then Dr. Delano murdered Del Delano."

"Does that make sense to you?"

"I'm a policewoman," she said. "I never disagree or find fault with my superiors." She took a sip of her wine just as the waiter was bringing in the dessert. "At least, not to their faces." After another sip she said, "Oh, by the way, I came to a decision on your wine. It's just wonderful. I take back what I said about plonk."

"Thanks. While you were gone, I came to a decision, too."

"What's that?"

"I am not going to be so wimpy about this conflict of interest business. I guess, Priscilla," he said, reaching across to hold her hand, "it's just that I have always been able to choose my own ground in the past. Even as a consultant for the police, I have always been able to take full charge of my aspect of a case. But in this case, you have treated me as a virtual partner in the whole murder investigation, even though I do not have the authority to be a partner, which does sting. But I am not going to whine about it any more. I am here to do a job for you, and I will do my job and leave. I will not complain because I cannot be Sergeant Sinclair."

In a way, he was right. Priscilla didn't quite understand how it had happened, but she had been using him as an investigative partner. Since he was clearly nothing of the sort, she wondered why she had put him in that position. Was it because she found it lonely—even scary—being in charge of her first murder investigation? Or was it something else? She had picked him by name because she had been attracted to him when she heard him lecture at a genealogical conference. She had built him up in her mind as a certain kind of man, and for the most part he seemed to match her preconception. Was she trying to make more out of the relationship than was really there? At this point, she honestly did not know. But he was holding her hand, and somehow it made her feel good. She felt confident when she was with him, if that was the right word.

To Mort she said, "You're right, of course. Let's just see if we can each do our job as painlessly as possible."

There was light dinner music in the background, and she was feeling comfortable, and did not want to leave. They had finished their meal, but Mort made no effort to leave either.

"More coffee?" he said.

"Just what I want."

He called the waitress, then sat silent with a relaxed smile on his lips, still holding her hand. "If you are going to Bay City tomorrow," he said finally, "maybe I can call Gorges and tell him I will take his assignment, get the background information from him, and take the ferry with you."

"Why don't you call him now?"

Mort had no sooner gone out to the phone than Sylvester Mann descended upon Priscilla. She greeted him pleasantly and asked him to sit down.

"I prefer to stand, Sergeant Booth," he said. "What is this damned outrageous story about your arresting my client Dr. Thomas Delano and having him dragged off to the mainland in handcuffs?"

"There were no handcuffs, and he was not dragged."

"Are you aware that Dr. Delano's wife can testify that he arrived at his home at exactly ten minutes past eleven o'clock, and they went directly to bed together, where he remained all night?"

Priscilla said patiently, "Corporal Dingley obtained a signed statement from Mrs. Delano, and we have all of her facts."

"Then Dr. Delano could not have done it. He would not have had enough time."

"Excuse me, Mr. Mann, but it would seem elementary that even if Dr. Delano started out of the pub five seconds after Tina Samson left, he still could have bashed in Del Delano's head as he left. You know as well as I do that there is nothing in the timing of this case that necessarily rules Dr. Delano out as the murderer.

"I know nothing of the kind. I demand that you release him."

"He's been arrested under suspicion of murder, and the matter is out of my hands in any case. You should know that, Mr. Mann."

Sylvester Mann's face, ordinarily ruddy, was beet red. Priscilla felt that his blood pressure must have gone up fifty points in the last three minutes. "All I know," he said, "is that you have no evidence at all against Dr. Delano."

"Please lower your voice, Mr. Mann. Why don't you calm down, get a good night's sleep, then you can talk to Lieutenant Bumpus about it tomorrow morning."

"You're goddamned right I'll talk to Bumpus about it tomorrow. With a habeas corpus in my hand." He turned and stomped off toward the lobby, where Priscilla could see his wife waiting.

"Did I miss something?" Mort asked as he returned to the table.

Priscilla told him what had happened. "Sylvester Mann has the reputation of being a hothead," she said, "and I suspect him of having watched too many Perry Mason reruns."

"Didn't you say he was once a suspect himself?"

"Still is, as far as I am concerned," Priscilla said. "Dr. Delano may have killed Del Delano in the heat of anger, but that wouldn't explain the three poisonings. Someone has to be the poisoner, and I frankly don't think it's Dr. Delano."

"No," Mort said, with a glint in his eye. "We know that Del Delano committed the three poisonings because Lieutenant Bumpus told us so, and we wouldn't think of disagreeing with Lieutenant Bumpus, would we?"

"Absolutely not," said Priscilla with a straight face. "But I'm still keeping my eye on Sylvester Mann. How did your call to the Senator go?"

"Satisfactory for my purposes. He is too busy to see me tonight, but he has prepared a curriculum vitae for me as a starting point, and I can drop by and pick it up from the butler. That means I can take the ferry with you. How about breakfast in the morning?"

"Not if we're going to catch the first ferry. It leaves at seven-thirty, the same time the dining room opens." They agreed to meet in the lobby at seven-fifteen and then, with considerable reluctance, left the restaurant.

◆   ◆   ◆

The crossing to Bay City was uneventful. Sylvester and Sylvia Mann sat at a table on the other side of the cabin from Mort and Priscilla, and Sylvester spent most of the ride glaring at them.

"He's not very pleasant, is he?" said Mort.

Priscilla answered, "I know him mainly by reputation, and his reputation is one of being extremely selfish, greedy, rude, and willing to go to any lengths to get what he wants. Still, he's not a bad lawyer. The police don't like him, but they respect his ability. They watch their words very carefully when he's around."

There was a double bump as the ferry landed. Sylvester and Sylvia Mann were among the first to rush to the exit, Mort and Priscilla the last ones out.

"Now I'll let you buy me a cup of coffee," she said, "and a doughnut if we have time. I'm to see Bumpus at eight-thirty, and the record offices you want open at the same time."

As they walked away from the pier, Mort said he could recognize only the police station, directly across the green. Priscilla pointed out that the city clerk's office—which held the vital records of interest to him—was in the large building to the left of the green, and the county registries of probate and land records were on the right.

"There's a coffee shop between the police building and city hall," she said. "Thus you conveniently have everything your heart could desire on this one square."

Following coffee and doughnuts, good even if eaten standing up, they went their respective ways. "I'm going back tonight," Priscilla called out as they were parting. "If we don't meet on the ferry, I'll see you at the hotel."

◆   ◆   ◆

Lieutenant Bumpus queried Priscilla as if she were the one under suspicion of murder. She felt wrung out when he finished, purged of everything she knew about the killing of Del Delano, and maybe more. At least the lieutenant was now fully abreast of the situation and ready to take charge as he sent one of the uniformed policemen to bring Dr. Delano to them.

"What was the nature of the original quarrel between you and Del Delano?" Bumpus asked his suspect, who sat resignedly in a chair in the center of the room.

Dr. Delano screwed up his features as if in deep thought. "The original quarrel? I think once at a family picnic I had to discipline my young cousin for eating all the hot dogs."

"Don't be facetious. You know what I mean."

"I know that I don't have to answer any questions until I have a chance to talk to my lawyer."

"But if you're innocent, as you claim, you shouldn't mind answering questions."

"Questions I don't mind. Insolence and attempts at intimidation I do."

Lieutenant Bumpus sighed. "What was the nature of the bad feelings between you and Del that existed immediately before you entered the pub that night?"

"There were no bad feelings between us."

"I can get other testimony that there were."

"You can always find gossipmongers on Fogge Island." The doctor pressed his massive shoulders against the back of his chair and stretched out his feet. "We were two different kinds of people, that's all. We belonged to two different generations. We had nothing in common."

"There was something about his dating Sylvia Mann before she married Sylvester Mann, wasn't there? As I understand it, Dr. Delano, you were somehow in the middle of a situation in which Sylvia left Del and went to Sylvester, and Del never forgave you for it."

"I can't speak for any lack of Christian virtue he may have had at the time."

"Then the facts are as I said?"

"Sylvia and Sylvester may have become engaged while staying at my cabin, but if Del held that against me, well, you'd have to ask him about it. I certainly didn't have any bad feelings against him."

There was a cat-and-mouse aspect about the interrogation that Priscilla found fascinating. She was glad of her role as a bystander, for she could take it all in with complete objectivity—or at least she thought she could. A feeling was coming over her that Dr. Delano was manipulating Lieutenant Bumpus, cleverly leading him into asking just the kind of question that Delano wanted him to ask. At first he would resist a question; then, when it was repeated, he let himself be "forced" into answering. Why?

"Because he's dead," Bumpus was saying, "I can't ask him, and have to ask you. When you talked to Del at the bar the night before last, did you discuss your role in Sylvia's leaving him?"

"I was very tired that night. I forget what we discussed."

The lieutenant changed tacks. "A witness has given us a signed statement that you yelled something to Del Delano about 'If you say anything, I'll kill you, I'll kill you.'"

"Is that a question?"

"The question is, is it true?"

"I don't recall saying anything like that, nor would I have had any reason for saying it."

"What was it that you didn't want Del Delano to tell?"

"This is like asking when did I stop beating my wife."

"You deny you said those words?"

"No."

"But you just said . . . ."

"That I didn't recall saying them. I didn't say that I didn't say them. Perhaps I did. I'd had a good bit to drink that night. Perhaps Del said to me, 'You're drunk, and I'm going to tell everybody.' Perhaps I was drunk enough to be argumentative. Perhaps I didn't want him to tell everyone I was drunk. I don't remember."

"Of course, of course. In fact, I have testimony that you'd been drinking heavily even before you entered the pub."

"One man's heavy is another man's light."

"Right, Dr. Delano. How many drinks did you have before going to the pub."

"Oh, a few perhaps."

"More than two?"

"Perhaps."

"More than four?"

"Perhaps."

"More than ten?"

"Perhaps."

"And where did you have these more than ten drinks?"

"I didn't say I had more than ten drinks. I don't know how many drinks I had. And I had them at home."

"Right. Corporal Dingley searched your home yesterday, Dr. Delano. You have an ample supply of Scotch there."

"Why not? Scotch is my favorite drink."

"Tell me, Dr. Delano, why did you go to the Admiral's Arms when it was almost closing time, when you'd had many drinks at home, and you still had a good supply of liquor at home? Why was it necessary to go to the Admiral's Arms?"

"I forget, Lieutenant Bumpus." The doctor straightened up in his chair. "After all, you've already established that I'd had a lot to drink. How would you expect me to remember?"

"Is that going to be your defense, Dr. Delano? You can't remember if you killed Del Delano or not because you'd been drinking too much?"

Delano quickly snapped to attention. "It's a fact, Lieutenant Bumpus, that I clearly remember leaving him alive. He'd gotten to his feet right after Tina left, and he sat down and nursed his bruised head. I looked at his wound and found it superficial, so I left. I know for a fact that he was alive, stable, and alert when I left."

The lieutenant's buzzer rang, and he picked up the telephone. After a moment he yelled back in the mouthpiece, "All right. Let him in!"

Sylvester Mann strode into the office. "Don't give them the time of day, Tom. They've charged you, so there's no habeas corpus, but I've just arranged for $20,000 bail." Turning to Bumpus, he said, "Lieutenant, I demand the release of Dr. Delano."

Bumpus shrugged, and Sylvester Mann led his client out the door.

"I knew that was coming," Bumpus said to Priscilla. "I was trying to get in as much as possible before it happened."

"What do you make of his testimony?" she asked.

"Booth, interrogation's been my business for more years than I care to remember. That very clever doctor thinks he's got me off the track. It's very obvious that he's more afraid of us finding out the real reason for his quarrel with Del Delano than he is about being brought to trial for murder. And you know something, sweetie, whatever it is, it doesn't have anything to do with that Sylvester and Sylvia Mann business. I'd stake my reputation on it. And on the fact that Dr. Delano wants desperately to keep something from us."

Priscilla wondered. Had Dr. Delano indeed been manipulating Bumpus? Or had Bumpus with all his experience been leading the doctor down a path of his own choosing? Bumpus certainly seemed convinced of his guilt. Could it be that Dr. Delano had committed all four murders after all?

Nine

Mort was recognized at the registry of Deeds by the clerk, a stately looking woman with blonde hair, an intelligent face, and a pleasant smile.

"Aren't you Dr. Mortimer Sinclair, the genealogist?"

Mort could not deny it, and the clerk introduced herself as Amy Hosmer. She was delighted to meet him—would he mind if she asked him a few questions? Mort's being recognized invariably cost him time, which, when he was in a hurry, as today, could be awkward. Still, the genealogist's cardinal rule was always to get along with personnel in record offices. They could be immensely helpful, if so inclined, or considerably harmful, if otherwise inclined.

This dependence on the good will of record office personnel had become even greater in recent years, with so many state, county, and local authorities now restricting access to public records, especially vital records. As governments and courts increasingly decided that lying could be in the public interest—themselves deciding, of course, where the public interest lay—life for the genealogist became more difficult. Human nature throughout the ages had been such that men and women lived together without benefit of marriage, that children were born out of wedlock or only a few months after the wedding, and that people sometimes saw fit to prevaricate about some aspect of their lives. The state determined that such foibles and peccadillos should be wrapped in a right of privacy, and that the state itself should take on the role of public liar when it came to adoptions. Thus the actual fact of parenthood was often nullified by the state for this or that individual as an adopting couple took on the responsibility for raising that individual's child, and records might contradict themselves, as some were legally altered to show the adopting couple as having conceived the child in the first place.

A typical rule was that only certain people could see the records for persons still living. But this time Mort found himself in the position of being able to see anything he wanted. Armed with both a power of attorney from Senator Gorges and a letter from Police Sergeant Priscilla Booth, he was given free access to all the records, and Amy Hosmer was quite happy to see that he got prompt service at all times. As a result, Mort was able to acquire a considerable amount of information in a relatively short period of time.

As he did his work with the various birth, marriage, and death records, Amy Hosmer came over from time to time to ask a question. "My sixteen-year-old son has taken a tremendous interest in genealogy. Are there any good books you could recommend?"

Mort told her that Donald Lines Jacobus's *Genealogy as Pastime and Profession* was as pertinent today as when it was first written, more than fifty years ago. As for texts on where and how to find genealogical information, *The Source* was particularly comprehensive. "And I would recommend as an excellent general guide both for beginning and experienced genealogists a two-volume set prepared by the American Society of Genealogists, *Genealogical Research: Methods and Sources.*"

She thanked him, and was back fifteen minutes later with another question. "What is the most important thing my son should do to become a good genealogist?" Again Mort interrupted his research. "Read the national genealogical journals. He can find bad genealogy in perhaps as much as ninety percent of the published family histories you find on library shelves. If he wants to see examples of good genealogy, he should go to the journals." Again she thanked him and went her way.

Mort gave her a vague "You're welcome," with his voice droning off to inaudibility, for his eyes had come across something of interest. He had seen and abstracted all the birth, marriage, and death records for members of Senator Atherton Gorges's family, and his genealogist's mind, trained to be especially watchful for chronological and other inconsistencies, had suddenly spotted a discrepancy. It was a small matter, and discrepancies were commonplace in public records, yet he knew it was well worth looking into. On the birth certificate for the murdered Ferdinand Gorges, the date of birth was given as 1 February 1961; on his death certificate the date of birth was 31 January 1961. Of course, the records he was examining were all clerk's copies, neatly typewritten from the original records. A good genealogist always tried to get as close to the original records as possible, and Mort decided he would have to see the originals before he left the office.

Amy Hosmer stood beside him again. "Dr. Sinclair, would German or Latin be better preparation for doing research in medieval European genealogy?" Mort patiently offered his opinion that Latin would be better for doing original research, which he recommended, but if a genealogist were to limit himself or herself to secondary sources, German would be more helpful. Time was passing, and there was so much to do. Mort finished his work at the City Clerk's office and hurried over to the county offices of probate and land records.

Wills and deeds being invaluable to the genealogist, Mort thought it unfortunate that most amateurs doing genealogical research overlooked these seemingly dry and uninteresting pages of inheritances and land transfers. What better proof could exist that John Doe had three sons and two daughters than his naming them in his will? So many relationships were given in these documents: children, grandchildren, spouses, in-laws, sometimes siblings and parents, often along with other details such as age ranges, marital status, and geographic locations. But if wills were a gold mine, then deeds were a diamond mine, for though perhaps ninety percent of deeds yielded no genealogical information, that remaining ten per cent more than made up for the total effort. A seller might describe land as having come to him via his wife, who received it from her father, who had in turn received it from his father, and so on. Deeds often encompassed broader relationships than wills. Together they were the genealogist's most powerful tools.

Mort meticulously made abstracts of those wills and deeds that interested him. Information from the wills of Fogge Island people greatly expanded his knowledge of living families. It certainly put him in a position of knowing what questions to ask when he got back to the island. When he got to the deeds, he was able to confirm in some cases, and supplement in others, a good amount of pertinent information.

It was now past noon. He was alone in the poorly maintained reading room, with its tired old furniture and lack of amenities, all others having gone to lunch except for a clerk behind the counter. He decided it was time for him to leave as well, for he wanted to spend the afternoon looking up old newspapers, but there was one more deed from the index that he wanted to look up: Gorges to Samson, 1953. He went to the shelves with their oversized books and selected the right volume number. Returning with it to his table, he quickly found the right page and scanned the information given there. Very interesting, he thought, especially when considered alongside with the previous deed for the same land. What he was reading also vaguely connected with something else he recalled from a conversation on the island. How could he get more information on this? Of course! It was a good thing he had gone to deeds before the newspaper office, for there could conceivably be something in the newspaper around the same date.

He was hungry. The single doughnut for breakfast had been hours ago and he knew he would not get another chance to eat until he was back at the hotel that night. As he walked out of the county offices, he looked to his right and left. Other than the doughnut shop across the square, the only thing he saw looking like a restaurant was to his left, on the corner across from the ferry building. Its sign read "Yorgo's Honest Food." That, Mort decided, was what he wanted, honest food.

It was served cafeteria style, with food-filled glass cabinets and plastic shelves rising above a long counter that accommodated the trays, and at lunchtime it was crowded. A young man with a black mustache rushed about his chores behind the counter, and above his head a menu board listed the available items: hamburgers, hot dogs, various sandwiches and subs, chili, soups, and soft drinks. Mort asked the man, "Where it says 'All Crab Meat,' under 'Subs,' does that mean 100 percent real honest-to-goodness crabmeat? Or this imitation stuff they've come out with?"

The mustached man said, "Look, I'm Yorgo. I own this place, and when I say 'Honest Food,' it's for real. Nothing but 100 percent pure king crab."

Mort smiled, and said, "Bless you, Yorgo, I'll take it. The world could use another million just like you." The sub was as good as the man's word, all crabmeat and delicious. As he ate, Mort mused that part of the reason for the high quality lay in the fact that the owner was not only on the premises but was the hardest-working person there.

"Mind if I join you?" the voice came from nowhere.

Looking up, Mort saw a familiar face—at least a face he had seen before, though he could not quite place it.

"There aren't any other seats," the voice said. It belonged to a paunchy middle-aged man in an ill-fitting business suit who seemed to have more hair in his brushlike moustache than on his head.

Mort smiled and beckoned him to be seated.

"I've seen you on the island," the man said. "I'm Mason Crosby, and I own the Samson Pharmacy."

Of course. Mort had seen him at both FIGS and at the Admiral's Arms, though they had never been formally introduced. Mort introduced himself, and they shook hands. Crosby was a quiet man, and they made only intermittent conversation as they ate their food. But Mort's companion did explain that he had brought his wife to the Bay City Hospital for some tests and he would be picking her up in the afternoon to take her back to the island.

"It's rough when you and your wife are the only ones running the store, except for the stock boy," he said. "I have to close up and leave a sign in the door telling people to come back later for prescriptions." He was attacking vigorously a pepper steak sub; between bites he said, "Good food here."

Mort agreed, finished his own sub and sipped at his mug of coffee, which was still steaming hot. "Tell me," he said, "how does a man named Crosby own a pharmacy named Samson?"

Crosby grinned. "Richard Samson used to own it, and I started working for him as a pharmacist when I got my degree." He went on to explain that Richard Samson had died in 1966, and that his widow tried to keep it going, with Crosby still as pharmacist, but she didn't have a mind for business and went bankrupt. "I must live right," Crosby said, "because just about that time some shares I inherited from my great aunt in the Ship Salvage Company—where both my father and grandfather had worked—suddenly went sky high. I didn't have many shares, but I made enough money selling them to put a good down payment on the pharmacy. After I bought it, I thought of changing the name, but the customers wouldn't have liked it. Tradition means a lot on Fogge Island."

Mort got directions from Crosby on how to get to the newspaper office. When he reached it, he found that they kept copies of the newspaper for only three months back. The older copies were on microfilm at the public library. Again he had to get directions, only to find out that the library was close to where he had started, in fact, just behind the police station.

There were a few teenage boys and girls in the library, probably doing homework assignments, but the adults for the most part looked as if they were seeking shelter more than knowledge. A half dozen poorly dressed, unshaven, unkempt men lounged about in various parts of the main reading room, as if they were trying to keep as far from each other as possible. The librarian, who seemed pleased to see a well-dressed man in front of her, was more than happy to answer his questions. Within minutes Mort was seated at a cubicle with a microfilm reader in front of him and a stack of thirty-five millimeter microfilms in boxes beside the machine.

Time was his enemy, but after glancing at a dozen or so issues of the newspaper, Mort saw his best hopes realized. The *Bay City Gazette* had for years followed the practice of featuring a "News from Fogge Island" page every Thursday morning. Looking up only one page per week, Mort might miss some headline or other big event, but the highlights of Fogge Island's everyday life could be skimmed without a major investment of time. For the most part he just wanted to browse, but this yielded him surprising insights into the island's people. He had but one specific purpose in mind and that was to see what happened, if anything, in 1953.

There it was! "Resident Hurt on Rocks." Deborah Samson, age twenty-five, had slipped while climbing on the rocks and badly injured herself. Most of the damage was to her face, which required twenty stitches. That was two weeks before the date of the land transaction Mort had abstracted at the Registry of Deeds. Another item some five weeks after the accident on the rocks announced that Deborah Samson, age twenty-five, had been appointed executive officer and librarian of FIGS, to replace Miss Elsie Crosby, who had decided to retire. Though very young to hold such a position, Miss Samson was considered to have an excellent background in genealogy and came from one of the island's patrician families. She had been elected to the position by unanimous vote of the trustees.

So, Mort thought, this was the sequence of events. Deborah Samson fell on a rocky ledge and injured herself quite seriously. He had wondered how she obtained that large curved scar jutting like a saber wound down her face, and now he knew—or at least he knew what the official version was. Then, about two weeks later, Atherton Gorges bought a house and land in Oldtown for twenty-seven thousand dollars. One day later, Atherton Gorges sold the same house and land to Deborah Samson for what was described as "one dollar plus other valuable consideration." Three weeks after that, the chief salaried employee of FIGS retired, and a very young Deborah Samson was appointed in her place by the board of trustees, of which the president was the father of Atherton Gorges. It was all very interesting, he thought, wondering what had really happened. No doubt it was another one of those island secrets Deborah Samson herself had declared to be more numerous than people. But was there anything here which might throw some light on the murders or on the motivation for the murders?

Mort continued rolling the microfilm through the years. Every now and then a headline would catch his eye, but if his quick glance showed it was not Thursday's paper, he continued turning the crank. All he had time for was Thursday's Fogge Island page. The living people—and the dead—who were connected in any way with the murders demanded all his attention, and they got it. There was an amazing amount of background information available just for the effort of cranking a microfilm reel, and Mort made notes until his hand positively ached.

All in all, it had been a fruitful day. Mort had gathered a significant part of the information he needed to complete his charts and had also made a start on his assignment for Atherton Gorges. Moreover, he felt sure there were leads in the information he had obtained that would help Priscilla beyond the genealogical charts per se. His work successful, his assignment would soon be over. Within the next few days he would be submitting his report and a bill, and could then go back to Salt Lake City. He would say goodbye to Priscilla, ask her to send him a letter when she had solved the case, and invite her to call him if she ever got out to Salt Lake City. One more episode in the life of Mortimer Sinclair would thus be ended.

Would his work really help Priscilla, or was all his effort just incidental to the murder investigation? The events concerning Deborah Samson in 1953 were provocative, but he admitted that Priscilla would be in a better position than he to exploit them. There was additionally an incidental item on Percival Mann that would seem to make an interview with Margaret Mann desirable. As he hurried down to the ferry, knowing that the schedule called for it to leave in ten minutes, he felt vaguely uneasy. There was something he was not doing, something that he should have done. There had been so many details that day, but what was it that he should have remembered? He heard the ferry's whistle, and walked even faster.

He was disappointed not to see Priscilla on the ferry. Had she caught an earlier one, or was she still in Bay City? The ferry departed on schedule, no delay this time. But then, he realized, there would not be the same need for a delay. They would not have had to hold the ferry for Senator Gorges; the Senator was already aboard sitting at his reserved table, drinking a mug of some kind of hot white liquid—malted milk, Mort guessed—seemingly oblivious to anyone else in the cabin. As Mort came in, the Senator suddenly looked up and noticed him.

He motioned him over. "Join me, Sinclair."

Mort took the seat across from him with some reluctance. The Senator asked if he had started the investigation.

Mort said yes; he had made a start in Bay City, and he had

telephoned a correspondent in North Carolina to check out the Senator's college years. "I am not doing anything at this time on your army service, especially the time you spent overseas. I will check again with you before I do, because it could be costly."

"Check out the army, too. I won't begrudge you any reasonable expense."

"Let's see what the North Carolina research shows first," Mort said.

He looked closely at the man sitting across the table from him. He was a strange man; he seemed to have it all. He was intelligent, well-educated and well-read; handsome in a formal way, seemingly in good health with a tanned face and good muscle tone; rich and powerful, ruler of all he could survey from his mountain-top aerie, a man for whom time had to stop, at least as far as ferry schedules were concerned. Senator Atherton Gorges was the epitome of the God-blessed aristocrat. And yet, Mort felt certain, Atherton Gorges was not a happy man.

The Senator returned Mort's appraising look with a wistful, saddened one of his own, his features losing some of their handsomeness. "You don't care for me, do you?"

"I don't know you. I'm sure you have your good points."

"That's nonsensical bullshit! You're not sure of anything of the kind. I probably bore you with my talk, but I doubt if you have anything better to do for the next half hour. You probably see me as everyone else does, born to wealth, arrogance, position and prestige, people waiting on me and cowering before me, trying to curry favor with me as if I had the whole world at my feet. The truth? I'm a sick man, completely dependent on medicine to keep physical pain away. My customary diet is pablum, and I haven't been allowed to touch alcohol for years. When it comes to mental pain, I sometimes feel like Tiberius Caesar: 'If you only knew what agonies I endure daily.'"

"Why tell me?" Mort said.

"We are very conscious of family on the island, we Gorgeses in particular," the Senator said. "More than anything else, I wanted sons to carry on my line. I was disappointed when Martha failed to give me more than one, but . . . ."

Mort stepped into his pause. "Are you sure it was entirely her fault?"

"I take your point," Gorges said. "I should have said that Martha and I failed to have more than one son, but at least there was hope for that one, and then, of course, I lost him, and there will be no descendants. After the loss of Ferdinand, I briefly transferred my hopes to Lettice, but you know what the situation is there. With her peculiar sexual preference, and her avowal never to go through pregnancy, realistically I cannot look for heirs there."

Mort could not help thinking of the Senator's niece, Esther, murdered while pregnant, and of her brother, Dudley, going around telling everyone that the Senator himself was the father. That would have been one way of carrying the line on, even if it could never have been revealed publicly, but of course that was a moot matter now.

"I still don't know why you're telling me all this," Mort said.

"I want you to understand how I feel about the murder of Ferdinand. Everyone seems to think I'm all power and no feeling. But I am powerless to get myself an heir. I'm powerless to change the past. And I do have feelings." The conscious Gorges seemed to be slowly receding, as if he were drawing further and further away from the present moment. Suddenly he looked over at Mort and said, "Do you know Kavafis?"

Mort, who was well acquainted with the poetry of Constantine Kavafis, merely said, "Yes."

"For some reason he is the only poet who can speak to me. In all my acquaintance with—and, yes, love for—literature, I have never been able to appreciate poetry, except for Kavafis. I discovered him long ago when I was stationed in Greece, and I've often wished I could read him in the original, but I know only the translations. There's a short poem that at times seems to have special meaning for me."

Dear God, was he going to start reciting Kavafis? Mort wondered.

"It's called *The City*, but I won't recite the whole thing, just the last line. It goes like this: 'Just as you have ruined your life here in this little corner, so have you destroyed yourself in all the world.'"

Mort repeated the line. "*Etsi pou ti zoi sou rimaxes edo stin kokhi touti tin mikri, s'olin tin gi tin halases.*"

"You know modern Greek?"

"Yes."

"I envy you." He took several sips from his cup. "More than you can imagine." He was staring fiercely at Mort.

Mort wondered, is he trying to confess something? Mort's first attempt at answering his own question was to theorize that the Senator was one of those types who enjoyed—or obtained consolation from—feeling sorry for themselves. In all his talks with Priscilla they had assumed that the Senator could not have committed the murders, since he had more to lose than gain by the loss of his son. Indeed, Priscilla's whole idea that inheritance was the motive for the killings assumed that Atherton Gorges was the person being acted on, not the actor. But now Mort began to wonder if they should not be paying more attention to this maudlin, melancholy multi-millionaire.

After a minute or so, the Senator let his eyes drop, and the two of them sat in silence until the ferry docked.

◆   ◆   ◆

As Mort passed the hotel desk, the clerk handed him a package about the size of a cigar box. It was addressed to him at the hotel, no room number, and was heavy. He was not especially curious, and he stopped by the bar for a beer before going on to his room. Turning on the TV to the news, he sat in an easy chair and slowly unwrapped the package. Whoever sent it had not been stingy with the plastic tape; it took a pocket knife to finish opening it. Inside was a cardboard box, and inside the box was something wrapped in newsprint. He finally unraveled all the covering, only to find a heavy flat stone with a note fastened around it by a rubber band. The note was penned in block letters and green ink on Mann Hotel stationery and read:

"Sinclair. This could of been a bomb! Get off the island or your dead."

Ten

IN THE MORNING MORT FOUND THAT Priscilla had left a message for him at the hotel. She would be tied up for a while but would like to have him join her at the constable's office at 1:00 p.m. He was glad in a way to have the chance to spend more time at FIGS. During his brief participation in this case he had gradually met and talked to a good number of people, checked records, asked questions, drawn preliminary charts, and made notes for himself; and now he felt that he was getting to be an expert on the genealogies of the island's families, that he might know more about the backgrounds of some of them than they did themselves. Now he was anxious to fill in any gaps that might prove significant—some dates here, a few missing family members there, had this one ever been married and to whom, did that one have children; did he have all possible probate information, both testate and intestate? There were still details to be obtained, and as usual in genealogy, those last few items were often the most difficult to dig out. So back to FIGS it would be.

Margaret Mann looked up from the librarian's desk and said Deborah was in her office. "Should I get her?"

"I might want to see her later," Mort said, "but for now I'll just occupy myself with some books."

As soon as he settled in with the first volume, Mort recognized Old Richie Crosby, said to be the oldest resident on the island, sitting half asleep at the far table. Having decided to start up a conversation, Mort found it easy to get Old Richie talking—for he loved attention, though his own attention span was quite short. Nonetheless, with great patience and carefully phrased questions, Mort was able to carry on a fruitful discussion with him.

Richie Crosby, at ninety-three, was fascinated by death. Having seen first his elders, then his contemporaries, and finally some of his juniors depart this earth, he took strength and, yes, even joy in being a survivor. "Tim Wheeler died on the mainland this week," he told Mort with a touch of pride in his voice. "He was ninety-four, and we went to school together. Last year he said he'd dance on my grave. Well, he's not going to do much dancing where he's going now, ha, ha."

Mort maneuvered the conversation back to island families. "Oh, yes," said Old Richie, "there was the influenza epidemic of 1919. They were dying faster than they could get coffins for them. Good thing it was winter and they could keep the bodies frozen in the shed by the pond. The mainland didn't want them. Couldn't get enough coffins there neither."

As the morning hours wore on, Mort was satisfied that he was learning more than enough to justify his time. Old Richie in turn seemed to be delighted with the opportunity of speaking out loud to someone who actually kept listening to him. His memory, of course, was far better for the years in which he had been young, and when he spoke of his contemporaries, the authority in his voice was unmistakable. On more recent events, he showed signs of vagueness. "Yes, those murders. Wasn't that young fellow Ferdinand Gorges, the son of Ferdie, Sr., poisoned last year?"

Mort gently corrected him, "The young Ferdinand who was poisoned was the son of Atherton Gorges and the grandson of Ferdinand, Sr."

Old Richie chewed that one over for a few seconds, and then said, "Oh, yes, Ferdie, Sr. died maybe twenty, twenty-five years ago. Young Ferdie was the son of Atherton Gorges and Martha Mann. Martha was the daughter of Samuel Mann. I knew Samuel real well. Used to work for him once, when he was manager of the Ship Salvage Company. My son, Nathaniel, used to work at the salvage company too. He was a diver. But my grandson went out and got himself a college degree and now he owns the pharmacy. Good thing Samuel married young, for he didn't last long after school. I went to his funeral."

Mort nodded his head in a friendly fashion and made occasional jottings on his notepad to show that he was listening. He waited for a pause, then said, "Now, your sister Lilly Crosby married Oswald Penrose. Did Lilly have any children?"

Old Richie paused again—Mort knew that if the time were sufficiently far back, the pause would not be a long one—and then said, "Only one, but he died without getting married, and my sister Elsie, who used to be the executive secretary here at FIGS, was an old maid. So the Crosby line continued only through me. You think about it, young man—anyone named Crosby on this island is my descendant. My grandfather was the first Crosby on the island, and he married a Gorges girl, so we also have the blood of Caleb Fogge, the founder, in our veins."

Every now and then someone would enter the library and greet Old Richie, whose response was likely to be "What, you still alive?" followed by raucous laughter. At times Mort had to wait twenty minutes or more to get the right kind of answer to a question, but at other times his pen was hard put to keep up with the plethora of details Old Richie could disgorge. This was the kind of information not usually found in public records, no matter how helpful they were. A will listed the heirs; a conversation with a knowledgeable old-timer could reveal why one heir was favored over another. Death certificates could yield the fact and date of death, but Old Richie could tell of the illness that had caused the death. His faint eyes could not see much in front of him, but behind the eyes a keen memory retrieved family feuds, broken love affairs, unsavory business practices, noble gestures, and scores of other human events that would never be chronicled.

More people entered the library and got books or talked together, and some of these Mort recognized and nodded to. Deborah Samson came out of her office a few times and gave him a wave and a smile. Finally, Margaret left for lunch, and Deborah took over the library desk. Old Richie did not seem to want to let go of Mort, and in truth, Mort was reluctant to leave, but the lunch hour was almost over, and he wanted to get at least a sandwich before going to meet Priscilla.

As Mort stood up to go, Old Richie said, "Do you know my granddaughter, Sylvia? I could tell you something about her and that young Delano fellow who got himself murdered if I had a mind to." Mort gently tried to coax more out of the old man, but although Richie enjoyed the renewed attention, he was not going to say anything more. Soon he started dozing, catching himself with a jerk at first but then slipping into a deep sleep. Mort left him and walked over to Deborah.

She looked up from the book she was reading. "We are having a trustees' meeting this afternoon which you might find interesting," she said. "I am sure the others would be pleased to have you attend."

"Thanks, but I doubt that I'll be returning to the library this afternoon." With which he left the building and headed for Meg's Muffin Shoppe.

◆   ◆   ◆

The first thing he noticed when he arrived at the constable's office was Priscilla's clothes. She looked charming in a light blue and white cross-striped kilt, a white blouse with triple cravat, and a navy blue velvet jacket.

"I didna ken ye were a Napier," he said.

"Are you trying to say that you didn't know I was a Napier?" Priscilla asked. "Well, I'm not."

"But you are wearing the Napier tartan."

"Oh, this!" she said, touching her kilt. "I didn't know what tartan it was. I just like the color."

"Hmmm. That wouldna do in Scotland, lassie. Those without a tartan of their own usually wear certain general ones, such as the Black Watch."

"What color is it?" Priscilla asked with genuine interest. "Probably a stupid question. Black, I suppose."

Mort walked over to a chair and sat down, "Blue and green."

"Oh, that's not too bad. How about Sinclair? I suppose there's a Sinclair tartan."

"Ay, that there is, lassie. Mainly red and green."

"Yuk! I think I'll have to look for a Napier to marry. I could never wear red and green. That's for Christmas trees."

They laughed and then were silent for a moment.

Mort said, "Want to see something crazy?" He took the note in green ink out of his pocket and showed it to Priscilla, explaining how it had come into his possession.

"Looks like the work of a crank," she said. "I suppose you checked with the desk clerk to see how it got there."

"It just appeared as if by magic on the desk, probably while the clerk was away for a few minutes. No idea who left it. Think there is a clue in the spelling?"

"Possibly. It could be an honest crank, if I can use the term. Or it could be something more sinister, someone giving you a warning but trying to disguise the way they normally write."

"Ben Mann, for example?"

"Oh, no. Ben would never do anything like this."

"Are you sure? He struck me as a little peculiar. Any chance he might be losing touch with reality? Someone like that could be dangerous."

"Ben might have some personal worries, perhaps finances, I don't know. But I've known him for years, and this just isn't his style. At any rate, do be careful, Mort. We've had enough killings here already, and they didn't get even this much warning." She took the note and put it in a file jacket, then locked the file in a desk drawer.

"That's what makes it look so funny, don't you think?" said Mort. "Four murders without warning, and suddenly this."

"How about three poisonings and suddenly a head bashing? Let's not freeze our thoughts on what the murderer might or might not do. But do be careful, Mort. Anyway," she said, her eyes brightening, "I'm glad you're here. Care to take a drive?" She pulled on a coat. "Come on."

She led him to a car that belonged to Constable Gorges and proceeded to drive down Gilman Street with all the fast abandon of a police officer on business. The island was close to being oval shaped, pinched in at the waist, and there were three roads that led to the opposite side from the three streets of Oldtown perpendicular to Sea Drive—all three roads were dirt and gravel by the preference of the Oldtown residents, who could not see raising their taxes to pay for paving roads used mainly by outsider hotels and villa owners. Priscilla wanted to show Mort the seacoast, and so they took the east road. On the way she explained that while she was gone Corporal Dingley had taken a telephone message from Michael Laszlo, a stockbroker who was spending a week by himself at one of the summer villas and claimed to have some important information about the murder of Delano Delano.

"I thought the villas were closed in winter," Mort said.

"Not exactly. The largest ones have off-season caretakers, and many of them are used for a week or two here and there by their owners or some of the owners' friends, especially during holidays but also at other times. Mr. Laszlo is staying at the Kincaid estate, one of the biggest. I brought along the portable typewriter, so I can take down his statement and have him sign it on the spot. You can witness it."

The sea route was lonely with gray skies, a few small pine trees, and mile after mile of gracefully sculptured sand dunes. Occasionally on the left, the land side, there would be a small house and signs of habitation—a pasture, fenced gardens, here and there a car, once even a barking dog. The sea side was clear of any human influence, the state having bought much of the land to preserve for an eventual park. After they had driven some five miles or so, the sand changed to huge rocks; perched on the rocks on the sea side, but considerably back from the sea, were large houses spaced far apart from each other, each house surrounded by a varying number of smaller outbuildings. The land gently undulated, forming small vales and coves, and Mort noticed that they were far from the sea now, the land surrounding the villas having taken up a significant corner of the island. Here and there on the right were private drives curving around to approach the villas, some tree-lined, some hidden on the other side of high walls. The villas all seemed to have one feature in common: they had obviously been built for privacy.

Before coming to the three-road intersection, Priscilla pulled into a rough gravel driveway on the right. The villa that was their destination was surrounded on the three land sides by a high stone wall. Priscilla had to stop for Mort to hop out and open a gate before they could continue past the gatehouse and on up a winding driveway. There had been no sign, no number, and no name at the gate, which itself was almost out of sight behind a baffle of hedges. "This is where the very public Kincaids come to spend the very private part of their lives," Priscilla commented. A bright orange BMW was parked outside the main entrance to the mansion.

By the time they parked their car, Michael Laszlo was standing in front of the door ready to greet them, a bent bulldog briar pipe clamped between his lips. A man of about forty, with regular features unremarkable except for the intensity in his eyes, Laszlo ushered them into a knotty chestnut-paneled den and invited them to sit down. After a few civilities, Priscilla asked him to tell the full story in his own words.

Well, he was not quite sure how to start. It was a bit embarrassing, but they were all people of the world, and he was sure they would understand.

"First, I think I should let you know that I'm separated from my wife, and have been for more than a year. We'll probably end up with a divorce." That preliminary disclaimer out of the way, he proceeded between puffs on his pipe to explain that he had come to the villa for a week of rest, but a few days ago the rest had turned to restlessness, and he decided to go to Oldtown that evening just to see what was happening there. "I'd had dinner by myself in the Talleyrand Room, then about nine o'clock I went over to the Admiral's Arms to have a drink before driving back to here. I didn't drink much, maybe two beers in almost two hours. I was sitting at a table by myself, and my waitress was a girl named Lucy." Out of loneliness, he had kidded around with her a little, but she seemed to think he was serious, and one thing led to another, and finally he asked her to go back with him to the villa. She declined, but he thought she was just being coy.

"Lucy was hard to read," he said, "but after a while I got the impression that she would like to go with me. Especially when it got near closing time and she suggested I go outside and she would leave in a few minutes. I looked at my watch and saw that it was fifteen minutes before eleven. I waited in my car, which was parked in front of the pharmacy. Several people left, and then I saw Dr. Thomas Delano go into the pub, which was strange, because it was closing time.''

"You know Dr. Delano?" Priscilla asked him.

"Oh, yes, he treated me once when I got a fishhook embedded in my arm."

Lazlo went on with his story. He'd waited there in his car, and finally saw a waitress leave, but it was the other waitress, not Lucy. The time was two or three minutes past eleven o'clock when he saw Dr. Delano come out, turn left, and walk up Sea Drive. Having nothing better to do, Lazlo watched the doctor go by Meg's Muffin Shoppe and turn into Gilman Street. He looked again at his watch and noted that it was five minutes past eleven.

He waited for Lucy another thirty or so minutes, but she didn't come out the front door. He guessed that she either lived there or had gone out some other door. Since the lights were still on, he decided to go in again and find out for sure what had happened to her. He got out of the car and walked toward the pub, but at that moment the lights in the front room went out.

"I could see there was still a dimmer light shining from the back of the building, but a minute later it went out too. I didn't ring the bell, but quietly tried the front door and found it locked." Again he looked at his watch and saw that the time was eleven-forty. He went back to his car and returned to the villa. There it was, the whole story. When he saw on television that Dr. Delano was being held for murder, he realized he should get in touch with the police.

Priscilla was writing fast. "Can you swear that it was Dr. Delano who came out around eleven o'clock?" Lazlo nodded. "Can you swear that you had Dr. Delano, and no one else, in your sight all the way from the pub to Gilman Street?" Again Lazlo nodded.

Mort of course understood what this information did to any police case against Dr. Delano. A good half-hour after Dr. Delano left, someone had turned out the lights and locked the front door. Dr. Delano's wife had stated that her husband came home at ten past eleven while she was watching the TV weather report and stayed with her all night. Michael Laszlo's watch could not be wrong, for he was right about the time Dr. Delano entered the pub and the time Tina left it. Unless his wife was lying, Dr. Delano could neither have turned out the lights in the pub at eleven forty nor locked the front door. Some other living person had been in the pub long after Dr. Delano left. Either that living person was Del Delano himself, or it was some person who wanted to remain unknown, most likely Del's murderer. In either case, Dr. Thomas Delano had a perfect alibi.

Priscilla asked only a few questions, for Laszlo had been quite thorough in his telling of the story. She quickly typed a statement and had Laszlo sign it.

◆   ◆   ◆

"Where to now?" said Mort, when they were back in the car.

"You've never seen Cobber Palgrave's beach house, have you? Well, you're going to see it now. Lucy Palgrave still lives there, and I not only want to get her corroboration for some of Laszlo's story, but I'm curious to see how she's coming along in the house now that she's the sole owner."

Mort recalled Priscilla's discovery that the late Esther Gorges had paid off the mortgage and bought the house from Cobber and then put the title jointly in her own and Lucy's names. Lucy would have inherited nothing from Cobber, who had more debts than assets, but at least thanks to Esther's peculiar actions, Lucy owned the beach house.

The dirt road to the house lay just a little beyond the entrance to the Kincaid villa. It descended into a crevice with steep sides and a gradual downward slope in the middle, ending in a small sandy beach at a rocky inlet from the sea. The house itself was more or less as Mort had imagined it, single-story, with somewhat dilapidated wood shingles, a small porch in front, and a crumbling brick fireplace to one side. The surprising thing was to see a black Mercedes parked in front.

Their knock on the door was answered by Lettice Gorges, who reluctantly let them in. "Lucy can't see *anyone*," Lettice said. "She's not *feeling* well."

"I'm sorry, but she'd have to have a doctor's certificate to avoid seeing me," Priscilla said.

Mort could see that there were but two rooms to the house, the front room in which they were standing, which was a combined living-dining room and kitchen, and the room where Lucy was, presumably a bedroom. An open door on the far side of the kitchen area led to the bathroom. The furniture, he noted in surprise, was all out of keeping with the quality of the house. If not luxurious, it was in excellent taste and quite new. Cobber had been killed more than six months ago. The furniture looked even newer than that—it even smelled new.

Lettice called Lucy, who came as far as the doorway between the main room and the bedroom.

"I'd like to talk to you alone, Lucy," Priscilla said.

Lucy looked bewildered. She glanced quickly at Lettice, who shrugged her shoulders. "Well, I guess it's all right. Do you want to talk to me in the bedroom?"

Lettice decided to try one more time. "I *insist* on being with her."

"You her attorney?" asked Priscilla.

"I can *get* one in a hurry," Lettice said.

"Good. Why don't you do that? Here, shall I open the door for you? Do hurry back. If you dawdle, we might be finished and gone." Toughness was not characteristic of Priscilla, but it was part of her training, and she knew how to use it when necessary.

Lettice, for her part, knew when to give way in a fight, and she did nothing further to interfere with Priscilla's entry into the bedroom. As she went through the doorway, Priscilla called back, "Dr. Sinclair, do keep Ms. Gorges company, please."

♦   ♦   ♦

Lucy sat on the edge of a new king-size, richly lacquered wood bed and offered Priscilla the one lounge chair in the room. Priscilla took out her notepad and pen. "Do you recall the night that Del Delano was killed?" she asked. She skillfully led Lucy into a sequential recital of her activities that night, without bringing up Michael Laszlo. Within a few minutes, Lucy alluded to him. "Tell me more about this customer who tried to pick you up," Priscilla said. "Can you describe his appearance?"

Lucy proceeded to describe Lazlo. Priscilla elicited more details, all of which coincided with the story she had heard earlier.

"I didn't want to get him mad," Lucy said, "because Del always tells us to string the customers along, but this guy kept bugging me. When I saw he thought I wanted to go out with him, I didn't know what to do, so I said I'd meet him out front. Business wasn't good that night, and I asked Del if I could leave a little early, and then I went out the back door. I've never seen him again, but I'd know him if I did. Did he do something, Sergeant Booth?"

◆　　　　　◆　　　　　◆

In the main room, Mort had declined Lettice's offer of a drink and watched her pour herself a straight Southern Comfort.

"You got a thing about ladies in *uniform?*" she said. "I think they're *gorgeous* myself."

Mort smiled without answering. "Did Cobber Palgrave leave much of an estate?"

"Are you *kidding?* He didn't leave enough money to *bury* him. Where'd you get that idea?"

"The furniture is all new," Mort said. "Looks like Lucy ran into a little money."

Lettice's drink went down the wrong way, and she coughed up whiskey on her blouse. "Lucy's a hard-working kid. Why can't people leave her *alone?*"

"Like you are leaving her alone?"

"Look, mister, I do a lot of *good* for Lucy. No one else gives a *damn* about her. I paid for this furniture, if you must know, because I wanted her to live in *decent* conditions."

Mort sensed the right moment and dealt her a blow based on sheer guesswork. "Just like you paid for the mortgage and fixed it for her to own this house?"

Lettice drew back her glass as if she were about to throw the rest of its contents in his face. "*Esther* paid off the mortgage," she said.

Mort took another calculated guess. "Esther didn't have that kind of money. After she blew her inheritance, your father gave her food and room and a minimal spending allowance. She might have signed the check that paid off the mortgage, but the money came from somewhere else, and it would have left a wide trail. Even if you gave her the money in cash, you would have done it by cashing a check around the same time that she deposited the money in her account. Money leaves tracks, you know."

Lettice thought this one over a while, then she poured more Southern Comfort into her glass. "It wasn't cash. She deposited my *check,* plus an extra *thousand* for her effort, and then paid the mortgage. There's no crime in that."

"I'm not accusing you of committing a crime, but you know how the police think."

"No, how *do* they think?"

"They are liable to ask how, when you let Esther put the title jointly in both her name and Lucy's name, you knew Esther was going to die."

Lettice's face paled. "They can't frame *me* for Esther's murder. I didn't know she was going to die. I let Esther make herself a joint owner because that was the only way she'd cooperate, and I had good *reasons* for not wanting to put it in my name."

"Your father?" Mort suggested.

Lettice said nothing.

◆   ◆   ◆

In the bedroom, Priscilla had finished questioning Lucy about Michael Laszlo, and was now going over some of the same territory being covered by Mort. "Lucy, what's your relationship with Lettice?" Lucy hesitated; Priscilla insisted and finally broke through her silence.

"We're good friends. She's kind to me . . . most of the time. She doesn't beat me. All my life people have been mean to me, and I've never had the good things other people have. Lettice gives me expensive presents, and she's kind to me."

"Are you lovers?"

Lucy hung her head.

"It's obvious, isn't it?" Priscilla said. "Did Cobber know?"

Here she hit an open nerve, and Lucy flared up. "That bastard told me to do it! That bastard told me I had to let her make love to me. It was all his idea, not mine."

"Then Cobber knew? And he didn't care?"

Lucy began crying, and Priscilla put her arm over her shoulder. Between sobs Lucy said, "Cobber sold me to her. That's what he did. She paid him for me. And she was a hell of a lot nicer to me than he ever was. I hated that bastard with all my heart!"

Priscilla apologized for having to inquire into Lucy's personal life and told her she would type up a statement about Michael Laszlo for her to sign. Lucy, still crying, agreed.

♦   ♦   ♦

As Priscilla and Lucy came into the main room, Mort was saying to Lettice, "I understand Ferdinand left a lot of money and a will, and named you his main heir."

Lettice said, "You know *you're* a dirty son of a *bitch,* don't you?" With which she threw her drink into his face, smashed the glass on the floor, and fled into the bedroom. Lucy ran after her and shut the door.

"What on earth were you two talking about?" Priscilla asked.

Mort drew her toward the outside door. "Come on, I'll tell you in the car. I'll bet we have some interesting notes to compare."

Eleven

"**N**OW THAT WE'VE EARNED OUR KEEP, there's not much to do in Oldtown on a Saturday night," Priscilla said, as they left the car in front of Constable Gorges's house.

"Have a drink, I suppose," Mort said. "Then have dinner, then I guess have another drink."

"Surely we can vary the routine a little more than that, Dr. Sinclair." She laughed and took his arm with both her hands, tugging on it as if she were prodding him to some action.

"What did you have in mind, Sergeant Booth?"

"Well, what could two normal, red-blooded American kids like us think up? Let's use some ingenuity."

"I think it would take more than ingenuity to make kids out of us. At least out of me. The last time I bled, my blood was still red. But I don't think I was a kid even when I was a kid. I went to college at fifteen and got my first degree at seventeen."

"Brainy little brat, weren't you? Didn't you ever do normal things?"

"Like what?"

"Like dance, play basketball, whistle at a pretty girl."

"Oh, I have done a little whistling."

They had reached the back of the church now and by silent

agreement were walking away from the hotel. The sea was quiet, the moon brilliant, and the weather not cold. They walked arm in arm down Sea Drive on the store side, crossed over in front of the gateway to the Gorges mansion and walked back on the harbor side. There was a bit more breeze now, but they ignored it.

"I suppose," Priscilla said, "we could go to my room and listen to a bit of music. I've got a mini-boombox with me and a handful of good tapes. Not exactly compact disc fidelity, but one can make do in an emergency."

"Sounds marvelous. Perhaps we could get a bottle of wine at the bar—some of that good stuff we had the other night."

"You're on, Dr. Sinclair. I knew we'd think of something."

"Sounds good. Are you hungry, or should we skip dinner?"

"I don't know about that, now. It's bad enough my having a man in my room in the first place. But factoring in a bottle of wine on an empty stomach sounds more risky than adventurous. I'd say discretion demands that we at least have dinner first. And besides, you'll love the Veal Oscar that's the chef's special on Saturday night."

Mort agreed that a well prepared Veal Oscar was mighty tempting, and they planned their meal down to the salad and dessert, deciding also to have Chardonnay with the veal but take a bottle of Pinot Noir to the room after.

As they entered the hotel lobby, Corporal Dingley rushed up to Priscilla. "For God's sake, Priscilla, where have you been? I've been looking all over for you."

She let go of Mort's arm. "What's the matter, Dingley? What's wrong?"

"I'll explain as we go. Come on. Bumpus sent the police boat for you, and he wants you immediately in Bay City."

She frowned. "I'm sorry, Mort. I guess you'll have to have dinner without me."

As he saw her disappear through the door, Mort let out a sigh. He walked toward the dining room, then veered to the left, entered the bar, and started to order, but couldn't think of what. Finally he decided. "I'll take a beer. Make it Sam Adams."

Twelve

ON SUNDAY MORNING MORT ENTERED THE Talleyrand Room for breakfast. Priscilla, he assumed, was still on the mainland, for he had called her room upon waking up and not gotten an answer. He was therefore surprised not only to see her at one of the tables but to see her with Ben Mann, who was perspiring and looking cross. As Mort passed close to their table, Priscilla asked if he would like to join them. Mort took a look at the expression on Mann's face, and said, "Thanks, but no. You seem about finished."

Priscilla looked apologetic, gave Mort her prettiest smile, and said, "Mort, can you drop by the office around ten? Something new has come up."

Mort nodded, took a window table, and spread the Sunday newspaper out before him. He ordered breakfast number three, with the eggs over medium. Not an overly curious man, he nevertheless wondered about this new development. Had he made a mistake in declining Priscilla's invitation to join them? He looked over at their table just in time to see Priscilla and Ben leaving together.

It was early, and he would probably finish his breakfast before nine o'clock. He skimmed the front section of the newspaper but couldn't muster much interest in the features. There would still be more than an hour before he saw Priscilla, a lot of time to wait, but not enough to accomplish anything constructive. But the weather was nice, and Mort decided to take a walk and see those parts of Oldtown he had never seen before. Walking down Wentworth Street, he became absorbed in the different styles of architecture, the lace-trimmed Victorians, symmetrical garrisons, and lopsided salt boxes, all displaying well-weathered wood; then the single brick, rather large, elegant center-hall Federal style mansion tucked in behind a six-foot-high iron fence. On the gatepost of this one a brass plaque read: "Sylvester D. Mann, Esq." Mort continued walking. When he reached the first intersection, he turned into a beautiful tree-shaded street called Coolidge. There the houses were more uniform in size, mostly smaller colonials, neatly painted with well-maintained yards. Crossing Center Street, he continued on until he reached Gilman Street and could go no further straight ahead.

Looking between the houses on the far side of Gilman, he saw that the land rose upward to a plateau and realized that this was the back of Senator Gorges's mansion; its grounds stretched for at least several blocks. He turned left and crossed to walk down Gilman on the far side, past a neat modern rambler where the mailbox in front was marked with the name "Thomas A. Delano, M.D." Still further down Gilman, several houses past Dr. Delano's, was a two-storied shingled Victorian whose mailbox had two names, "Margaret S. Mann" and "Tina Samson." At the next corner he came to a red colonial that must have been one of the oldest houses on the island, the mailbox indicating "Deborah W. Samson." A sign attached to the house showed that it had originally been built by Micajah Fogge in 1672 and was registered with the state's Historic Preservation Commission.

The cross street was called Winthrop, and Mort noticed that the houses on it were obviously less expensive, not so well kept up, with even a few dilapidated and abandoned. He was deliberately not walking fast, so as to take in as much as possible and not finish his stroll too early. All the same, impatient to find out what Priscilla had been talking about, a few minutes later he terminated his tour abruptly and proceeded at a faster pace up Center Street, reaching Sea Drive at nine forty-five.

In Constable Gorges's office, Priscilla and Benjamin Mann were talking. She smiled at Mort as he entered, motioned him to be seated, and turned back to Ben.

"Are you sure that you weren't in any way steered toward taking a particular one of those two glasses? You know I trust you much more than Dudley Gorges."

Benjamin Mann's face was pale, and he looked extremely serious and tired. "It was a matter of pure chance, Priscilla. I could have gotten the poisoned one just as easily as the good one." He shuddered. "When I think of it! I'm not overly suspicious like Dudley Gorges, and unlike him I did drink out of my glass. If I had given Dudley the other one, I'd be dead now."

Priscilla told him she would prepare a statement later and have him sign it at the hotel. Mann passed in front of Mort and left without saying a word to him.

"What's up?" Mort said to Priscilla.

It seemed that someone had tried to poison Dudley Gorges at a meeting of the FIGS trustees. Dudley, being of a suspicious nature, had refused to drink his drink and brought it over to the constable's office yesterday while Priscilla and Mort were on the far side of the island. Corporal Dingley had the presence of mind to seal it and send it to the mainland for analysis. As soon as the lab results came in, Bumpus hit the ceiling and began yelling for Priscilla. The drink contained much more than enough cyanide to kill a person.

"I spent the night in Bay City, then the police boat bought me over this morning so I could do some interviewing while memories are still fresh.

"What kind of a maniac are we dealing with?" said Mort. "You would think with all that has been going on, you would find a pattern. But after three poisonings, suddenly the murderer goes in for head-bashing. And after four successful murders, the killer goes back to poison, this time unsuccessful."

"Dudley Gorges is convinced that his uncle, Atherton Gorges, is the murderer. He made the accusation to Corporal Dingley yesterday, and he's coming to see me at ten this morning. That's why I wanted you to come here. In fact, I think that's Dudley now."

Dudley's attitude was quite different from what it had been when Mort saw him at the Admiral's Arms. He was neither sure of himself nor blase. "My freaking uncle is trying to kill me!" he shouted.

Priscilla tried to get him to talk in some kind of logical sequence, but his conversation jumped and darted in every whichever direction. "I was suspicious when he invited me to become a trustee. FIGS is his thing and he thinks I'm a wing nut. Just like he killed Esther to try to cover himself. He keeps us all dangling like puppets on his purse strings. Something told me something was wrong about that drink. And that proves it."

When he came to his first pause, Priscilla asked, "And you mean he killed his own son, too?"

"I don't know why he killed Ferdinand, but he must have. There can't be two poisoners loose on the island."

Having had a good part of the story from Benjamin Mann, Priscilla was able to coax Dudley into some degree of coherence.

She then put the two versions together so that Mort could understand what had happened. The trustees' meeting had been scheduled for yesterday afternoon. In the morning, Senator Gorges told Dudley that he would like to have him attend the meeting and said he was proposing Dudley as a trustee to replace Dr. Thomas Delano, who had resigned. Dudley told his uncle that he was honored on the one hand but perfectly aware that the Senator had never before shown any confidence in him, particularly when it came to positions of responsibility or prestige. Senator Gorges agreed that he found a lack of dedication and purpose in Dudley but explained that it was important to keep a Gorges on the board, and he, the Senator, could not be expected to continue forever. Dudley, if brought in now, could gradually learn the workings of the board and perhaps be in a position to become its president some day.

Dudley, who thought of the trustees as a bunch of grown-ups playing little kids' games, would have preferred to turn down the dubious honor. But Uncle Atherton was the keeper of the purse, and a dependent could not be choosy. On the other hand, he had made no attempt to hide the fact that he thought Uncle Atherton was the father of Esther's child—and that, rather than let her expose him, he had murdered her. Atherton Gorges had shown admirable restraint in dealing with Dudley's wild accusations. It was neither nice nor proper to go around accusing one's uncle of incest and murder, and the Senator announced that he would not be responsible for the consequences if Dudley continued. Dudley did continue, but the Senator, instead of taking any open disciplinary action against him, paved the way for his nephew to take over a very prestigious position. Dudley's first thought was, "He's trying to buy me off"; the second, that prestige went a long way but a little bit of money would go further. "If he wanted to buy me off, the old goat should have tried coin. You can't do much partying with prestige."

The trustees' meeting began at two o'clock in the back part of the FIGS library. Business as usual was taking place in the front, and there were two visitors making use of library facilities—Mrs. Beeton on her afternoon off, and Sylvia Mann, who was passing time while waiting for her husband, Sylvester, one of the trustees. Margaret Mann sat at the librarian's desk, while Deborah Samson sat with the trustees ex officio. Aside from Deborah and Sylvester, the other trustees were Atherton Gorges, his wife Martha, Benjamin Mann, and the pharmacist Mason Crosby. Atherton Gorges brought Dudley along with him, and Dudley sat between Benjamin Mann and his Uncle Atherton. When Deborah offered to serve them cold soft drinks, everyone accepted except Senator Gorges, Ben Mann, and Dudley. The Senator drank plain water. Ben Mann brought with him his customary flask of bourbon, which he offered to share. Only Dudley accepted Ben's offer, and they both asked for a glass with ice and a little water. Deborah brought in the glasses. While Ben was adding whiskey to the water, Deborah presented to the board the matter of purchasing a set of reference books that cost considerably more than her spending authorization. Since this was a second series, someone suggested that they take a look at the first series, which the library already owned. They got up from their chairs, walked to the shelves furthest from the trustees' table, and looked at random volumes in the indicated set.

Although FIGS was generously endowed, the trustees never gave Deborah her way on purchasing books without a fight. If precedent was followed, most likely Deborah would get approval at some subsequent meeting but would be voted down at this one. Sulking, she led the way back to the table. The others were talking to each other about a variety of topics. Dudley, the last to reach the table, carried one of the books back with him, trying to act as if he were seriously interested in the matter. Ben Mann then took one of the two whiskey drinks and gave it to Dudley, who placed his glass on his left, between himself and his uncle, without tasting it.

Dudley dropped his book on the floor and reached over to retrieve it. Then, as he was lifting his head, his eye caught a quick motion of his uncle's hand near his glass. That was it as far as Dudley was concerned. He was convinced beyond all doubt that his drink had been poisoned, and that his uncle had done it. He turned to his uncle and suggested that he drink the whiskey. Atherton Gorges refused and asked Dudley what was wrong with him. Dudley first yelled that his uncle knew damned well what was wrong, then stormed out of the library, taking the glass of whiskey with him. He proceeded directly to Constable Gorges's office, found Corporal Dingley there, and insisted that Dingley have the contents of the glass analyzed.

As soon as Dudley had finished his story, Priscilla typed a formal statement. Dudley signed it and left.

"There you have it," she said to Mort. "It sounds like the stuff of fantasy, but the fact remains that there was poison in that glass. Thus we have several possibilities: Dudley is right, and his uncle put the poison in the glass while Dudley was picking up his book. Or, Dudley himself put the poison in the glass after he left the library so as to make it look as if his uncle were the criminal. Or, and I really cannot believe this, Ben Mann put poison in the drink before he handed it to Dudley."

"There's a fourth possibility," Mort said. Priscilla raised her eyebrows. "Or some other person put poison in that glass either before or after Dudley took it out of the library."

Priscilla laughed. "Good. That certainly covers everything. But the most logical possibilities are that either Dudley or his uncle did it."

"You put a great deal of trust in Benjamin Mann, don't you?"

"I've known him for years, and he's always been a very decent person. He's not been himself recently, but after what he went through yesterday, what can you expect? I won't shut my eyes to evidence, Mort, but there's no evidence at all that he did it."

"Priscilla, if you think of it, there is no evidence at all that any given person did it."

She shrugged her shoulders.

"Another thing," he continued. "We keep talking about cyanide, but that is a general term. Do we mean hydrocyanic acid or potassium cyanide or sodium cyanide or one of the other cyanides? Or don't we know?"

Priscilla said, "In some cases, as you undoubtedly know, it's very difficult to be sure which. But in Esther's case, where we had the bottle of absinthe with cyanide still in it—and in Dudley's case, where we had the whole glass available—the analysis was conclusive. It was hydrocyanic acid, HCN, and we think it was hydrocyanic acid in the case of Ferdinand and Cobber, too."

"I thought that might be the case, judging from the way Ferdinand died. The fastest way. HCN is one of the most powerful poisons known. How about accessibility?"

Priscilla apologized for not going into more detail on these matters with him earlier. "Remember," she said, "I thought of you then as knowledgeable about genealogy, not poisons."

Priscilla described what she knew about hydrocyanic acid. It was a colorless, transparent fluid with an odor like peaches or bitter almonds. Most of the other cyanides were solids or gases and considerably slower to act. Some suicides favored slower forms such as potassium cyanide or sodium cyanide because this allowed them enough time to get rid of the evidence after swallowing it, thus making their deaths look like murders for insurance purposes. But HCN was fast. Its victims had convulsive seizures and died in seconds, their respiratory systems completely paralyzed. Less than half a teaspoon of a 2 percent solution of hydrocyanic acid had been known to kill a person, and the deadliness of a more concentrated solution could be measured in drops.

"It's not readily available to the average person," Priscilla said, "but there are many kinds of people who can get it easily enough— doctors, pharmacists, and chemists, to mention a few. At first Lieutenant Bumpus felt that Cobber had killed Ferdinand with HCN and then used a slower cyanide on himself, but the murder of Esther ruined that theory."

"Back to Dr. Delano," Mort said.

"Or even Mason Crosby. And of course Senator Gorges, with all his industries, presumably would have no trouble obtaining HCN. And I doubt if Sylvester Mann would find it difficult."

"Ben Mann?"

"He could probably get it, too." She frowned. "I want to call in a report to Lieutenant Bumpus, and then let's question Mason Crosby.

◆   ◆   ◆

The balding pharmacist seemed surprised to see them. He did not invite them to his apartment upstairs but ushered them into the pharmacy and talked to them from behind the counter as if they were customers. It was uncomfortable standing, but there was no place to sit. The interview was short. He saw nothing out of the ordinary. He couldn't say if Dudley were telling the truth or not. No, he had no cyanide in his store. Perhaps the hardware store might carry it.

"Really," he said, "I don't know nothing. I just mind my own business. I don't make trouble for others. And I don't want them to make trouble for me."

"Let's hope," Priscilla said, as they walked away from the pharmacy, "that our interview with Deborah will be more informative."

"It should be. With the items I found on her accident and on her appointment as FIGS executive officer, we'll have more to talk about."

They visited Deborah at her house, the one registered with the state's Historical Preservation Society, which Mort had passed earlier. They were a little late for their appointment, and Priscilla had to start by apologizing to Deborah. They sat in the original room in front of the fireplace and all its cast iron hangers, hooks, pots, andirons, and other accouterments. On one side of the fireplace was an antique wooden settee with straight lines and a high back, and though Mort could admire its authenticity, he knew it would be quite uncomfortable as a seat. Fortunately Deborah had a sofa and two easy chairs of wingback colonial design and comfortable modern construction; he and Priscilla sat on the sofa, Deborah facing them in one of the easy chairs.

She professed complete surprise as to why they would want to see her. "Surely you do not suspect that I had anything to do with these murders!" The silver of her pompadoured hair caught the light, and she looked almost regal, as a larger-than-life Queen Victoria might have looked giving audience to Disraeli, someone she liked but who could also cause her surprise at times. She had such commanding presence that even the scar running down her face aided the impression of authority.

Priscilla explained their dual purpose, first to discuss the attempted poisoning of Dudley Gorges, then to delve a bit in Deborah's background.

Deborah's lower lip jutted out and she sat firmly upright in her chair, as if daring anyone to displace her. "So that's it," she said thoughtfully. "My background. I suspected you might be getting around to that. Suppose we discuss the attempted poisoning first, and then we shall see if we can go any further."

Priscilla agreed, and Deborah told them more or less what they had already heard. All the trustees were seated at the table when she got up to get the refreshments. It was easy, for all she had on hand was Seven-Up. She knew the Senator would just want plain water. She should have known that Ben Mann would have his customary bourbon and water, but since he had not spoken up in the beginning, she had to go back and get two more glasses for him and Dudley. She put ice cubes in, filled them with water to the halfway mark, and brought them in on a smaller tray, which she placed in front of Ben. She saw him take out his flask but paid no attention as he poured. Then she led the group to the shelves to see the first series of the books she had talked about, and on their return she was the first one to sit down again at the trustees' table. She recalled that Dudley had been the very last. She noticed nothing more concerning Ben, Dudley, or the Senator until Dudley started casting loud accusations at his uncle.

Priscilla thanked her and switched to the events of thirty-five years ago.

Deborah's lips tightened. "I don't have to answer this type of question, you know."

"I think it will be easier this way," Priscilla said.

"We have certain facts from old newspapers and deeds," Mort said.

"Very well," Deborah said after giving the matter due consideration, "you are probably right. I will tell you the story, and you will see that it has absolutely nothing to do with these murders. After all, this was thirty-five years ago. So I trust that once I have told you everything you will be able to keep it quiet and not let it become one more story to titillate the gossip mongers of this island."

Mort reflected to himself that Deborah referring to others as "gossip mongers" was akin to a crooked lawyer calling his opponents "pettifoggers."

Deborah hesitated, as if wondering where to begin. "I guess I should mention first that my father died while doing research in South America for a book when I was still a young girl. It was all my mother could do just to support us. She was well educated, and she gave private tutoring lessons to bring in some money. She had to mortgage our house, which had been in the family for generations. There was no money for me to go to college, but my father had left many books, and my mother gave me my education." She stopped and looked up at Priscilla. "Do you know that I have never set foot off this island?"

Priscilla and Mort paid her the compliment of astonishment. "I did not even go with the rest of the children to high school in Bay City. When I finished grammar school, I was so far ahead of the rest of the children that the authorities agreed with my mother that sending me there would be a waste of time. My mother gave me the equivalent of a university education. I was in my early twenties when she died, and she left a small amount of money for me. It was gone by the time I was twenty-five, the mortgage on the house was foreclosed, and I even had to sell my father's books at auction— Senator Gorges's father bought many of them. I used the money from the books to rent the family house from the new owner, but I could not hold out much longer.

"Atherton Gorges returned from the university shortly before my mother died, and we started dating off and on over several years. At one time we sort of had an understanding, an unofficial engagement. It was never announced—just a possibility we talked about. And then suddenly it was formally announced that he was going to marry Martha Mann. He had his choice between beauty and brains, and he chose beauty. Not," she said quickly, "that I was so bad-looking, but Martha was stunning. I was hurt, but there was nothing I could do about it. I did not want to leave the island, but I had no family, no money, no job, and no training for the kind of jobs that were available—and I was about to lose my home. One day Atherton suggested that we take a walk together. Dared I hope that he had changed his mind? I went with him full of anticipation. But all he wanted was sex. He raped me. At knife point—a switchblade knife. He flicked it open and threatened to use it if I did not submit to him. When he had finished, he threatened me again, and made wild slashing motions in the air with his knife. One slash came too close, and you can see the result running from my forehead to my chin. We were on a grassy knoll, and I fell backwards, rolled down the hill, and passed out.

"Some time later, Atherton Gorges and his father came for me with a truck and put me in the back. Gorges, Sr. washed my wound and gave me first aid, all the time assuring me that I would not be hurt, that I need not be afraid. I believed him and calmed down. When I was calm, he said, 'Debby, you have two choices. You can tell the authorities what happened and ruin my son and gain nothing. You will be destitute, and people will even look down on you and make your continued stay on this island unbearable. Or, you can forgive or at least try to forget what happened, and I will make it up to you. If you wish, I'll have Atherton buy the house you live in and give it to you so that you will have a home all your life.'"

"I was still scared, but I gave some thought to what he said." She laughed bitterly, and her voice lowered half an octave. "I was also a practical one. I cried out something to the effect of wanting to know how I could be expected to feed myself and keep up a house with no means of support. Gorges, Sr. thought for a moment and then said that Elsie Crosby was eligible for retirement as FIGS executive officer. He could encourage her to retire now, and I would be selected, at the wise old age of twenty-five, to replace her. My first thought was all those books. I could have my house, a paying job, and be surrounded by books.

"The books persuaded me, and I accepted his proposition, his hush money, if you wish. We prepared a story—I had been by myself and fallen from the rocks. They took me to a doctor, who did the best he could for my face, but he was no plastic surgeon. Gorges, Sr. kept his word. He had Atherton buy my house from the man who had obtained it in the auction following the foreclosure, then transfer title to me. And a short while later the FIGS trustees elected me executive officer.

"So there you have the whole sordid thing, Priscilla, and you, too, Dr. Sinclair. You know now that not only was Atherton Gorges a mean and unconscionable creature, but Deborah Samson had no honor and was little better than a blackmailer. But that was all long ago. Surely no purpose would be served in raking it up now."

◆   ◆   ◆

They were back at the office. "Sometimes," Priscilla said, "I feel like a fly on the wall of some foreign seaport house of prostitution, witness to all the multitude of filthy acts that humans are capable of. My father did not bring up his daughter to be a policewoman."

"Granted," said Mort. "But policewoman you are. The issue now is to make the best determination as to whether the story we just heard from Deborah Samson might have anything to do with the crimes you are investigating."

"Why on earth?" asked Priscilla. "Don't you believe her?"

"Oh, I want to believe her. And the facts are probably as she told them. But though she declares herself without honor, is she equally without any desire for revenge? How she must hate Atherton Gorges! Can you be certain that the thought of retribution has never once entered her mind during these thirty-five years?"

Thirteen

T HE QUESTIONING OF THE WITNESSES WHO WERE
at the library during the trustees' meeting continued into the next
day. Though the witnesses were more or less cooperative, little was
added to the known facts. No one other than Dudley had seen the
hand of Atherton Gorges provocatively close to Dudley's drink, but
no witness—saving Sylvester Mann, who, as Gorges's attorney might
be biased—could say that the Senator did not have the opportunity
of poisoning the drink.

The Gorges's cook, Mrs. Beeton, impressed Mort as a strong-
minded woman, full of old-fashioned virtue and capable of showing
considerable righteous indignation if she felt the occasion called for
it. They interviewed her in the kitchen of the Gorges mansion. She
seemed ideally matched to her master, as if she, too, knew that there
was an order to things. If she burned the soup, she would expect to
apologize to her employer. If her employer brought people to dinner
without previously advising her, she would expect an apology from
him. She answered Priscilla's questions with the aid of one determined
to do her part even though she was being imposed on.

She had finished serving lunch at the Gorges's mansion around
one o'clock and, since it was her afternoon off, gone immediately to
the FIGS library to do as much research as possible. She had forgotten

that there would be a trustees' meeting; had she known, she would have arranged for some other afternoon off. "I don't like to be there when they have their meetings. It's impossible for a body to concentrate, what with them scurrying around like mice and sometimes yelling their heads off." In and out of the stacks during the meeting intent on researching her own genealogical interests, she had paid no attention at all to what was going on in the rear alcove. She knew nothing about the poisoning incident until she heard Dudley's loudly voiced accusation.

Priscilla looked to Mort, as if to say that she was ready to terminate the interview unless he chose to continue it.

He did. "You have a very attractive daughter, Mrs. Beeton," he began. Sensing that nerve ends all over her body were already bristling with suspicion, he tried to put her at ease. "I had a pleasant talk with her while I was waiting for Senator Gorges. She said there were hopes of an operation to correct her foot."

Mrs. Beeton's leathery red face relaxed a little. "God willing!"

"Does it seem possible?"

"It's all a question of money. Them that has gets, and them that hasn't goes without."

"You mean there's no money for an operation?"

The last question started her talking. Dr. Delano and Martha Gorges were trying to get Senator Gorges to pay for the operation, but it would cost up to a quarter of a million dollars, and the Senator was not willing to be that charitable. Mrs. Beeton's own savings were about ten thousand dollars, and Martha could raise fifty thousand. Dr. Delano had already paid for the examinations and travel necessary to see that an operation was possible and likely to succeed. That left it entirely up to the Senator, who would not give a flat no but would not say yes either.

"I hope he changes his mind," Mort said. "Incidentally, you are related to Martha Gorges, aren't you?"

"Not closely," she said. "We're third cousins. I was a Delano before I married Mr. Beeton, who died many years ago. My mother, Keturah Ewer was a second cousin to Martha Gorges's mother, Elizabeth Ewer."

"Then you are related also to Dr. Delano?" Mort already knew the answer, but he wanted to know how Mrs. Beeton would react.

Clearly she did not like the turn the questioning had taken. Her mouth quivered as she paused. Finally she said in a monotone, "Dr. Delano and I are first cousins, once removed."

"And?" Mort persisted.

Mrs. Beeton's eyes appealed to Priscilla, but only for a moment before she responded. "It seems you know my family as well as I do. Yes, Dr. Delano's my nephew, too, even though we're almost the same age. My older sister was his mother."

Was she embarrassed because of the implications of inbreeding? "Thank you, Mrs. Beeton," Mort said. "You know if you go far enough back in any family you're bound to find marriage between cousins. My own paternal grandparents were doubly related like that."

Mrs. Beeton gave him a curious look. "Are you through with me?"

Mort nodded to Priscilla, who thanked Mrs. Beeton for her time and help.

The interview with Martha Gorges in the front of the house was shorter. Pale and gaunt, she motioned them to be seated and then gracefully slipped into a chair herself, perking her face up in reserved anticipation. She was wearing a gray plaid business suit and a pink blouse buttoned high about her neck. Her makeup looked as if it had been professionally applied, expertly obscuring wrinkles and bringing out her good features. In answering Priscilla's questions she pointed that she was a FIGS trustee only because her husband insisted on it, but she did not in fact care for genealogy at all. The implication was clear that she did not care for genealogists either. She noticed nothing of interest during the board meeting, which she found as boring as usual. Of course she believed her husband, and not her nephew.

When Priscilla finished, she again turned the questioning over to Mort.

Mort had nothing to ask about the library matter but again asked about Belinda Beeton. "That's a very attractive daughter your cook has," he said. "Do you think she will ever get her foot corrected to normal?"

Martha Gorges looked at him sharply and turned to Priscilla. "Do I have to answer his questions?"

"Dr. Sinclair is an official consultant to the police," Priscilla said, a note of apology in her voice.

"Does that question have anything to do with the case under investigation?" Martha wanted to know.

"I guess not," Mort said. "I suppose I was just trying to ease into a conversation, Mrs. Gorges, and I'm sorry if I offended you. I have nothing else to ask."

As the witness rose from her chair and stood guard-like to usher them out, Mort started to ask another question but then thought better of it. More importantly, he remembered what he had neglected to do in Bay City. Vaguely aware that Martha Gorges was saying some last words to them, he missed the sense entirely, for his thoughts were focused on the discrepancy in the vital records on Ferdinand Gorges. He was not sure what it signified, but he knew he would have to visit the Bay City clerk's office again as soon as possible.

Martha Gorges closed the door behind them with a bang. "She doesn't seem to like you," Priscilla said as they walked down the driveway.

"I may be about to become the most unpopular person on Fogge Island," Mort said. "You do see what is happening, don't you?"

She shook her head.

"It's true that there are more secrets than people on this island— and our investigation is beginning to uncover some of those secrets. It's unfortunate because many of them will turn out to have nothing to do with the murders, but we can't avoid uncovering them until we know for sure. Martha Gorges is right. My role in this investigation has necessarily become that of the muckraker. And the only justification is that I feel certain some of the material we are or will be uncovering will lead us to the murderer."

◆   ◆   ◆

Early that evening they interviewed Margaret Mann at her home on Gilman Street. Tina Samson, Margaret explained, was spending the night with friends in Bay City, where she had gone to look for a job. "You never see the fallout from these things in the beginning," Margaret said. "Lucy and Tina are both out of work with the Admiral's Arms closed down. I offered to let Tina stay here indefinitely without paying rent until she comes up with something on the island. The room doesn't cost me anything extra, and the little food she eats is no drain on me. After all, someone will undoubtedly buy the Admiral's Arms and open it up again, probably under a new name. I've even heard that Sylvester Mann is interested in it. But Tina is determined to get a job now at any cost, even if it means taking the ferry each day back and forth to Bay City."

Margaret had seated them in her living room and served them Earl Grey tea. Mort looked around and decided the room was what an audiophile would call well damped. The thick gold and maroon wool carpet on the floor looked Persian in origin, old but durable. Dark brown velvet draperies covered two high pilaster-guarded windows on one wall, and on two of the other walls were hung large variegated woven tapestries with scenes from Greek mythology, one of fleet-footed Atalanta stooping to pick up a golden apple and the other of Diana with bow in hand accompanied by a hound chasing the stag. The massive wingback lounge chairs were covered in a thick golden-brown pile fabric, sturdy, comfortable, and deep seated. Bric-a-brac collected over several lifetimes was displayed on the tops of small tables all over the room and on the mantle above the fireplace. The overall effect of the room was dark but pleasant, a quiet room where one could relax and think.

Priscilla asked the routine questions and got the routine answers. Margaret had been busy either at the librarian's desk or returning books to the stacks during the board meeting. She had not been in a position to see what was happening at the trustee's table, though she did remember them coming out en masse to look at some books.

Mort continued the questioning. "Margaret, the other day when you were telling me about your husband's death, you didn't mention that he died under somewhat mysterious circumstances."

She looked surprised. "Well, I didn't think it was an official police interrogation. I was more or less gushing over a big-name genealogist and saying anything that came into my head."

"Could you tell us more about it now?"

"I guess. I don't really know what to tell. My husband fell ill, but we didn't think it was anything serious, and then quite suddenly without any warning he died."

"You said he died of some kind of flu."

"Well, the flu had been suggested. But no one really knew what it was."

"The newspaper item used the word 'mysterious,'" Mort said. "The doctor could not diagnose the illness and gave the cause of death as heart failure. Apparently Dr. Delano did not handle the case, and there was no autopsy."

"Percival was being treated on the mainland by Dr. Timmerman, who's dead himself now. There was no sign of foul play, and so it was decided there was no need for an autopsy. Percival was ill for a while, and then he had a heart attack. The only mysterious thing was that Dr. Timmerman could not recognize the kind of illness. It resembled a type of flu but was not contagious."

"How did he know that?"

"He checked with the communicable-disease people in Atlanta. They couldn't find anything contagious."

Mort digested the import of her answers for a moment, then began again. "Some time before his death, your husband was involved in a lawsuit with Senator Gorges. The newspaper item said that as a result of losing the suit, he lost his shipyard as well."

Margaret frowned. "Yes, he did—Atherton cheated Percival out of a lot of money. Because of that loss Percival ultimately couldn't keep the shipyard going, and right after he lost the lawsuit he came down with his illness. But the lawsuit was a mistake, for Percival really had nothing to go on. It was only after he died that I heard something that might have changed the decision, making it a criminal matter instead of just a civil one. Percival might have been able to get evidence to prove what I had learned, but I didn't know how to go about it."

"What did you learn?"

"Atherton had information that another company wanted to buy a certain division of the shipyard, called the Ship Salvage Company, because it had some valuable real estate options. That much Percival suspected but couldn't prove. The shipyard lawyer was also the executor of the will. Remember, Percival and Benjamin were minors when their father died, and it was only years later when Percival took over the shipyard that he realized what had happened and brought the lawsuit. The executor had had to sell off something to realize cash for various expenses, and as it turned out he sold the Ship Salvage Company to Atherton Gorges. It was then discovered that the Ship Salvage Company was the most valuable part of the entire shipyard conglomerate. Atherton bought it for two million dollars and sold it six months later for eight million to the company that wanted the real estate options."

Mort emitted a low whistle in appreciation of the magnitude of the profit. Then he asked, "What was your information?"

"The shipyard lawyer who was also the will executor had a third position. He was on Atherton Gorges's payroll. Atherton paid him a fortune for telling him how valuable the division was and then selling it to him cheap."

"Where did you get your information, and how do know it was true?" Mort asked, recognizing with these questions how similar genealogy and police detection work could be.

Margaret's face showed she clearly did not care for the question. "Deborah Samson told me, but I don't know where she learned it. And of course, you're right. I don't know that it's true. All I have is Deborah's say-so."

"Who was the executor?"

"Sylvester Mann, Percival's own cousin. He was just barely out of law school at the time. Percival's father took him on at the shipyard and a year later made him executor of his will. Atherton Gorges also gave him a position, but a secret one, and paid him a small fortune for double-crossing his uncle and cousin. Incidentally, Sylvester then blew all his ill-gained profit in the stock market, losing everything. It was then that Atherton Gorges officially retained him as a lawyer."

"Then at the very least, Atherton and Sylvester were responsible for your present economic situation. Even as a widow, you should have been a rich widow."

"If what Deborah told me was true. But even so, Dr. Sinclair, you may have your values, but I have mine. The money was not important to me. My husband was. Anyway, I couldn't prove anything. Everyone knows now that Sylvester works for Atherton, but I don't think anyone could prove exactly when he first started working for him. All I have is Deborah's word." From her expression, it was obvious that Margaret was trying hard to keep herself in check. From what? Showing emotion over a reliving of painful past events? Or lashing out at Mort as a hateful meddler?

Mort did not relish his role. He was not cruel by instinct, but he had his priorities in order, and his first priority was to help Priscilla solve these crimes. "One more thing," he said. "Other than the crooked business deal, did anyone stand to gain financially from your husband's death?"

"No, I don't think so. By the time he died, he had no money left."

"How about insurance? Did your husband leave any?"

"Oh, yes." Margaret's face brightened. "He had a policy for $50,000. It saved the house for me." Then she jumped quickly forward as the full import of his question reached her. "But surely you don't think my husband was murdered. You can't think I would have murdered my husband for a $50,000 insurance policy!"

"No, Margaret, of course we don't think that," Mort said. "What I am getting at, I guess—although I am doing it awkwardly—is to raise the possibility of your husband's having been killed. But I don't mean by you. In retrospect, it certainly seems convenient for Atherton Gorges and Sylvester Mann that Percival died when he did. Perhaps it was convenient for someone else, too. The mysterious nature of your husband's death makes me wonder if he could have been murdered for reasons that are equally mysterious."

The idea, Margaret said, had never occurred to her, or to anyone else that she knew of. "Dr. Timmerman suggested that perhaps Percival just didn't have the will to live after the lawsuit. He seemed to have no desire for anything. When he was in the hospital in Bay City— that's where he died—the nurses couldn't get him to do anything. He refused even to eat or drink for them, and it was only during my visits that he could be induced to take any nourishment."

The interview had revealed much more than Mort had expected. He gave Priscilla a look intended to convey the message that this would be a tactful time to leave, and Priscilla got his message. Standing up, she thanked Margaret for her helpfulness, and they walked to the door.

It was dark when they left Margaret's house, and the heavens were bright and clear. The three brilliant stars in the belt of Orion lay ahead of them in the southwest sky, reddish Betelgeuse also especially noticeable in the hunter's right shoulder. "You certainly did your homework over in Bay City," Priscilla said to Mort. She linked her arm with his as they walked along Coolidge Street. "I'm glad we're working together."

Mort reached a hand over to clasp hers as it rested on his other arm. "I guess we can add one more person to the list of people on this island with reason to hate Atherton Gorges," he said.

◆   ◆   ◆

Their next appointment, the last for the day, was with Sylvester and Sylvia Mann. Though they lived on the opposite side of Oldtown from Margaret Mann, even walking slowly it did not take Priscilla and Mort more than ten minutes to get to their house. A large German Shepherd patrolling the yard behind the fence began barking and charging at them, stopping only when the closed iron gate made further assault impossible. Priscilla reached for the bell, but Sylvester Mann was already at the door and called back the dog. Opening the gate, he led them to the house.

The house was richly furnished in the showy, impersonal manner of a professional interior decorator. Nothing reflected the personality or individual interests of the owners, unless it was intended that they be shown as cold, acquisitive, and ostentatious. It was the incongruity that struck Mort the most. In the reception room, a dozen Tanagra statuettes with their backs to a giant Steuben vase full of long-stemmed artificial flowers on the huge marble mantel looked about as much at home in this place as did the elongated Lladros tucked away by the dozens in a glass-walled curio cabinet. The self-portrait of Geralis, obviously painted shortly before he committed suicide—with his intense dark eyes shining maniacally at the viewer and the

sunlight behind his left ear revealing blood vessels in the lobe—might
have been appropriate in a spacious art gallery, but in a private home,
competing for attention amid hundreds of other expensive items, it
looked obscene. Expensive glove-leather upholstery could do little
for chairs and sofas standing on chrome legs in long-limbed bird-like
pose.

"We might as well be comfortable while we're enduring this,"
their host said. "I'll take you to the club room."

The club room had pine-paneled walls which held a dart board,
and too many framed "Ape" and "Spy" lithographs from *Vanity Fair,*
a squat round glass-and-chrome table surrounded by six leather-and-
chrome club chairs on gigantic casters, an antique oak bar, a huge bar
mirror advertising Hampden Ale, bar stools of chrome and leather—
apparently their host had a passion for chrome and leather—and, in
one of the corners, a forty-inch television set. Beneath the bar mirror was a variety of bottles that would have done justice to the best
of commercial drinking establishments. The labels told Mort that the
owner at least had taste when it came to laying in liquor.

"What'll it be?" asked the proud owner as he stepped behind the
bar, got out some glasses, and fingered his mustache to see that every
whisker was in place.

Priscilla asked for club soda and got Perrier. Mort, spying a bottle behind the bar that made his heart quicken, found himself unable
to refuse the offer and said he wouldn't mind having a Usquaebach
straight up, no ice.

When Sylvester handed him his glass, Mort sniffed the aroma
lovingly and then took a cautious sip. "Ah," he said, "now this is a
drink!"

"Would you like to know how much I paid for a bottle of that?
Sure you don't want ice?"

Mort said, "At least fifty dollars, maybe more, and no ice, thank
you. I couldn't put ice in the finest blend of all malt whiskey ever to
come out of Scotland."

"Seventy-five dollars a bottle," Sylvester said. "I don't care for
Scotch myself, but some happen to like it cold. *Chacun à son goût.*"
He poured a generous glass for himself from a bottle of pre-mixed
martinis, "made with Beefeater."

Sylvia Mann entered the room wearing a wide-legged pink satin lounge suit just in time to say that she would have a "Chin-Chin and soda."

Mort savored his drink with unabashed self-indulgence while Priscilla led off with questions about the alleged attempt to poison Dudley Gorges.

"The Senator could not have done it," Sylvester Mann said. "I sat across from him during the entire meeting, and I could not possibly have missed seeing him put something in Dudley's drink. But he didn't. I don't know what Dudley's game is, but he's definitely trying to pull a fast one."

"You're retained by the Senator, Mr. Mann?" Priscilla asked him.

His face flushed. "One of a number of attorneys retained by him or his companies."

She tried another tack. "Could anyone have lingered behind when the rest of you went to look at the books?"

"I guess so. Why not? But I don't see what good that would do. If any poison had been placed in one of those glasses at that time, there could have been no way of predicting whether Dudley or Ben Mann would be drinking it. The earliest the poison could have been put in was after Ben Mann was in complete control of the glasses."

"You're not suggesting Ben did it," Priscilla broke in.

"No, of course not. I'm just trying to make you see the facts. Ben Mann was a possibility for doing it, not a probability, but Atherton Gorges was not even a possibility—I can testify to that. My view is that Dudley himself did it after he left the meeting."

Sylvia Mann contributed nothing to their knowledge of the event. "Now, look, all I know is that I was sitting in that stuffy library bored as all get-out waiting for Sylvester to leave the meeting. We were planning to catch the three o'clock ferry, and Sylvester was going to leave before the meeting was finished. I sat at my table and glanced at some silly picture book about the fauna and flora of Fogge Island." She sighed. "Dudley Gorges ruined my whole afternoon."

Sylvia Mann looked like a woman who had been told all her life that she was pretty, had always believed it, could not imagine being anything except pretty, and by sheer conviction maintained her prettiness. Her dark yellow hair was brushed straight back in waves, her

small nose was turned up at the end, her lips were daintily curved
and bright red, and her golden eyes were big and babyish. Mort knew
she was some years older than her husband, but not from looking at
her. Sylvester was about forty-five and Sylvia could easily pass for
forty, if one did not look too closely.

When Priscilla signaled Mort to begin his questioning, he skipped
over Sylvester and went directly to his wife. "You were a registered
nurse?"

"Yes."

"Could you tell us about leaving Fogge Island and then coming
back again?"

"Say, is this a fishing expedition?" Sylvester demanded. "I don't
know what right you have to ask questions in the first place, but I'll
be damned if I will let my wife be subjected to that kind of shotgun
approach."

"Look here, Mr. Mann," Priscilla said, "someday there's going to
be a trial in this case, and you and your wife could be witnesses. A
district attorney can ask questions one way to a cooperative witness
and another way to an uncooperative one. The police can be tough,
too. Either you're going to be cooperative or you're going to be uncooperative, and I'm going to remember which."

Sylvester jerked back in his chair but did not say anything.

Priscilla turned to Mort. "Go ahead, Dr. Sinclair."

"Let me put it this way," Mort told Sylvia. "You were Dr.
Delano's nurse. You left him to take a job in one of the big Boston
hospitals. Did Dr. Delano feel that you had let him down?"

"Far from it," she said. "Dr. Delano highly recommended me,
and it was his recommendation that got me the job."

"All right. You then married a wealthy doctor there and stopped
working. Your first husband died, and you came back to the island.
Then you started dating Delano Delano?"

"I wouldn't call it dating," she said. "We were friendly. And I'll
tell you that meant something to me, because a lot of the people here
were not very friendly when I returned. But I never got serious about
him. Who could get serious about a bulldog-looking kid like Del
Delano when there was a handsome hunk of man like Sylvester
around?"

"Del Delano apparently thought his cousin Dr. Delano had something to do with your rejecting him and marrying your present husband."

Sylvester looked as if he were about to burst, but Sylvia touched his arm to reassure him. "Just what are you getting at, Dr. Sinclair? Come out with it. Quit beating around the bush."

"I guess all I am trying to say is that you were a good nurse to Dr. Delano and you left him. Rather than resent it, he seemed to want to do you every possible favor."

Sylvia jumped as if she had been kicked in the stomach. "Now wait a minute," she snapped. "If you're implying that there ever was anything between Dr. Delano and me, you're crazy."

"I think this line of questioning has gone on long enough," Sylvester said.

"All right," Mort said. "I have no more questions for your wife. Now let me ask you one. You were the executor of the will of Percival and Benjamin Mann's father. You sold off one of his companies to Atherton Gorges?"

Sylvester Mann jumped to his feet. "That's enough!" he shouted, then turned to Priscilla. "I think you must admit, Sergeant Booth, that my wife and I have been fully cooperative, as reasonable as you could wish. But this kind of slanderous questioning has got to stop. If you have nothing more to ask bearing directly on your investigation, well, it's getting late."

He walked to the gate with them, keeping his dog at bay, and let them out. Mort could sense how much Sylvester would have loved to let the leash drop from his hand. Again they walked along slowly in the cold air.

"Was it necessary to hit Sylvia with that question about Dr. Delano?" Priscilla asked cautiously.

"I don't really know. There is something that bothers me about Dr. Delano, some kind of . . . character discrepancy, you might say. And we have never had an answer for this fight he had with Del Delano—which in itself is bothersome."

"You know that all charges against him in the Del Delano murder have been dropped."

"I take it he is doing business as usual?"

"That he is, Mort. Dr. Delano really is a very nice man. Everyone on the island loves him."

"Del Delano didn't."

"The exception that proves the rule." She put her arm through his again, and said in a softer tone, "I guess we should call it quits for the night. We'll tackle Senator Gorges tomorrow morning."

Mort stopped walking and turned to her. "Would you mind conducting that one alone?"

"I guess not. But why?"

"I want to go to Bay City early tomorrow. I think I can do us much more good there. I made a mistake a genealogist should never make, and I've got to correct it."

Fourteen

SYLVIA MANN SAT AT HER MAKEUP TABLE AND LOOKED intently into the mirror. The wrinkles on either side of her mouth could not be hidden by cosmetics, and her skin had lost some of its resiliency. She told everyone, including her husband, that she was in her "forties," but she was fifty-one, and age was taking its toll. Her true age, of course, was a matter of public record, but she hoped no one had taken the trouble to look it up. The police were a different matter. She could not imagine their exposing her for fibbing about her years, especially since it had nothing to do with the serious crimes they were investigating. But Deborah Samson knew her true age— and much more. Deborah was dangerous, and Sylvia knew she would have to keep her appointment with her. Sylvester must never find out.

How convenient after the interview that he had decided to catch the last ferry to the mainland. Of course, he would have to stay over-night. Did it have anything to do with the police questioning, or was it a different kind of need? Sylvester was never really open with her, though when some deal was a success, he would tell her about it after the fact. If not successful, she would never hear anything about it, at least not from Sylvester. They had unspoken rules in their marriage, and she tried to play according to the rules. Of course, the way it happened tonight was perfect. She had been wondering what excuse she could give Sylvester to get out of the house. The rules did not work both ways. Sylvia had to account for her movements, but at least tonight she would not have to make up some whopper and take the chance of being caught in it.

Were they just deceiving each other? Actually, if Sylvester had to go to some whorehouse, as long as he was discreet about it and took sound prophylactic measures, she did not particularly mind. So long as she was the one he really loved. She could not stand the idea of possibly losing him. Sylvia even welcomed his little tirades of jealousy as signs that he still loved her, but she worried about aging. And she worried about Deborah. She looked at her watch and saw that it was time to leave. As she got up from her chair, she hoped Sylvester would not telephone and find no one at home.

As Sylvia walked past the Mann Hotel she saw two island couples leaving, late diners at the Talleyrand Room. One of the wives waved to her; she waved back and hurried on. What excuse could she give if one of them casually mentioned to Sylvester that they had seen her? She noticed that the grocery store next to the Samson Pharmacy had just closed, and some of the clerks were sweeping up inside. She could always say she had needed some coffee, or bread, or something. Even if the late diners said, "Oh, we just happened to see Sylvia shortly after the grocery store closed," not that they would say such a thing, she could say she had hoped it would still be open but got there late. She crossed in front of the church and continued to the other side. The FIGS building loomed in front of her, a gleam of light showing in one of the windows underneath a drawn shade.

Deborah and Sylvia confronted one another across the desk in Deborah's corner office. The FIGS executive officer was calm, composed, and in full command of the situation; Sylvia was nervous, apprehensive, and sitting at rigid attention. Sylvia wore a mink stole over a sleek dress that emphasized her slim curved figure, the hem of the dress of a length to show off the legs that had gained her many a compliment. She had finished her face with care before leaving the house, and her dark gold hair was beautifully arranged.

Deborah wore an old sweater and slacks, and her normally silvered hair seemed grayer than usual. Had her visitor been a man, she might have dressed and made up with some care, but she knew she had no need to primp for Sylvia and nothing to fear from her. Being in no hurry, she made polite conversation, aware that her patter made Sylvia all the more nervous. "It is so much easier to concentrate at night when there are no interruptions, don't you think?"

In her younger years Sylvia might have waited her out, might have thought "Well, it's your nickel. Speak your piece."

Only it would not be a nickel these days, would it? There were some pay telephones on the mainland where the charge was still a dime, but any time now they'd jump it to a quarter. Why were all these silly thoughts crowding into her head? The perversity of the human mind, she guessed. "All right, Deborah," she said finally, "so you know. What is it you want?"

"Want?" said Deborah. "Why, I only want to be your friend, Sylvia. We are friends, aren't we?"

"I guess so," said Sylvia. What the hell, with charge cards you didn't even need coins for a public telephone anyway. "Yes, I want to be friends, Deborah. You won't tell, will you?"

Deborah laughed. "Of course we're friends. We all have our little secrets, don't we? I know something that you don't want told, but I'll bet you know a lot of other things that I don't know. Isn't that one of the main occupations on the island, guessing what secrets each person does and does not know?" Without waiting for an answer, she asked, "Would you care for a cup of tea, Sylvia? Tea somehow makes things so cozy."

As Sylvia passed the Mann Hotel again on her way home twenty minutes later, she saw Lettice Gorges walking up the hotel steps, but Lettice paid her no attention. At home, Sylvia poured herself a double shot of Jack Daniels. How she wanted to wash the taste of that tea out of her mouth. Oh, what a tangled web we weave . . . She wished she could stop thinking those thoughts.

The sour mash smarted as it went down her throat. She had taken it without ice, without even thinking about it, just like that genealogist who followed Sergeant Booth around like a puppy. She did not like that genealogist. Hell, she hated all genealogists.

◆   ◆   ◆

In one of the smaller rooms of the Mann Hotel, Dudley Gorges sat in a chair and nursed a can of beer. He wondered if she were coming. Cheap bitch! After all he had done for her. Serve her right if her father did cut her out of his will. Not that he had any reason to think he had, but he laughed as he thought how just the idea would give her such a fright. He felt like walking, but the room allowed only a few paces back and forth, and soon he sat down again. Then Dudley heard footsteps outside his door, followed by a gentle tapping. He jumped to his feet and threw the door open. "Letty, thank God!"

"Well, you've certainly fixed *yourself* up, *haven't* you?"

"Did you bring money?"

"One hundred dollars," his cousin said. "*All* I could raise at the moment." She withdrew a small wad of bills from her pocketbook and threw them on the bed. The ten bank notes scattered in every corner, two on the floor.

"Was that the best you could do, Letty? I'm leaving this damned island tomorrow, and I need money to tide me over until I can get a job."

"*You*? Get a job?" She laughed uproariously as she crossed over to sit in the other chair. Putting her feet up on the table so that her full-skirted dress draped toward the floor, she made a display of her panty hose. Then, watching her cousin, she laughed again and said, "Don't get any *ideas*, Dudley. You're not my type."

"Don't flatter yourself, you slut. You're not capable of arousing that kind of interest in me." He took his seat on the opposite side of the table. "But we do have something in common."

"I can't imagine what. Now that daddy's *thrown* you out, we don't even have *meals* in common."

"I heard that he's revising his will."

"To cut *you* out."

"Ha! You don't know? I just wish I could see your face when they read that will one of these days. Aren't you aware that he cut me entirely out of his will after Esther was killed? He told me what he'd done when he threw me out. So what do you think he's doing now? Putting me back in?"

Lettice took her feet down from the table and crossed her legs. "He wouldn't *dare*. I'm all he's *got*."

"Okay, don't believe me. But just mull it over all the same. Maybe the two of us could put on a dance act for a living. How about 'The Gorgeous Gorges Cousins'"?

She got up, lifted her handbag from the table, and proceeded to the door. "Don't forget," she said, "I have an independent income."

"Don't leave me, Letty," Dudley said.

"I've got a *date*," she said, turning up her middle finger in an obscene gesture.

"Come on, Letty, can't you get me any more money? I'll starve!" "This afternoon I called everyone I know, and only one of them is willing to lend me anything, and I don't even know how much that will be. Where can I get enough to live on?"

With a sigh, Lettice opened her purse again and rummaged through it. I don't know *why* I should do *you* any favors." Taking out two one-hundred-dollar bills, she threw these, also, on the bed. "But here, Dud, take these and get by the best you can. Maybe I can work on daddy to get him to forgive you."

◆   ◆   ◆

It was late at night, and Benjamin Mann was not feeling well. His head ached, and his stomach was upset, and he could not control his diarrhea. He reached up to feel the top of his head and found his hair damp with perspiration. The pain in his head was spreading throughout his body. The Alka Seltzers hadn't helped, and he had nothing else available. He did not like the idea of calling Dr. Delano at such an hour, but he doubted that he could get through the night this way.

When the telephone rang sometime after midnight, he found himself hoping it might be Dr. Delano. He would have settled for anyone, anyone at all who might offer him comfort. The voice was a familiar one. "I'm not sure if I understand what you're saying," he said, "because I feel so horrible. Yes, it's more of the same that I had yesterday . . . ." It helped a little just to talk about it. "Would you? That would really help . . . . Yes, please hurry. Please."

Ben knew he must throw on a coat and bundle up, that it was cold outside and he would be especially susceptible now to a chill. The last thing he wanted was to make matters worse than they already were, but he could hardly think to recall what it was he had been about to do. Oh, yes, put on a coat. He had several coats, but the only one that came to mind was a lined parka hanging in the vestibule of the hotel. Somehow he made it downstairs, clutching the rail tightly as he negotiated each step. He put an aching arm in a sleeve and tried to throw the rest of the coat around his back, but the other arm was not reaching. Hard work, but he tried again and again. The night was quiet, the silence broken only by the whir of the furnace fan, but now he thought he heard a car outside and moved to the outer door, still with only one arm in its coat sleeve. He was feeling giddy, no longer capable of trusting his senses, but somehow he managed to open the door and continue outside. He reached for his keys and tried to lock the door, then after exhausting too much effort in a futile attempt, dropped the keys in his pocket, leaving the door unlocked. The car was there, and the door on the driver's side opened. Firm hands helped him finish putting on his coat, then guided him into the front passenger seat, where he collapsed in relief. The hands again helped him, this time putting a seat belt around him.

Ben continued for a timeless period somewhere in that wretched state between awareness and unconsciousness. He could sense the car's motion, and it made him feel even sicker to his stomach. His head seemed to be bobbing back and forth. At times the sense of pain and discomfort almost went away, and he seemed to be floating on his stomach, as if he were resting on a billowy cloud. The headlights dancing on the dirt road seemed to be pulling the car onward, and a vague sensation of something going wrong came over him, something wrong other than his illness. He tried to talk, and the words came out so slowly. "Long . . . way, long . . . drive. Too . . . long."

The car came to a gentle stop. He heard a gurgling noise, and then the hand was there in front of him, offering him a most welcome cup of liquid. He tried to reach for the cup but could not grasp it. But the cup came closer to his lips, and it promised relief to his tortured mind. Eagerly he tightened his lips around the edge, then he swallowed with abandon. He was unaware that the lid of the cup was being screwed on again and the cup put away. He was unaware of the car's motion now. The hands had given him a kind of relief. Seconds later Ben was even unaware of that relief. He was no longer aware of anything.

◆   ◆   ◆

Tina Samson was thinking of the dawn long before it came. She lay in bed staring at the ceiling and wondering what she could tell Margaret. Not that it was any of Margaret's business what she did. Certainly Margaret knew that she had been sleeping with Del Delano long after they got divorced. But it was nice of Margaret to let her have a room and not make any fuss about whether she used the room at night or stayed all night elsewhere. Tina had spent two whole days scouring Bay City for a job, and she had said she'd be back this night. Well, she had come back, if not exactly the way she expected. And as for a decent job, she didn't think there was such a thing in Bay City. There had been one opening at a fast-food place, working with a bunch of teenagers for less money than she had been earning at the Admiral's Arms—and it would have meant ferry fare and all the extra travel time, too. Then there was one as a waitress in a cheap dock-side bar, finishing at one o'clock in the morning, long after the last ferry left for Fogge Island.

There had to be something on Fogge Island besides just the summer jobs. She could accept Margaret's offer, keep the room without paying rent for another three months, then get a live-in job at one of the hotels on the other side of the island, but that would just be for the summer and then she'd be out in the cold again. After all, she had her pride. It was one thing to accept an occasional extended helping hand and quite another to be a moocher.

How she wanted the dawn to come! And yet, what would she do? Perhaps a cup of coffee at Meg's, then wait until the first ferry came over? Then she could pass by the FIGS library, tell Margaret she had missed the night ferry and stayed on the mainland, and go to her room. But she wanted to get out of here. It was smelly, and she did not feel right. It was on the ferry coming back last night that she'd met Mason Crosby and unburdened herself while the older man listened patiently and muttered appropriate words of sympathy about her job hunt. Then she was willing to listen patiently in turn as he told her how he had taken his wife that morning on the ferry for a few days in a hospital in Bay City. Kidney trouble, he said, then described the stench in her bedroom.

"You can't imagine what's it's like," he'd said. "Every day other people come in and tell you about their problems, but you just don't realize it could happen to you." He said the doctor told him Mrs. Crosby would be a permanent invalid.

Gradually, as they talked, Tina realized that Mason's wife would not be able to help out in the pharmacy any more. The pharmacy stayed open something like twelve or more hours a day, six days a week, plus Sunday mornings. And at times it was very busy, even in the winter, for it was not just a pharmacy, but also sold newspapers, beer, small convenience groceries, some hardware items, even toys. Mason could not possibly handle that store all by himself. Tina asked, "But what'll you do, Mason, without your wife to help you in the store? And I guess as long as she's in the hospital, you'll be going over frequently for visits."

"I haven't given much thought to it," he said. His head was hairless on top in a tonsure, and the fringes were long, thinning, and pointing in all directions. " Of course, this morning I just closed up all day. Probably got a lot of people mad. But I can't help that. I put a sign on the door telling them in case of emergency I'd be back on the last ferry, and they could get prescriptions filled then. I'll bet I'll have an hour's work waiting for me."

Tina was quite sympathetic, and then, as if the idea had just occurred to her, she came out with it. "Say, isn't that a coincidence? I'm looking for a job, and you're going to need a helper in your store."

Mason looked at her. "Well, I don't know." His eyes squinted, and he seemed to be thinking it over.

Was he wondering how much she had made at the Admiral's Arms? She made good tips there. Of course, he knew she was a hard worker. After all, many a night after closing the pharmacy, he'd drop in at the Admiral's Arms for a few drinks before going to bed. And he knew she didn't irritate customers or talk back. People told her she had a nice personality. And she wasn't bad-looking. She had a good figure. She must be twenty years or so younger than Mason and his wife, so she could certainly keep up with the work. He wouldn't be able to get any teenager to work like she could.

Tina could sense the dawn just minutes away. Well, she got the job. She was Mrs. Crosby's replacement behind the counter, and, at least as far as this night was concerned, in bed, too. She had never thought much about Mason Crosby before. He had been just another customer at the pub, certainly not anyone she would ever look upon romantically. Life was full of surprises. She and Mason had negotiated her salary, and when he put his hand on her leg and she did not move, the bargain was sealed. The work would be quite satisfactory, but she wondered about the other job. It was not what she had looked forward to.

She still could not believe that Del Delano was dead. They had grown so close that last year in the pub, closer even than when they were married. They had planned to get remarried as soon as he could straighten out that mess he had gotten into, and Del had even agreed that she could have children. Somehow they would have found room above the pub for a nursery. All her grown life she had wanted children, and then she lost the first one, and after the divorce, she thought she might never have another chance. Tina had never really fallen out of love with Del, and now he was dead. She had never really known Mason Crosby before, and now she was sleeping in his wife's bedroom, with him snoring in the thin-walled adjoining room. Mrs. Crosby's room had a bad smell to it, and she could not wait to leave.

◆   ◆   ◆

It was a beautiful morning, and Dr. Thomas Delano walked briskly into his office. He opened the flowered chintz drapes to let sunshine flood the room. The rays fell directly on the row of certificates hanging on the wall to the right of the massive dark oak table he used as a desk. He crossed over with his hands clasped together behind his back and stared at the glass-entombed pieces of paper that told so much about his life: B.S., Bowdoin, 1947; M.D., Harvard, 1951; Intern, Massachusetts General Hospital, 1951-1953; Captain, U.S. Army, 1953-1957; Fellow of the American College of Surgeons, 1965; and that final framed parchment, in the position closest to his desk where he could conveniently reread it when it so pleased him, a copy of the Hippocratic Oath. He glanced now at the Oath, his eyes glued to one spot as his lips continued from memory: "Whatsoever house I enter, there will I go for the benefit of the sick, refraining from all wrong-doing or corruption, and especially . . . ." He stopped, cleared his throat, and went back to the door. "I'm ready, Miss Putnam."

The first patient was Old Richie Crosby. His pains were keeping him awake at night. Could he have some more of that medicine? Dr. Delano made a superficial examination of Richie's abdomen only because Richie expected it. Richie was dying of cancer that had already metastasized from the colon to the lungs, and, considering that the man was a frail ninety-three, there was nothing that could be done to cure it or even slow it down. For some reason, the doctor was reminded of an explanation once given him of the Russian word *nechevo:* If you tell me that your grandfather died, and I say *nechevo,* it means "Well, I'm really sorry for him, but after all he was an old man and had to go sometime." As he counted out some morphine tablets, he repeated silently to himself, *Nechevo,* Richie, *nechevo.* Aloud he said, "Try to make these last as long as possible, Richie."

Dr. Delano had finished with his last patient of the morning, Mrs. Cooke, who stood behind a portable partition as she put her clothes back on. The nurse knocked on the door, as she always did when it was necessary to interrupt him while he was with a patient, and entered when she heard no verbal prohibition, "It's Mrs. Gorges on the telephone, doctor. She says it's urgent."

"Is it all right to come over, Thomas?" Martha Gorges asked him.

He'd prefer that she not, but he couldn't tell her so. "Yes," he said, "if it's urgent." He turned to see Mrs. Cooke wave him a thank you as she went out.

It took Martha Gorges no more than ten minutes to reach the office. He was looking out the window as she walked up Gilman Street, and he went to the reception room to tell his nurse, "Mrs. Gorges has been having headaches, Miss Putnam. Show her right in."

"It's that horrible detective-genealogist, Thomas," Martha said. "He either knows or suspects something."

"Suppose you tell me all about it."

Martha relayed the details of her interview the previous day with Dr. Sinclair and Sergeant Booth. "He keeps talking about Belinda. Is there anything that he can find? Do you think he could ever prove anything?"

Dr. Delano leaned back in his chair and crossed one leg over the other. "Well, I don't know. There's Sylvia Mann, I suppose."

"But she's loyal to you." Martha's words were as much a question as a statement. She tapped her slender fingers nervously against the arm of her chair.

"I suppose loyalty has its limits, but let's hope you're right," he said. Then, "You've got to work on Atherton, Martha. It's now or never. I just hope it's not too late."

"I don't care for myself, you know."

"I know. Go home and do what you can."

Martha rose and took a step toward him, squeezed his arm gently, then walked very slowly out the door.

Fifteen

IT WAS EARLY AFTERNOON. MORT STOOD AT THE cabin front window watching finely beaded white spray leap up as the ferry surged closer and closer to the island. It had been a profitable morning's work, and he felt the way all genealogists feel when suddenly one important discovery more than compensates for hours and days of fruitless searching. He was too old and too reserved to jump up in the air, click his heels, and yell "Whoopee!", but that was the way he felt. He wished the ferry weren't so slow.

The people in vital records had again been most helpful. He had been ushered into a vault, to which Amy Hosmer brought the gigantic, leather-bound original register of births for the year of his interest, 1961. Here every birth as reported to the city clerk by the hospitals or doctors was recorded exactly as given, line by line, one line to a birth, with each line showing in columns across the page the surname of the baby, given name, sex, mother, mother's age, mother's birthplace, mother's occupation, and mother's address, with other blanks for the same information on the father, except that there was no place for the father's address. In a pluralistic society, blanks in official forms had to cover all conceivable possibilities but in a very impersonal way, so as to offend no one. In this the state was probably more realistic than genealogists. The genealogist assumed every child had to have a father and a mother. The state assumed only a mother. Information about the father was not mandatory, nor, as far as an address was concerned, even desirable.

In the present case, Mort had no interest in such sophistries. He was concerned with discrepancies, for his experience had taught him that although on the one hand human beings were fallible creatures and easily made little mistakes in ages, dates, and such; on the other hand, a discrepancy in vital records was sometimes a warning sign that there was something significantly wrong in the events themselves. The death certificate of Ferdinand Gorges had a space for his date of birth, given as 31 January 1961, but his birth certificate showed he had been born on 1 February 1961. Typographical error? Possibly, though an error of one day in the same month was much more likely than an error straddling months. The certifying doctor for both birth and death information was Dr. Thomas Delano, although the actual information supplied to the city clerk could have come from some employee using the doctor's records. When he saw the original records spread out in front of him, the picture they conveyed was a somewhat different one from that shown in the transcribed certificates. Mort was reminded of the Emperor Claudius, who said, "Let the record be erased, but let the erasure show."

◆   ◆   ◆

Success often came in pairs, and on his return to the hotel, Mort found a message telling him to call his correspondent in North Carolina. Blasingham Sharpe was young in age but old in experience, and though his rates were higher than average, he could often accomplish more in one hour than many an ordinary professional genealogist could in a day. He did not waste time on the telephone, either, but came straight to the point and gave Mort the highlights of his research on the college years of Atherton Gorges, adding, "I'll send all the details in a written report with my bill this afternoon." A quick "See you at the Salt Lake conference," and he hung up. There was no need to catch up on news and gossip of friends and acquaintances over the telephone; they could do that by letter or wait until they met in person. Telephones, to Blasingham, were for business.

The first thing Mort noticed when he reached the hotel was Sylvester Mann standing behind the counter, talking to the clerk. Sylvia Mann sat in the lobby, impatiently waiting for her husband. Neither one seemed to want to notice Mort, who left the hotel and started walking over to the constable's office. The weather was fairly warm for February, and people younger and bolder than Mort were out in the air with only light clothing. He caught himself making funny noises with his lips, then realized that he had been trying to recapture in whistling form the third movement from St. Saen's *Third Violin Concerto*. His lips did not a violin make, he decided, and he stopped whistling but allowed the music to keep playing in his head. How he would love at that moment to be at an Isaac Stern concert! Would it not be wonderful if they had all-violin-concerto concerts, offering three or even four. What four would he prefer? St. Saen, yes. Certainly Tchaikovsky. Beethoven?—how he loved Beethoven!—but for a violin concerto he would choose others. Dvorak, yes, though he preferred his cello concerto, but still if it were to be all violin, Dvorak should be there. Finally, Mendelssohn? Wieniawski? Lalo? Brahms? Bruch? Bruch, he decided. He remembered something he had read about Bruch, that in his long career he had been struck by genius just once, when he was composing the second movement of his violin concerto. It was sad that genius had paid so brief a visit, but still it was much more than ever happened to most mortals.

Mort was trying again to whistle a complex tune when he entered Priscilla's office, but he stopped when he saw the look on her face.

"What's wrong?" he said. "Did you see Atherton Gorges this morning?"

"No," she said. She got up from her desk and crossed over to him. "He's missing, Mort. Both Atherton Gorges and Ben Mann are missing. They're not to be found anyplace."

She quickly brought Mort up to date. Ben Mann had disappeared from his room at the hotel. His parka was missing, but his car was still there. He had last been seen when the bar was closing at eleven o'clock; he'd come down to ask for Alka Seltzer, taking a whole package to his room. He had also been seen by the desk clerk, who had just finished his accounting for the day, and was preparing to go to his personal quarters in the hotel. The bartender had locked up the hotel, leaving only a night light on in the lobby. The door was found open in the morning, and Ben and his parka were gone without a trace.

Following his usual early breakfast with his wife, Atherton Gorges had said he was going out to take a walk and would be back in an hour or so. When it was time for lunch and he had not returned, Martha telephoned around to see if she could locate him. The desk clerk had seen him at the Mann Hotel early that morning, before it was known that Ben Mann had disappeared. He thought Atherton might have gone upstairs, but he was so well known that the clerk had not paid particular attention to his movements.

Martha telephoned Nehemiah Gorges. No, Nehemiah had not seen him, but then he was investigating the disappearance of Ben Mann. Did Martha think there was a connection? She did not know what to say. She telephoned the ferry office and was told that Atherton had not taken the ferry that day. She called every store in town, and though a few people mentioned seeing him early in the morning on Sea Drive, no one knew where he had gone. Like Ben Mann, he had just disappeared.

Finally Martha called Priscilla, who was already feeling as if the world had caved in on her with the disappearance of Ben Mann. "We don't know what on earth is going on," Priscilla said. Martha did not feel consoled.

Lieutenant Bumpus apparently learned about Atherton's disappearance around the same time Priscilla did, for he telephoned as soon as she put the receiver down from Martha's call. "What are you trying to do, Booth? Get rid of the entire island?"

Mort could not keep back a smile as Priscilla repeated Bumpus's words; they conjured up a vision in his mind of all the familiar faces on the island disappearing into thin air one by one. But he rapidly changed his smile to an apologetic frown when he saw Priscilla's expression. He was not on the spot; Priscilla was.

"Perhaps this may cheer you up a bit," he said. "It does not by itself solve the murder, but it sure accounts for some of the secrets." He explained what he had discovered in the Bay City vital records.

Priscilla's lovely eyes lightened with hope. "If only we could confront Atherton Gorges with what we learned from Deborah on Sunday, plus your suspicions regarding Ferdinand's birth . . . ." Her hope was not long-lived. "But we can't even find him."

"I am not sure that we would want to confront Atherton Gorges at this moment anyway. I suggest we have a talk with Dr. Delano. He seems to be the central player in these theatrics."

◆   ◆   ◆

Dr. Delano sat behind his oak table with his hands clasped together and his head lowered so that he could not see their faces. "Dr. Sinclair has observed some irregularities in records where you were the certifying source," Priscilla said.

Without looking up, Delano raised his open palm and said softly, "Can we just get to the point?" Then his head suddenly rose. With his lips pressed tightly together and his chin jutting out, he seemed to be daring them to do their worst.

"All right," Mort said. "I'll come straight to the point. Who was Ferdinand's father?"

"John Beeton."

Neither Mort nor Priscilla seemed surprised. "And who was his mother?" Mort said.

"Alice Beeton."

"And who was Belinda Beeton's father?"

Delano lowered his head again briefly, then raised it to the side, taking a quick glance at the framed Hippocratic Oath on his wall. Arms widespread and palms firmly pressuring the top of the table, he slowly raised his body upright from the chair and leaned forward. His presence loomed over them as if they were in a small dinghy and he a leviathan from the deep poised in some fearful act of retribution. "I am Belinda's father."

That one was not expected. Mort looked to Priscilla, and she, with her forehead wrinkled in a deep furrow, returned a quizzical glance. They both seemed to be wondering, can we take a brief recess to collect our thoughts and make sure we don't ask the wrong questions? But they knew they couldn't. They had cornered Delano, and, either because he thought they knew more than they did or perhaps because he no longer wanted to evade and lie, he had started to blurt out the whole story. They must not say anything now to make him change his mind.

Delano was silent, awaiting some further response from them.

Mort took a calculated risk. "The mother was—is—Martha Gorges."

"Of course," the doctor said. "Martha had burned her hand, and I was coming to her house each day to change the dressing. Atherton was spending all his days on the mainland trying to make his millions beget more millions. He had little time for her, and she was lonely. And I was only human, and found her attractive—and, by God, believe me, she was attractive! I was also married then, but one thing led to another and she became pregnant. Atherton was sleeping with her regularly enough so that the pregnancy seemed to him to be the most natural thing in the world. In fact, it improved their relations. She was going to give him another chance for a male heir, after already having given him Lettice."

"But the child turned out to be another female," Priscilla said.

"With a clubfoot," said the doctor.

"Excuse me," said Mort, "but if you were both having relations with Martha, how could you be sure Belinda was yours?"

"Ha, ha! Atherton was not that regular! He was consumed with business deals and plots. Martha noted dates, and there could be no mistake. We knew it was my child long before the actual birth. I suspected it was a girl, and we both knew Atherton would be displeased, but when it turned out to be a girl with a clubfoot, Martha was ready to commit suicide. She just knew Atherton would divorce her and, if you know the man at all, you'll understand she wasn't overreacting."

Mort and Priscilla both nodded.

"Well, you can guess the rest. Circumstances at the time conspired to make it possible for us to do what we did. Atherton was in Europe. Martha was in my clinic—there had been a severe winter storm making transportation difficult, and her labor pains were coming on too fast to risk sending her to Bay City. I have two beds for patients back there—and Alice Beeton, whose husband had died after she became pregnant, was also in the clinic, having just given birth to a healthy male child a number of hours earlier on Tuesday afternoon. Belinda was born in the early hours of Wednesday morning, the first of February. Martha was desperate. I was racked with guilt feelings. And Alice, oddly enough, was not especially happy to be a mother, not so soon after losing her husband. She knew she was facing a rough life and would probably have to leave Fogge Island to find work. And then the idea took hold of me."

Priscilla said, "You switched the babies, of course, but did Mrs. Beeton know?"

"Oh, yes, it was a three-person conspiracy. Her child, Ferdinand, would be brought up by the Gorgeses and given all the advantages of being born rich. She would be hired as a cook by Martha at a good salary, and she could bring up Belinda in the Gorges household. I promised on Martha's behalf that everything possible would be done to ease any burden, and, if feasible, to correct the defective foot. Keep in mind that Martha and Alice were distant cousins, they had known each other for years, and Martha had always been very friendly and helpful to Alice. Alice readily fell in with the idea. The two births, even though on different days, were so close together that no one else knew—except for my nurse Sylvia, now Sylvia Mann."

"That explains a good bit about Sylvia," said Mort.

Priscilla asked, "Did you help get Sylvia that job in Boston?"

"Yes, but I'll go into that later. It could have been a foolproof scheme had I not telephoned in a birth registration as soon as Alice Beeton had Ferdinand. The people in the city clerk's office in Bay City were used to my giving them information on the telephone, knowing that the next time I was in Bay City I'd drop by to sign the forms. Early the next morning I went to Bay City and told the registry officials that I'd made a mistake. It was easy, there was no reason for them to suspect anything. They crossed out the entry showing a male baby born to Alice Beeton on 31 January and added an entry showing a female baby born to her that date. Then a new entry was made showing a male baby born to Martha Gorges on 1 February 1961. That's how you caught on, no doubt," he said to Mort.

Mort said, "Of course, it would not show in the transcribed records, but the cross-out was there on the original pen-and-ink register. Did you know you made a mistake in filling out Ferdinand's death certificate?"

Dr. Delano's face asked a silent question: how?

"You put down 31 January as his date of birth, I guess because it was the true date and it had made an impression in your mind."

"We always seem to slip up when we're most relaxed. When Ferdinand died, that part of our little deception was over. I was grieving more for Ferdinand than worrying about having to be consistent in all the details of his birth." He looked from Mort to Priscilla and asked, "Does Atherton Gorges have to know about this?"

"Not necessarily," Mort said, hoping Priscilla would back him up. "But tell us about Sylvia."

"Sylvia was a young, impressionable girl longing for all the things young girls long for. She was loyal to me, but I couldn't be sure for how long. I wanted to get her off the island, and so I arranged with some friends in Boston to get her a more glamorous nursing job, if you can call nursing glamorous at all. It certainly suited her, for it led to a marriage with a very wealthy doctor. I not only got her off the island but I put her under more gratitude to me. You can imagine I was not pleased when she came back to the island after her husband died. But I helped her in her ambition to marry Sylvester Mann, and so she was all the more under obligation to me."

"She wasn't blackmailing you?" Priscilla asked.

"She's not the type to ask for blackmail, and, believe me, I'm not the type to pay it." He waited a minute, then went on. "Martha's worried sick about this. In fact, she's been worried sick about you," he said, indicating Mort. "She just knew that you would discover our secret, and as it turns out she was right."

Priscilla asked, "What was the difficulty between you and Del Delano?"

"He was threatening to tell you people about the switch of babies. He thought it might have something to do with the murders."

"How'd he find out?" she said.

"Sylvia told him. They were still friendly even after she married Sylvester."

"How about the bad feelings between you and Del over your lending your cabin to Sylvia and Sylvester?"

"Nothing to it, really. By the time I lent my cabin to Sylvia and Sylvester, Sylvia and Del were already finished. Del wasn't in love with Sylvia. He wanted to remarry Tina." The doctor moved his hands in front of him and spread open his palms, as if to say that he was giving them everything.

"Del and I had no serious trouble until he told me one day that Sylvia had told him about switching the babies and that he thought it might be important for the police to know. We had a few bad words on several occasions, and then one day he said he could hold off no longer. That night I drank too much at home. Not ten or twelve drinks, but maybe four or five. Anyway, I worked myself up and then rushed over to have it out with him at the pub. I very stupidly said something about killing him if he told, and then he went and got himself murdered. Which didn't make things look very good for me."

"What about Belinda's foot?" Mort said.

"That's the damned pity of it! Alice and Belinda came into the Gorges household, and after a few years Martha suggested that Atherton pay for an operation. He refused. She brought it up as often as she dared, and the answer was always the same. Now the costs for an operation such as that have soared so much that it's out of the question that he'd ever pay it. And, of course, now if he has to find out that Belinda is mine and Martha's, well, that puts finish on it."

"Just suppose that you told him the truth about Belinda," said Mort. "But not the whole truth, only that part which is so strongly backed up by the crossed-out record?"

"I don't get what you mean," said Dr. Delano.

Priscilla was looking at Mort questioningly, too.

"Suppose you tell him about the switch, the reasons for it, the way it was done, and so on. But without telling him you are the real father. Let him think he is the real father. I take it you and Martha did not make a confession to either Mrs. Beeton or Sylvia about your fathering Belinda?"

"Of course not. They only knew about the switch. There was no need to tell them about Martha and me."

"Exactly. And there would be no need to tell Atherton about Martha and you. Let him think that Belinda was his baby. What would the result be? An egomaniac like him wanting desperately to carry on his line loses a supposed son who turns out not to be a son and gains a living daughter, albeit one with a clubfoot—what would his likely reaction be?"

"You mean after he had a chance to think it all over?" asked Priscilla.

"Yes. Admittedly it would come as a shock initially. But he is a cold, calculating man, and what would his sober second thoughts be?"

The doctor's face lit up in a smile. "You mean—and you're right—he would welcome another chance to have heirs, and probably be damned glad to pay for an operation on a girl he thought was his daughter."

"I think you were a bit despondent when we walked in, and you gave away more than you needed to," Mort said. "I had discovered information relating to the switching of babies, but neither Priscilla nor I could have known anything about your being Belinda's father. For my part, I have already forgotten it, and I don't think there's anything in Priscilla's code of ethics to require her to make a report on some gossip she overheard which apparently had nothing to do with the matter under investigation. Am I right about that, Priscilla?"

"About what? You know I'll have to include in my report the baby switching, but when Martha tells that to Atherton, it will probably become a public matter anyway. That's the only thing I heard this afternoon." She sat back with a smile, then added, "Of course, we're all assuming that the disappearance of Atherton Gorges, not to mention Ben Mann, is just a temporary one."

As Mort and Priscilla stood up, the doctor came from around the desk and put his arms around them. "To think how I dreaded your visit this afternoon!"

As Mort was ushering Priscilla through the door, Delano called after them, "I can't say more, but Sylvia Mann might also be receptive to some well-intended counseling."

"About this matter?" asked Mort.

"Sylvia has her own matters."

As they walked back to the feed store, Priscilla said, "That was like something out of a novel by Fielding."

"The older we get the more we see how much stranger than

fiction truth can be. And as far as Atherton Gorges is concerned, it certainly shows that genealogy can be a very inexact science, doesn't it? As the saying goes, it's a wise child who knows its own father." He paused to think and then said, "It also both answered some questions and didn't answer some questions."

"What didn't it answer?"

"Oh, little things, such as who murdered Ferdinand Gorges, Cobber Palgrave, Esther Gorges, and Delano Delano—and caused the disappearance of Atherton Gorges and Ben Mann."

"Oh, those little things," Priscilla said. "Yes, well, I'm afraid we've still got a long way to go. Let's take stock of the problem. What have we got?"

"Do you want to go victim by victim?"

"Why not? First we're assuming that just one person is behind it all. If we find the murderer of one, we've found the murderer of all."

"Reasonable."

"Well," Priscilla began, "let's take the murder of Ferdinand Gorges. We've been assuming that we could eliminate Atherton Gorges because Atherton would not have terminated his male line, no matter how much he might otherwise have disliked his son. Thus, no matter how despicable Atherton might be, he could not be our murderer. But if Ferdinand were not Atherton's son, and if—this is a mighty big 'if'—Atherton knew he was not his son, then Atherton can't be eliminated."

"We don't have any reason to suspect that Atherton knows, but can anyone really be eliminated at this time as Ferdinand's murderer?"

"Well, I'm eliminating you, Mort, at least on the basis of present evidence."

"Thanks."

"I don't see how anyone at that reception could be eliminated, and I don't see how anyone not at the reception could be a suspect. Of the people who figure into the various murders, I think we can eliminate Tina Samson, because she was working at the Admiral's Arms at the time Ferdinand was murdered. Of course, we could also eliminate Cobber Palgrave and Delano Delano, because they were also murdered—if, of course, we're right in thinking that one person killed all the victims. Now, Dr. Thomas Delano was at the reception, and in fact he was the one who pronounced Ferdinand dead, but, as my department found out the hard way, Dr. Delano could not have murdered Delano Delano. Therefore he didn't murder any of them and is not a suspect."

"Let's say that at this time he seems to be in the clear. Now let's take the killing of Cobber Palgrave. Is there anyone we can eliminate as a suspect?"

"It was someone having a friendly drink with him," Priscilla said. "Is there anyone who under no circumstances would have been drinking with him?"

"Cobber was a petty blackmailer, and he wasn't fussy about who provided him with cash. Anyone coming to pay him blackmail money might have sat down first and had a talk over a drink before killing him. Further, we can't even be sure when the poison was put in his glass, because he drank so much he was always passing out. He could have had a drink with his murderer and then passed out. The murderer could have put the poison in Cobber's glass with some gin, knowing that whenever Cobber woke up, the first thing he'd do would be to go for that glass again."

"You mean even his wife Lucy could have put poison in the glass while he was sleeping before she went to work?"

"Exactly. Now let's take Esther. Either the murderer was someone who lived in the house with her, or it was someone who did not live in the house with her."

"How self-evident can you get?" she said.

"I am merely trying to divide the problem into its two different aspects. Anyone in the house presumably could have gotten into Esther's room and put poison at any time into the bottle of absinthe. But if the murderer were someone outside the house, it would have been more difficult. How could it have been done?"

They passed by the feed store, crossed the street, and continued walking up Sea Drive along the sidewalk by the sea wall. Mort instinctively put Priscilla on the inside, but as he saw her getting more than her share of the spray leaping above the wall, he changed positions again. Priscilla put her arm inside Mort's as they strolled along their way. It was early evening, and they could see in the distance the glare of lights from Bay City illuminating clouds above. A shrill whistle rose above the noise of waves lapping the sand below the wall, and they knew a ferry was making its way toward the island.

"Easy," said Priscilla. "Someone could have given her a bottle of poisoned absinthe and said, 'Here's a present, Esther. Take it home with you.'"

"Exactly. That is possibly why it was absinthe. An ordinary drink might have been disposed of in an unpredictable way, but Esther would have been more selfish with a rare drink."

"Absinthe makes the heart grow fonder."

"It did have a reputation as an aphrodisiac, you know. It was all the rage in Hemingway's Paris in the nineteen twenties."

"I know, but the wormwood in it is said to dissolve brain tissue or something, and most countries now outlaw it."

"Something like that," he said. "At any rate, it is not easy to get. The point is that someone could have given Esther that bottle outside without even having to enter the house. Is there anyone who could not have given her that bottle?"

"Her brother Dudley. He would have kept it for himself and given her a bottle of cheap wine, such as that Premium Pinot Noir of yours."

"Premiat Pinot Noir. But Dudley would have been inside the house anyway, and so he wouldn't have needed the ploy of a bottle of absinthe. Which, of course . . . ."

"Is just what I'm saying, Mort."

"Do you really think we can eliminate Dudley?"

"No, I guess you're right. As far as Esther's death is concerned, we can't eliminate anyone."

"Now, when it comes to Delano Delano, we can eliminate Dr. Delano, but that seems to be all. Anyone could have entered the pub after Dr. Delano left. Furthermore, we have no right to assume that the murderer entered with the intention of killing him. Someone could have entered with another intention and then killed him on the spur of the moment."

"Suppose the murderer were really two people," Priscilla said. "Can we really eliminate Dr. Delano and Tina Samson? Maybe they were having an affair and for some reason still unknown to us decided to murder some people. Very cleverly Dr. Delano poisons Ferdinand, and we eliminate Tina because she wasn't there, and then Tina bashes

Delano Delano over the head, and we eliminate Dr. Delano because he has a perfect alibi."

"You're right. We cannot completely eliminate them. Now, how about the disappearance of Atherton Gorges and Ben Mann?"

They were at the end of Sea Drive now, to their left was the wide wood-covered pier leading to the ferry slip. The ferry had just docked. Passengers were disembarking and walking up the pier to Sea Drive, and Priscilla and Mort stopped to let them by.

Suddenly Priscilla cried out.

"What is it?" asked Mort.

"There! See them?"

Mort's surprise matched hers. Walking side by side up the pier as if they were in no hurry and talking in a friendly fashion were two men. The older one was Atherton Gorges; the younger, Dudley Gorges.

Sixteen

As far as the police were concerned, Senator Atherton Gorges had a lot to explain. As far as he himself was concerned, he saw no need to explain anything.

"Am I charged with some criminal offence?" he asked Priscilla. "Am I under arrest? Do you have a warrant against me? Am I even a material witness in some way? You do realize that I may be the next governor of this state."

He agreed reluctantly to be interviewed by Priscilla and Mort later that night at his house. He would not visit the police office at the feed store unless they produced a warrant.

On questioning Dudley Gorges they found him more cooperative, though not necessarily more helpful. They walked across the street with him as he checked back into his hotel, his only luggage a small knapsack slung over his shoulder.

At the bar he offered to buy them a drink, but Priscilla said, "No, thanks, I'll pay for my own."

Dudley ordered a Miller's beer, and Mort asked for Glenfiddich Scotch, straight, no ice. Priscilla ordered a glass of club soda, noting that they still had to question Atherton Gorges that night. In fact, they might not have any other chance to eat, so she ordered a hamburger. Mort changed his own order to club soda and a hamburger.

"It's all very simple," Dudley said. "I've become a remittance man."

"A what?" said Priscilla.

"That's what your uncle calls it?" Mort said. "Where is he sending you?"

"You know what it is, huh? Australia. I get my remittance once every three months as long as I stay there and don't make any trouble for him."

"That might be called compromising a witness," Priscilla said.

"If I were a witness to anything in the first place. I was just shooting off my mouth with those wild accusations against Uncle Atherton. Why, Uncle Atherton's the salt of the earth, and I can't imagine anyone saying anything nasty against him." Dudley threw his head back and laughed. "I was hysterical," he said. "I'd been drinking earlier, and I just said anything that came into my head. You know I couldn't prove it, and you certainly didn't seem to take my accusations too seriously, since you didn't arrest him."

The talk with Dudley at least cleared up the reason behind the disappearance of Atherton Gorges. Atherton had gone to the hotel in the early morning to make Dudley his remittance offer. On learning that Dudley had just taken the ferry for Bay City, Atherton got a man who worked for him and owned a powerful boat to take him across to Bay City and beat the ferry. He was on hand to meet Dudley as he stepped off the ferry. They went to Atherton's Bay City office, where they talked and negotiated all morning. They had lunch and went back to the office, where Atherton had a lawyer draw up a legal document for Dudley to sign. Atherton did not want Dudley in the house again, but he was free to go back with Atherton on the late afternoon ferry, stay at the hotel, and the next morning pick up from the house the rest of his clothing and any other possessions he might want to take to Australia. Dudley showed Mort and Priscilla his copy of the legal agreement, in which he promised not to disseminate in any way, verbally or in writing, anything untrue against his uncle. The agreement specifically noted that it was not intended to bind Dudley in any way from telling the truth in any criminal matter; however, the burden would be on Dudley to prove that it was the truth. He would not make any accusations he could not prove.

Priscilla asked if she could make a photocopy of the agreement, and Dudley agreed. The clerk at the desk made the copy for her, she returned the agreement, Dudley put the paper back in his pocket, then excused himself and went to his room.

Priscilla decided she had better check with Lieutenant Bumpus before Dudley left the island again, but, as she told Mort when they were alone, she did not see how they could stop him. Though he was one of many people present at the reception when Ferdinand was poisoned, he was not really a witness to that event or to any of the murders. As for the poisoning attempt against himself, she thought an able lawyer would easily defeat any efforts by the police to detain him. Besides, with four actual murders to solve, Priscilla did not take an unsuccessful murder attempt—if it were even that—as seriously as she might otherwise.

◆   ◆   ◆

Priscilla and Mort met Atherton Gorges at his house. He led them to the library, his attitude markedly different from what it had been a few hours earlier. His hands were shaky, and he looked as if he had a severe headache. His eyes were focused far away from them, and Priscilla had to ask, "Are you ill?"

"No," he said. "I just had a talk with my wife, and she's given me a lot to think about. In fact, this whole thing tonight is inconvenient. Could we make it tomorrow sometime?"

Priscilla was adamant. They were not going to chase him any more; he either would answer questions now or she'd indeed have to get a warrant. Gorges nodded and sat down with them at the table, still looking as if he were miles away.

The accusing witness having withdrawn his testimony, the attempt to poison Dudley had lost much of its import. Gorges maintained that he knew nothing about any poisoning attempt, that they had all moved about during the meeting, particularly to see some books, and that Dudley had dropped a book and leaned over to pick it up. No, he did not recall seeing Dudley actually take a drink. Could Ben Mann have poisoned the drink? Certainly it could have been possible, but why?

When asked for his suspicions as to what had really happened, he said, "Well, frankly, I think it was a prank of Dudley's. He always was a prankster, but it was a joke in bad taste. If there was poison in that drink—and I have no reason to doubt the laboratory report—Dudley must have put it in after he left the building." He looked at Priscilla. "I hope the police won't feel it necessary to bring charges against him."

"I wouldn't worry," Priscilla said. "Either way, whether we bring charges against Dudley for falsely reporting a murder attempt, or against the person he accused of making that attempt, a competent attorney could put enough doubt in a jury's mind to get the defendant off. I had to question you routinely on this, but now that I've done it, we're putting the so-called attempted murder on the back burner and concentrating all our resources on the four actual murders and the disappearance of Ben Mann."

Atherton had heard about the disappearance of Ben Mann but had no light to shed on it. "Any more questions?" he said as he started to rise from the table.

"Not questions," Mort said, "but you did commission me to see if I could find anything in your background that might be embarrassing if you were to run for governor. I would advise you not to run."

Atherton Gorges glared at Mort, then slowly sank back into the seat of his chair. "You've found something?"

"When you were in college, you were the head of a fraternity. During some particularly rough hazing of some pledges, one of them died—he couldn't hold his breath under water as long as the others. You were one of three fraternity members whom the police held responsible. It was a messy case, all the more so because there were charges in the newspaper that your father bribed some officials to get you off. Just the kind of thing that would derail an election campaign, and neither the opposition nor the media would have much trouble digging it up."

Atherton pursed his lips and tapped the fingers of one hand against the table top. Finally he said in a monotone, "How much do I owe you?"

"Three hundred dollars."

"That's pretty cheap." Atherton took a checkbook out of his jacket pocket and began writing.

"It was a cheap case," said Mort. "But there is more at no extra charge."

Mechanically Gorges thrust the check toward Mort, who folded it and put it in his pocket without looking at the amount. Instead he watched Atherton Gorges watch him.

"Neither would it be difficult," he said after a long pause, "for the media or for your opponents to learn that some years ago you raped and severely injured a girl on this island, and again used money and influence to cover it up."

"That's a lie!" yelled the accused man, standing up. "If you dare publish that kind of accusation, I'll have you for libel."

"Truth is a perfect defense to libel."

"That's not the way it happened. Rest assured, I'll sue."

"Relax—libel suits sometimes backfire. If Oscar Wilde hadn't started one, he'd never have had the chance to write *The Ballad of Reading Gaol,* would he?"

"I am not an Oscar Wilde."

"Oscar Wilde might have said that he was not an Atherton Gorges. And there's more, Senator. About ten years ago you were involved in some shady business transactions. An attorney on your payroll, Sylvester Mann, as executor of the will of Ensign Mann, sold you a company for a fraction of its true value, and if that little conflict of interest doesn't smack of criminal conspiracy, all my law training was wasted."

"I made a shrewd purchase. And Sylvester Mann was not working for me at the time. It was more than two years after the purchase that I first retained him as a lawyer."

"Tell that to the judge when you bring your libel suit."

Atherton Gorges was still standing, and now Mort, too, got to his feet. "In short, Senator Gorges, you have about as much chance of being elected governor of this state as Richard Nixon has of being appointed the next Supreme Court Justice. Oh, by the way, do you have any idea how that agreement you signed with Dudley would look in the newspapers, especially coming on top of everything else? Now, I think, we will leave you to your thoughts." Mort reached for

Priscilla's arm, and the two of them started to go.

"Wait!" came the voice behind them. "Do you want to know what really happened in that so-called rape case?"

Mort and Priscilla turned and waited.

"It was all so long ago. You're talking about Deborah, of course. I know you won't believe me, but she led me on. She made the advances. After I followed through in a natural way, she suddenly jumped up, ripped her clothes, and threw herself to the ground. She miscalculated and hit a sharp rock, which is what gave her that scar. But even that suited her purpose, because it was well known that I owned a switchblade knife. She was yelling, and I tried to quiet her down, thinking at first that she had gone crazy. Then she told me what she wanted. A house and a lifetime job. I left her hiding there until I could get my father. My father promised her in writing that he would give her what she wanted, just to keep the thing quiet.

"Afterwards he was furious with me. He said he didn't know if he could believe me or not, but in either case I was to blame for allowing myself to get into that kind of situation. He ordered me to join the service. I was incapable of disobeying my father, and so I joined the Army and got a commission. I spent four years in the Army, much of it in Greece. To me it was exile. Finally, after four years, he let me resign my commission and come home." He was silent for a while. "You don't have to believe me, but let me give you some advice. In dealing with Deborah Samson, be very, very careful."

"If it came down to it," Priscilla said, "do you think people would believe your version over Deborah's?"

"Probably not," Gorges said. "When you're Tiberius Caesar, people are only too willing to believe the worse of you."

Outside, Priscilla asked, "Do you believe him?"

"I don't know. Do you?"

"In a case like this," Priscilla said, "who can know who's telling the truth? In any event, one thing impresses me. Have you noticed, Mort, how everything seems to revolve around Atherton Gorges? The murder victims were respectively his son, his cousin's son, his niece, and his nephew by marriage. His blood nephew accuses him of trying to murder him and of being the father of the murdered niece's unborn baby. He injured Deborah Samson and Percival Mann directly,

Margaret Mann and Ben Mann indirectly. Sylvester Mann is his attorney. Granted, he conceivably could have been the injured party in the Deborah Samson matter, but when you consider the pattern of his entire life, I'm inclined to believe her."

The night was dark as they walked down Sea Drive, and fog was rolling in from the sea. The few widely spaced street lamps gave off an eerie halo. A lone motorist disappeared around the corner, but the street was otherwise deserted. Most of the buildings were unlit inside, Meg's Muffin Shoppe, FIGS, the church, the Admiral's Arms. Only the grocery store and the pharmacy seemed open for business, and they noticed Tina Samson behind the pharmacy counter, gazing out the window, looking bored. There were lights on, of course, at the Hotel Mann in the distance, and the chill in the air made them both eager to reach their destination quickly.

"You have recited a list of circumstances," Mort said, "but as far as all the murders revolving around him, you are overlooking something. Atherton Gorges stands out because he has so much influence on this island, but with everyone being related to everyone, you could pick out any of our suspects and say that the case seems to revolve around him or her. The truth of the matter is that we have no better idea now of who the murderer is than when we first started. Now, you may be right that Atherton Gorges could conceivably be the killer, but consider what that does to your theory of inheritance as the motive."

"I see what you mean," she said. "Do you think we'll ever solve this case?"

"I don't know. But I have a feeling we will—for one good reason. We seem to have a murderer who has a purpose and who cannot stop. It's a bit like ciphers. If you send messages with completely random characters, no one could ever decipher them because they make no sense anyway. But if you intend to convey some kind of intelligence in those messages, sooner or later a pattern will show up, and once that pattern is understood, the cipher can be cracked. So far we have four victims."

"Possibly five."

"All right, maybe five. And I hate to say it, but it's almost as if we need another victim or two before we will be able to detect the pattern. I wish it were otherwise, but I'm afraid there are a number of other people at risk. And without a hint of what the pattern is, I could not even guess who they might be, or how high a priority they might occupy on the murderer's list."

"You think the murderer has a list?"

"Oh, yes," he said. "There has to be a list. If we only knew who might be the next intended victim, we could probably make a better analysis. At any rate, I plan to spend some time at FIGS tomorrow, and I expect to complete the work you assigned me. Then there will be no longer any reason for me to stay here."

"Do you have to finish tomorrow, Mort?"

"Would you have me take advantage of your employer?"

"I don't see it that way. You've been giving me immeasurable assistance in this case far beyond the preparation of genealogical charts and legal inheritance interpretations. Stay on. Please."

"Well, we can probably justify at least one more day."

"I'm truly worried about poor Ben," Priscilla said as they approached the hotel. "The fact that the Senator has shown up but Ben has not leads me to fear the worse."

"You like him."

"Of course I like him, Mort, but not in the way you mean. I don't love him and I wouldn't ever marry him, but he is a very good friend."

She thought back to the time years earlier when she and Ferdinand Gorges were sophomores at Bennington, and Ben Mann was a senior. She drove to Williamstown with Ferdinand and another couple for Sunday afternoon dinner at the inn there. Then they toured the Clark Art Institute and rode back, with Priscilla and Ferdinand in the back of the open convertible and Bill and Liz in front. Ferdinand became increasingly insistent as he attempted to make love to her; Priscilla became increasingly alarmed as she resisted him. Liz was laughing and shouting over the seat, "A little fighting makes it more fun, Priscilla, but you shouldn't overdo it." And then Ben and two friends, like the Lone Ranger with two Tontos, came up behind them fast in another car and pushed Bill's car to the road shoulder, bringing it to a halt. There were words between Ferdinand and Ben, and then she got into Ben's car and was safe. The bad feelings between Ferdinand and Ben had never ended, and Ben had never stopped letting her know that he was available, even when she married George . . . .

"I didn't mean to get personal," said Mort.

"I know."

They went to the desk to check for messages, then turned toward the dining room.

"Dinner?" said Mort.

"I don't know. We had that hamburger. I'd only want something light."

"Me too."

"I've got some cheese and crackers and fruit in my room. Why don't we get a bottle of that wine of yours and have a snack in my room and see if we can listen to some good music without anyone knocking on the door to announce another murder?"

Mort smiled. "I cannot think of anything I would rather do." Taking her by the arm, he led the way to the bar.

Seventeen

T HEY ORDERED TOAST, COFFEE, AND ORANGE JUICE
for breakfast, the waiter pouring the coffee from an insulated jug
which he left on the table.

"Thank you for a lovely time last night," Priscilla said, as they
waited for their order.

"On the contrary, I should thank you," Mort said, reaching over
to touch her hand. "You provided the music."

"Ah, but you provided the wine."

"Cooperative endeavors are always best," he said.

"That depends on who you're cooperating with."

"You have a way of putting profound truths in just a few words."

"Well, I went to kindergarten at age five and graduated from high
school before I was twenty."

He laughed. "You do like to throw my words back at me, don't
you?" After a pause, he said, "What is the order of the day?"

"We want to talk to Sylvia Mann. Remember, Dr. Delano hinted
that she might have something on her mind of interest to us."

"Good, let's do that, and then I want to go to the library to finish
up."

Sylvia was not happy to see them. She agreed on the telephone
to their coming over but said she wasn't sure it was right, since her

husband had gone to Bay City. She did not think he would like her talking to the police without his being present. "Sylvester is very protective of my rights, you know," she said as she conducted them into the house.

Priscilla's first questions were perfunctory. She led Sylvia into repeating everything she knew about the history of the murders, one by one, as if she were drawing fingers over Sylvia's responses, gently searching for a soft spot. The soft spot seemed to appear whenever the name Delano Delano came up. Priscilla filed the reaction away for future reference, then asked a sharp question about Ferdinand Gorges. "You were the nurse at the time of his birth?"

Sylvia obviously knew she had made a mistake by not insisting that her husband be present, yet just as obviously she now felt it might be a greater mistake to break off the interview. Every time she gave an evasive answer, Priscilla showed that she knew the correct one. It was demonstrated to Sylvia over and over that the truth about Ferdinand's birth was known and that she was just digging a hole for herself by trying to deny it. During the next fifteen minutes, she confirmed Dr. Thomas Delano's story, insofar as she knew the details, but, more subtly, she also allowed herself to become convinced that it was useless to try to lie to Priscilla.

Priscilla now charged full speed ahead. "We want to hear about your relationship with Delano Delano." The look on Sylvia's face showed that Priscilla had been right on target.

"You seem to know all about it," Sylvia said.

"We want to hear it from you."

"All right, I'll tell you the whole story. But does Sylvester have to know?"

"I don't have to tell him," Priscilla said.

Mort recognized and gave her credit for the equivocation. Priscilla didn't have to tell him, but—depending on what Sylvia revealed—someone might have to.

"Del and I were married in New York," Sylvia said. "It was more an elopement—we weren't going to tell anybody until we got back." She went on to explain that by the time they got back, they had good reason to continue keeping it a secret. They were not in love at all. Sylvia really wanted to marry Sylvester. Del really wanted to remarry his ex-wife Tina. Sylvia felt it had something to do with their age difference, for she was more than twenty years older than Del. "At any rate, after the first few nights, we knew the marriage was a mistake, and all the way driving back to Bay City, we discussed what we could do about it."

They planned to get a divorce, with Del going some place far away, perhaps Reno, so no one would have to know. Then came Sylvia's sudden opportunity to marry Sylvester, and she could not take a chance that he might refuse to wait if she hesitated. "So that's my little secret. I married Sylvester without benefit of divorce from Del." Of course, she knew that with Del dead she was in no danger of facing a bigamy charge. Her only concern was Sylvester, and the fact that she was a few years older than he worried her constantly. If she understood the law correctly, she had not been legally competent to marry Sylvester since she was already married at the time to another living person. Therefore, her marriage to Sylvester was not valid, even though her other marriage to Del had subsequently been terminated by death.

"Of course," Mort said, "you and Sylvester are free to get married again any time you want."

"If he'll have me," Sylvia said. "That's what I'm so damned afraid of. What if he decides that it's an easy way of getting rid of me?"

Priscilla put her arm around Sylvia's shoulder and patted her gently on the back, while Mort looked around him. He had seen the outside of the house, the grounds, and a number of the richly furnished rooms. "I take it that it is your money that bought and furnished this place?" he said.

Sylvia looked up and wiped her eyes with her fingers, smudging her makeup in the process. "Mostly, I guess. Sylvester has a good income as a lawyer, but he has expensive tastes, too. We bought this place and most of the furnishings after we got married."

"His previous place was not so well furnished?"

Sylvia laughed. "Neither the old house nor its furnishings suited him, and we sold them. If you're trying to get an idea of our relative worth, the return from my capital is more than three times his income, and when it comes to capital he has almost nothing."

"That is what I was getting at. Frankly, I do not think you should have any trouble in getting him to remarry you, but what you do is up to you. I know that Sergeant Booth would keep her promise not to tell Sylvester, but I suspect you will not be able to keep it a secret forever. The sooner you tell him yourself, the better. How many people know it besides those in this room?"

Sylvia said that both Tina Samson and Deborah Samson knew. "Deborah tried to blackmail me."

"Blackmail?" Priscilla's ears popped up.

"Well, perhaps not blackmail. There was nothing of monetary value involved. But Deborah found out about my horrible position— as she usually finds out about everything that goes on in this island— and hinted to me that she would not say anything if I told her something she wanted to know."

"What was that?" Priscilla said.

"What you asked me about when you first came in, the switching of babies. In fact, I thought Deborah was probably the one who told you about it."

"Do you have any idea why she was especially interested in that?" Mort said.

No, Sylvia did not know. She supposed that Deborah was just adding to her treasury of secrets. Deborah acted as if her position both at FIGS and as one of the island's social leaders depended on her knowing more unsavory details about the islanders than anyone else. She exchanged gossip on a daily basis the way a bank receives and pays out money.

"As for Tina, she and Del were going to get remarried, but Del told her about me because he was determined he was not going to make the same mistake I made. He intended to shut down the pub for the rest of the winter and go away with Tina, then come back divorced from me and married to her. Of course, he was murdered first. It was a dreadful shock for Tina."

Sylvia seemed relieved to get them out of the house. They both knew she was fighting a fierce battle with herself as to whether or not she should tell Sylvester about their visit. She called her dog to come to her so as to allow them safe passage to the gate and smiled at them as they departed.

Mort and Priscilla had different destinations, he planning to go

to FIGS, and she to Constable Gorges's office; but as they passed by
the Mann Hotel they noticed a number of bystanders at the top of the
steps looking in the doorway. Priscilla rushed up the steps. Less at-
tuned to the significance of gawking onlookers, Mort waited on the
sidewalk, expecting Priscilla to rejoin him in a moment. It was more
than a moment, though, before she reappeared, and when she did,
she remained at the top of the steps.

"For heaven's sake, Mort, come here! There's been another murder!"

Eighteen

DUDLEY GORGES HAD BEEN POISONED IN HIS ROOM at the Mann Hotel. It was mid-morning by the time the chambermaid, who assumed he had checked out, got around to cleaning the room. The door was locked; she opened it cautiously, then pushed her cart in. When she looked up and saw the horror the room held, she screamed. She heard running on the steps and knew it was the desk clerk, who rushed into the room and leaned over the body of Dudley, fully dressed but with his shoes off, lying on the floor face up.

The desk clerk telephoned Constable Nehemiah Gorges's office, but no one answered. Finally the manager of the feed store found Nehemiah next door at Meg's with a mug of coffee and a plate of cheese Danish in front of him. Nehemiah arrived at the hotel three minutes later out of breath but within seconds in complete charge.

This much Priscilla learned when she arrived at the hotel a few minutes later. This time Nehemiah had not thought to call the mainland, so Priscilla telephoned the news to her section.

She left a message for Lieutenant Bumpus, who was not in his office, then turned back to Nehemiah. "Now tell me everything you've done . . . ."

Mort stood silently beside her ready to give whatever support she might want.

Viewing corpses did not affect Priscilla, who had seen too many of them. The fact that this one was a person she had known and talked to only the night before saddened her but did not deter her from her duty. Dudley's waxen face seemed more animated in death than it ever had in life. He seemed angry, as if in the moment before death he had suddenly realized what was happening to him, and, perhaps, who was doing it to him. Priscilla's eyes took in the three-quarters-full bottle of bourbon and the can of Coke on the table, the broken glass on the floor beside the body. She searched for a room key but could find none.

Tiptoeing out of the room, she said to Mort, "We'd better leave everything just as it is until the experts have a chance to do their thing."

Using Ben Mann's office behind the reception desk as her base, Priscilla called in the people who had worked at the hotel the previous night and questioned them one by one. The last time Dudley had been seen alive was around 9:00 p.m., according to the night room clerk, the bartender, and a waiter. Dudley had come down from his room around eight o'clock and ordered fried shrimp for dinner by himself in the Talleyrand Room. Before and during the meal he ordered two bourbons with Coke. After he finished eating, he bought a full bottle of bourbon from the bar to take to his room. Then he went to the hotel desk to request a wake-up call for eight o'clock the next morning. The clerk called at the appointed hour, but Dudley failed to answer.

While Priscilla was finishing her preliminary questioning of the hotel staff, she got a telephone call from Bumpus's office. His receptionist informed her that Bumpus had started out for the island in the police boat, along with Corporal Dingley and the technicians.

"I suppose," she said to Mort, "this could mean that I might be relieved from the case even before you finish your part."

Somewhat to Priscilla's surprise, Lieutenant Bumpus did not seem to hold her personally responsible for the latest murder. He told her he had no present intention of removing her from the case and even commented that he would be lucky not to be removed from his own job. Fogge Island was becoming known as Murder Island. Both the mayor and the governor had asked for daily reports on the progress of the investigation. The latest murder would certainly make the national newspapers, and they could expect another flood of reporters and television people on the island.

"Frankly, Booth," Bumpus said, "I don't want to be around when the reporters register for rooms in the island's only hotel and discover that even the hotel owner is missing and presumed dead."

The medical examiner gave a preliminary report that Dudley had probably been killed by poison, and that he must have died around ten o'clock the previous night, give or take an hour. The room was searched and the contents of Dudley's pockets made available to Bumpus and Priscilla. Priscilla noted that Dudley had his room key in his pocket. His possessions were modest and not unusual, except for the $10,000 in travelers' checks and almost $5,000 in cash he had been carrying in his pockets and knapsack.

A ballpoint pen had been removed from Dudley's shirt pocket and placed on the table with the rest of his possessions. Priscilla used her handkerchief to hold up the pen, twist it open, and draw a short line on the back of her hand. The ink was green. Well, that answered one question. She put the pen down, making a mental note to tell Mort about it.

Bumpus requestioned the night staff to find out who might have gone upstairs in the evening, especially between nine and eleven. Other than hotel employees and the registered guests, only one person had been seen going up the stairs during those hours, Lettice Gorges. She had come into the hotel about nine-thirty, gone upstairs without stopping by the desk, and stayed about fifteen minutes. She was seen coming down and leaving the hotel at nine forty-five, an exact time since the desk clerk had been asked the time by a guest one minute earlier.

Bumpus asked Priscilla, "Is it all right to send Constable Gorges to bring in Lettice Gorges? You know, the same name and all? What is he, her uncle?"

Priscilla said it would be all right. "He's a first cousin, once removed. And he'll have a much better chance of finding her than Corporal Dingley, who doesn't know the island that well."

It did not take Nehemiah Gorges long to find Lettice. After telephoning the mansion and learning from the butler that she was somewhere "in town," he patrolled Sea Drive on foot and inquired of a few passersby if they had seen her. She had been seen with Lucy Palgrave, unlocking the front door of the Admiral's Arms. Nehemiah proceeded to the closed pub, rang the doorbell, was admitted by Lettice herself, and told her she was wanted for questioning at the hotel. Lettice and Lucy were apparently among the few people in town that morning who had not yet heard of Dudley's death. The news devastated Lettice; her face froze in horror for a second, and then her body seemed to crumple. Lucy helped her to a seat, fetched a glass of brandy from the bar, and put an arm around her while she sipped it.

"How did he die?" she asked when she was calmer.

"Someone put poison in his drink," Nehemiah said, "the same as Ferdie and Estie."

Lettice flinched again on hearing the words.

Lieutenant Bumpus took over Ben Mann's office and he questioned Lettice there with Priscilla and Nehemiah Gorges present. Lucy waited in the lobby with Mort and Corporal Dingley.

"You went up to Dudley's room last night?" Bumpus asked of Lettice. "What time?"

Lettice said she'd visited Dudley around nine-thirty. He had telephoned her and said that her father was paying him to go to Australia. He wanted to repay Lettice the three hundred dollars he had borrowed from her the previous night. She went to his room, he gave her the money, and then they discussed his future plans for a short while. She told him she was sorry she could not stay longer for his last night on the island, but he had caught her at an awkward moment.

"Did he mention anyone else?" Bumpus said.

"Well, *yes*," she said, lapsing into her affected accent as she recovered her composure from the initial shock. "He said it was all *right* if I left, because he was having another visitor soon."

"Did he mention a name or give you any possible idea of who that visitor might be?"

She shook her head.

"What were his exact words?"

"Well, as near as I can *recall*, he said 'That's okay, Letty, someone else is coming. Just three hundred and fifty dollars more, and my last debt in this damned place will be paid off.' "

"But no inkling as to who?"

"Someone *else* he had borrowed money from, I guess."

Bumpus asked Priscilla if she had any questions. She said, "Lettice, Constable Gorges told us he found you at the Admiral's Arms. Could you tell us what you were doing there?"

Lettice almost smiled. "Looking it over. I might *buy* it, put it back in business, and make *Lucy* manager."

"One last question," said Priscilla. "Dudley was known as a practical joker. Would you know anything about his writing a threatening note—in green ink—to Mr. Sinclair?"

"Oh, that." Lettice couldn't stifle a chuckle. "Well, what difference does it make now? Yeah, poor Dud. He told me what he'd done . . . thought it was a big joke to frighten the hell out of your genealogist and maybe stir up a little suspicion against Ben Mann. But it was just a joke, nothing more."

Priscilla told Bumpus she would explain what this was all about later.

"I read your report," Bumpus said. "I never let that threat bother me in the first place."

You wouldn't, thought Priscilla. It wasn't your life being threatened.

Bumpus dismissed Lettice and said he had no need to question Lucy at that time. The two of them could go. Nehemiah Gorges reminded Bumpus that he would not normally be working that afternoon—did the lieutenant want him to put in overtime? No, the lieutenant did not. "Just let me know where we can find you, and you can go, too."

With Lettice and Nehemiah gone, Bumpus and Priscilla went over the information available to them. Obviously if Dudley had been expecting another visitor—yet no one had seen any likely visitor go upstairs—that unknown visitor was the prime suspect. Most likely it was not a guest or hotel employee, for none of these people was a suspect in the other murders, and both Priscilla and Bumpus felt that the theory of just one master murderer was still valid. But in that case, how had the murderer reached Dudley's room without being observed?

Priscilla said, "If, as I suspect now, Ben Mann has been killed, and if there is but a single murderer, he or she would probably have Ben's keys to the hotel. There's a rear door, you know, and back stairs near it. The hotel staff were at their stations, the front desk, bar, dining room, and kitchen, and so it would have been easy for anyone with a key to come in the rear door, go upstairs to Dudley's room, have a drink with him and poison his drink, then sneak out the back way again. Remember, the maid found the door locked, and Dudley's key was in his pocket. That suggests the murderer had a master key and locked the room door after the deed was done."

"You're right, of course," said Bumpus. "It could have happened that way. But there's at least one other possible explanation. Lettice Gorges herself might have done it. She had the opportunity. Damned convenient—wasn't it?—Dudley's telling her that he was expecting another person but not mentioning any name. The evidence in the case indicates that Lettice, among the people who could have killed the others, was the only one who went up to Dudley's room last night . . . . Unless," he added, "it was Dudley's doing away with himself."

"Why didn't you arrest Lettice?"

"I guess because I don't think she'd have been that stupid. The murderer's not a stupid person. So far there's no real clue as to who killed the others. It just doesn't fit into the previous pattern that Lettice would have openly gone upstairs and let herself be identified as the only person visiting Dudley just before his death."

The next ferry had arrived, and already reporters were scrambling to get rooms from the desk clerk.

"Let's go to the constable's office," Bumpus said.

Mort, sitting in the lobby reading a newspaper, approached them, but Bumpus suddenly faced him and said, "What, are you still here? I thought you finished your job long ago." Then, turning to Priscilla, "Booth, I hope this genealogist's fees are going to be within your original cost estimates."

She started to protest, but Bumpus turned his back and continued walking out of the building. Priscilla had just time to tell Mort, "That note in green ink came from Dudley, after all," before running to catch up with Bumpus.

◆   ◆   ◆

Life is not fair, Mort told himself for perhaps the ten thousandth time since his first awareness of that fact as a young boy. Priscilla was doing a competent job of investigation, but she could not help it if the murderer left no obvious clues. The murderer had made but one small mistake, washing a glass and putting it in the wrong place at Cobber Palgrave's beach house. But that was the only time the murderer's performance had been flawed. Was that in itself a clue? The murderer had to be a very intelligent and shrewd person, which to Mort's mind ruled out, say, Lucy Palgrave and Tina Samson. Belinda Beeton? Perhaps. She was highly intelligent, but with that clubfoot could she have moved around as efficiently as the murderer had? Mrs. Beeton? Again, perhaps. She was a clever woman. Martha Gorges? Oh, yes, certainly clever, as were Deborah Samson and Margaret Mann. Lettice Gorges and Sylvia Mann had brains, too.

Why was he thinking in terms of a woman? Because of the poison, he supposed. Poison was a woman's weapon. A man would have been more likely to use a gun or a knife—or did that kind of thinking belong to a bygone era? Women used guns and knives nowadays, and some of the most famous poisoners in history were men. And bashing in Del Delano's head was not exactly the type of thing one would expect from a dainty creature like Martha Gorges. Why was Del Delano's death different from the others? Where was Benjamin Mann? Probably dead. But if so, why had his body been hidden? What was different about Ben Mann? If he knew that, Mort had the feeling he would know the reasons behind the whole thing. In their way, these were all clues, but the element that might enable him to make sense of them was missing.

It was a busy day at the FIGS library, and people came and went during the course of the afternoon. Mort continued working on his genealogical charts, now about as complete as he could make them. Some of the time Deborah Samson was at the librarian's desk, at other times Margaret Mann. As additional people came in, Mort gathered his papers in a neat pile to make more room for others. Old Richie

Crosby entered the room, looked around, and walked over to sit at Mort's table. Later Mrs. Beeton came in, and though there was no place at the other table but one empty seat at his, she took the empty chair from his and moved it over to crowd in with the people at the other table. Late in the afternoon, Richie Crosby left, and Constable Gorges came in and sat across from Mort.

Nehemiah seemed to think it necessary to explain himself to Mort. "My afternoon off. Nothing further I can do on the murder of Dudley. I'm the Gorges family genealogist, you know."

Mort assembled his papers and put them in his briefcase. He had finished, not only the day's work but the assignment. If Priscilla were taken off the case, he wondered if any use would be made at all of the work he had done. Even if she remained in charge, would it be of any real value to her? Well, at least it was done, and Priscilla would not have to worry about what she might be overlooking, genealogically speaking.

He looked at Deborah behind her desk and wondered: how much more does she know? When it came to intelligent women, there were few who could hold a candle to her. He observed the self-satisfied smile on her face as she jotted down notes on the paper in front of her. On an impulse, he walked over to her and asked if he could talk with her privately.

She smiled and said, "Why, certainly, we can go to my office. It's quiet in there." She stood up and called across the room to her assistant, who was putting away books. "Margaret, dear, can you take over the desk? Mr.—I mean, Dr.—Sinclair wants to have a private word with me."

Once in her office, the conversation could not really begin until she had made and served tea. "Tea makes things so cozy, don't you think, Dr. Sinclair?"

Mort agreed that it did indeed. This being the first time he had been in her private office, he was surprised at how modestly she had furnished it. There were a desk and chair, just one other chair for a guest, a five-drawer filing cabinet, and a rectangular table. On one wall was a photograph of an intelligent-looking woman in her late twenties, possibly Deborah's mother, wearing a flounced dress and the marcel-waved hairstyle typical of the pre-World War II period.

On the wall facing Deborah was an embroidered sampler bearing the words "Faith and Hope are Meaningless without Charity."

Once Deborah had the tea steeping, he said, "I have been hearing a great deal about you ever since I have been on the island."

"Nothing bad, I hope."

"Far from it. People tell me you are the fountain of knowledge around here. I have certainly found that to be true in my talks with you. I have now finished my assignment for the police, and I doubt that I could have done it without some of the information you have given me."

"Kind of you to say so, Dr. Sinclair."

"With my part of the work done, I will be leaving soon—with a certain reluctance, I admit. I have been so closely involved in this case that I will naturally be sorry to leave before it is solved."

She smiled, her lips tightly sealed, then poured out the tea.

"Of course, Dr. Sinclair, I can understand how you feel," Deborah said. "But do you think these murders will ever be cleared up?"

"I don't know. I've never participated in a case quite like this. Of course, I don't know the people as you do. Do you think the murders will be cleared up?"

Deborah sat with one hand on top of the other on her desk. She released a hand briefly to take a sip of tea, then replaced it. "It would depend, wouldn't it?"

"On what?"

"Well, among other things, on whether the police are more clever than the murderer, or the reverse. It could depend also on whether the murderer makes a mistake."

"Tell me," he said, "do you suspect anyone?"

"Oh, I'm just a genealogical librarian. How would I know about these things?"

"You are a very clever person. Probably more clever than anyone working on this case."

"Does that include you, Dr. Sinclair?" Now she was more relaxed.

"Most certainly," Mort said. "I accompany Sergeant Booth and run all over the island, but I doubt that I learn half as much as you do just sitting here at FIGS."

"Well, one hears things, of course. But weren't you the clever one to add up two and two when you found the deed from Atherton Gorges and the newspaper report of my accident?"

"You know that was routine for a genealogist."

"Of course you suspect that there's more to it." she said.

"More to it?"

"You're wondering what part of what I told you was true and what part might not have been."

"I would never call you a liar."

"Oh, I know that. And under the circumstances, no one would ever take Atherton Gorges's word against mine."

"He did, of course, protest that the story was not the complete truth."

"Knowing him, I suppose he said I forced myself on him, fell on the rocks to injure myself on purpose, and then threatened him with a rape and deadly assault charge if he did not give in to my demands?"

"Would you be capable of doing something like that?"

"It's not what I'm capable of, Dr. Sinclair, is it? It's a matter of what I actually did or did not do, is it not?"

"You're right, of course."

She nodded and smiled. "Does it really matter now exactly what happened thirty-five years ago?"

"Hardly. I'm sure Atherton Gorges has never been a paragon of virtue."

"That I assure you, he has not. None of us is without sin, I'm afraid."

"There are little sins and there are big sins—like murder. I only want to help Priscilla Booth solve the murders on this island. Do you know anything at all that could help? Some clue, perhaps, that the rest of us have overlooked?"

She waited a long while before answering. "What kind of clue would you have in mind, Dr. Sinclair?"

"It occurred to me that with as many murders as we have had, some pattern should emerge. I have racked my brain to see if I could find one, for I'm sure it exists, but it eludes me. I cannot quite see what is in front of me, if you do not mind my confessing."

"Not at all, Dr. Sinclair, not at all." She was now positively glow-ing. "May I see the charts you have been working on?"

Mort reached into his briefcase and extracted some of the charts that he considered most important, those covering the Gorges, Mann, Delano, Samson, and Crosby families.

Deborah bent over them in silence for a long time. Then she lifted up her head and said, "I see you have me down here, too."

"The Samson chart would hardly be complete without you."

"Of course, of course." She scrutinized the charts once again, then abruptly stopped, shuffled them together, and handed them back to Mort. "No, Dr. Sinclair. I am sorry but I see no pattern in your charts. Nothing other than facts of purely genealogical interest."

"I appreciate the time you spent with me," he said, standing up.

"Oh, there's no need for thanks, Dr. Sinclair. And if there were anything there, with my experience I am sure I would have noticed it. There's the pity. If one could only have youth and experience together. I envy you, for you are at a happy medium between the two. You have ample experience, and yet, really, you are still in the prime of life."

Mort thanked her again and left.

In a way he was amused. She had finished their conversation by telling him that, in effect, if he persevered he might one day be on her level as a genealogist. Well, maybe she was right. What had he expected of her? Some clue that would allow him to solve the crime and present it gift-wrapped to Priscilla? But had Deborah seen some-thing on those charts that he himself had missed? He had the impres-sion during one brief moment while she was looking them over that she was going to share with him some significant observation. But then she looked puzzled, and that was when she abruptly handed the charts back to him and terminated the interview.

If there were some clue on those charts that might help with the solution, Deborah now knew that it was also available to him. She would realize that what he did not know now, he might discover later. Or was he reading too much into it?

◆   ◆   ◆

The sun was starting to sink below the horizon on the mainland side as Mort arrived back at the hotel. To the casual eye, everything looked normal again. No curious gawkers, no policemen scurrying around, no sign of confusion on the part of the staff. The hotel was back to its business-as-usual efficient self. People were drinking at the bar, a lot of them, some by themselves, some talking and laughing together. A few early diners—but more than usual—were scattered around the Talleyrand Room. Looking them over, Mort realized what the difference was between this night and previous nights. There were a lot of new guests at the hotel. The media people had arrived, as a block larger in number than all the other registered guests put together. They would be interviewing and photographing each other, and second-guessing the police, for the next few days at least. They were a part of the island now, an important part.

He recognized Ken Fusetti sitting in one of the booths in the bar and talking to an attractive young girl whose cobra-hooded hair style indicated that she might be an anchorperson for one of the news programs. The girl had a large silk scarf draped around her shoulders. Hadn't he seen her before? Then it came to him. Of course, he had seen her on TV in Boston, and New York, and Washington, and Charlotte, and Atlanta, and New Orleans, and St. Louis, and Denver, and Salt Lake City, and San Francisco—she or her many twin sisters. They all looked like light, bland, caffeine-free, low calorie, no-cholesterol, Wharton-MBA-packaged clones of one another. Fusetti himself was wearing a necktie in the de rigueur color combination of red, white, and black.

Fusetti recognized Mort and said, "You're a heel for not leveling with me. Why didn't you tell me you're a big-name genealogist and police consultant?

Mort spread his hands, palms up. "What can I say?"

"At least now I don't owe you anything." Fusetti said. "I've got to leave tomorrow with a good story, and I have two possibilities. Either the police will break the case by then, or my story'll be a front-page sizzler on police incompetence. They deserve an 'A' for giving a woman a chance to take charge, but apparently they picked the wrong woman. She's going to get crucified."

"You don't know what the hell you're talking about!"

"Oh? Something else for my story?"

Mort bit his lower lip. "Forget it!" He turned to the bar, willed his muscles to relax, and ordered a Portland Lager. But he couldn't resist turning sideways and glaring a few more times at Fusetti, who by now was again fully engrossed in conversation with his companion.

Taking a healthy swig from his glass, Mort told himself to concentrate on something else. Concentrate on the beer. It had a full malt flavor, somewhat more than Sam Adams, though not so hopsy. Sometimes he preferred the one, sometimes the other. It would be nice to have a beer combining the strength of each, heavy on the malt and heavy on the hops. The God-damned son of a bitch!

He thought of having a second beer, changed his mind and told the bartender that he wanted a bottle of Glenfiddich to take upstairs with him.

Some part of his conversation with Deborah seemed to be pricking at his mind, but he could not be certain which part it was. Something was knocking at the threshold of his brain and wanted to be admitted, but he didn't know how to open the door.

The bartender handed him the bottle of Glenfiddich Scotch. "Last one," he said, "almost full. I can give you a special price."

"Sounds good, put it on my bill," Mort said, leaving two dollars on the counter as a tip. He assumed he would be eating alone, since Priscilla was tied up with Bumpus. But no, she was just entering the hotel. He lifted his head so she could spot him, and she started walking toward him.

What had he been thinking about? Something about Deborah. Something Deborah had said.

Priscilla sat on the bar stool next to him. Bumpus was taking the police boat back, she said, and her work was done for the day, at least she hoped it was. She quickly explained to Mort how she had confirmed that Dudley was the author of the green ink note, then said, "Let's have something to eat. That is, unless you've made other arrangements."

They agreed to meet again in twenty minutes. He went to his room, brushed his teeth and washed his face. Several thoughts were competing for attention in his brain, and he found it difficult to sort them out. He did not look forward to telling Priscilla at dinner that he had completed his assignment. Nonetheless, he would bring the finished charts with him and explain them to her.

Somehow he felt as if he were on the verge of some great discovery. It had something to do with the conversation he had had with Deborah. And it had something to do with the classics. But there was also something else competing for attention in his mind, something more negative, more menacing than the other thoughts. Well, he would sort these things out one at a time. The thing he wanted to concentrate on right now was Priscilla.

Nineteen

THERE WAS A LIGHT SPRAY OF ICY COLD RAIN coming down, and people passing the Samson Pharmacy were trying to hunch themselves into as much of a ball as they could, shoulders sunk to maintain a low center of gravity, hands in pockets, coat collars turned up against their necks. In the course of an hour perhaps seven or eight passed, some with hats, a few with umbrellas. Tina's fixation on the front window yielded her little pleasure, for there was not much activity when the weather was like this. She was, nonetheless, quite happy. Mason Crosby had left for the mainland in midmorning, saying he would return before closing to fill any prescriptions. "Tell them to telephone first to make sure I'm back."

At the time he left, there had been considerable doubt that the doctors would release his wife that day. Tina was not much for praying, but she had closed her eyes, folded her hands together beneath the level of the counter—so no one coming in would notice—and prayed for Mrs. Crosby: "Dear God, please let her be better and come home." Tina had heard that God answered all prayers but sometimes the answer was "no." But on this day the answer was "yes." Mason had telephoned after lunch to say that his wife would be released in the afternoon and they'd catch the ferry just as soon as he could arrange to buy a wheelchair. They had arrived back at the island on the early evening ferry, Mrs. Crosby bundled in blankets that made her look like a cocooned nun.

"I'm so glad you're back, Mrs. Crosby," Tina said. "You look so cold. Can I make you some coffee?"

Mrs. Crosby grunted her responses, which Tina understood to mean she did not want coffee. The ferry ride had been tiring, and she wanted to go right to bed. Mason and Tina helped her up the stairs, Tina observing that the stay in the hospital had not eliminated the odor associated with the diseased kidney, but that just made Tina count her blessings all the more. She had spent the past two nights in Mrs. Crosby's smelly bedroom at the beck and call of that coarse, inconsiderate man, and tonight at least she was free to go to her own home. And probably tomorrow night, and the night after, and . . . Tina prayed again to ask that God keep Mrs. Crosby well and at home for a long, long time. Mr. Crosby had quickly finished preparing the few backlogged prescriptions, dashed over to the hotel to buy a bottle of bourbon, and then gone up to his apartment above the pharmacy, leaving Tina to mind the store and close up at quitting time.

Tina gazed out the window and watched the occasional passersby hurrying back and forth on the street. It would not be long before it was time to close up. As she watched the minute hand of the clock make its slow quantum movements, her face contained a slight smile that masked the greater smile within. She looked, in fact, like a self-satisfied cat patiently staking out a mouse hole.

◆   ◆   ◆

Mort and Priscilla had noted Mason Crosby come into the bar and order his bottle. "Well, the old lady's back and in bed," they heard him tell the bartender. "She's got her medicine, and I've got mine." The bartender slipped the bottle into a paper sack and handed it to Mason, who tucked it under his arm and left.

"So Mrs. Crosby's back," Priscilla said. "That should be interesting for Tina."

Mort wasn't paying much attention. He was deep in thought.

Charts. Deborah. Classical Greece. Glenfiddich. Priscilla. Newspaper reporters. Priscilla. He looked up and saw her smiling at him from across the table.

"You were going to show me your charts," she said.

"Yes, of course." He must seem like a bumbling fool with his hesitant speech and inability to pay attention. He was glad for the opportunity of keeping her busy with the charts. Almost too eagerly he took them out of his briefcase and spread them on the table in front of her.

If he could only concentrate on one thing at a time. Glenfiddich. What was there about the whiskey, the bottle of whiskey? Yes, that was it. The bottle! "Excuse me a moment," he said to Priscilla and walked quickly over to the bar.

"Did anyone else ask for Glenfiddich Scotch today?" he asked one of the bartenders. Ben Mann had told him that none of the island people ever asked for all-malt Scotches, but with the flood of media people coming in, Mort thought it best to eliminate all possibilities.

"Not since I've been here. But ask Charlie—he was by himself all day until they called me in to handle the extra load."

Charlie said the same thing; no one had asked for Glenfiddich. "We hardly ever get a call for that stuff. Too expensive. Some of the summer crowd perhaps. You like it, huh? Can you taste the extra cost?"

"Try it and see what you think the next time you get a shipment in," Mort said. And then, in a moment of extraordinary generosity, inspired no doubt by his success in recalling the significance of the bottle, he handed the bartender a five-dollar bill. So there had only been two bottles the day he checked in the hotel, both unopened, and Mort had bought one for his room. That one was now finished, and Mort had bought the second bottle only an hour or so ago. But that second bottle had no longer been unopened, a small amount being gone from the top. Ergo, someone had opened it, not Mort, and apparently not the bartenders.

"Priscilla," he said, back at the table, "tomorrow morning I want to give you a bottle of Scotch whiskey. Can you have it sent securely to the mainland and tested for poison?"

"Of course," she said, looking up from the charts. "But—oh, no, surely you don't mean someone is trying to poison you, too."

"I mean exactly that. I think somebody wants me out of the way."
He explained why.

"Let's hope there's some less threatening reason for that bottle's
being open. Could Ben have decided to try it?"

"It's a possibility. But we can discuss it after you get it tested."
Perhaps he was getting jumpy. But then everyone on the island was
getting jumpier and jumpier with each succeeding murder. He could
not imagine why anyone would want to poison him—unless they
were dealing with a maniac who was just killing people randomly for
the thrill of it, or unless Mort was doing something to make the murderer consider him a menace. "Anyway," he said to Priscilla, "are
the charts what you expected?"

"I think you've got everything down here, Mort, including a lot
of people I've never heard of before. Now what about the legal
ramifications of inheritance?"

"That is a separate report," he said, taking another thick stack
of papers from his briefcase and handing them to her. He thought he
had covered all the legal permutations of the inheritance picture, like
a computer doing "what-ifs." What if Atherton Gorges died and left
Martha as his heir, and then Martha died? Who under those circumstance would be Martha's heirs? Suppose one or more of those
heirs were dead, how would that change the picture? What if Martha
died first, and Atherton left his estate to this person or that person,
and then suppose this person or that person predeceased Atherton,
and then Atherton died before he had a chance to revise his will?
What if Atherton and Martha died simultaneously? What if Atherton
left everything to Lettice, and then Lettice died intestate? The possibilities seemed endless. He had even covered the possibility of Atherton leaving everything to Belinda as his supposed daughter. But did
it really matter? Would Priscilla be able to make any use of all these
facts and speculations?

"Some of those papers have to do with the possibility of Dudley
being an heir," he said, "so they can be discarded now."

"If your inheritance report is anywhere near as complete as your
charts, it will be of great help."

"That is," said Mort, "if our murderer is a rational person and if inheritance is the motive."

"Can you think of any other motive, Mort? Why else would so many people in the prime of their lives be murdered?"

There it was again! That was what Deborah had said. Classical Greece. Plato. "Plato stated that the prime of life for a man was thirty years," he said.

Priscilla wondered if she was hearing him correctly. "Did you say Plato?"

"The prime of life. Thirty years." He moved his chair to her side of the table and grabbed the charts again. "Look at them. Look at each of the murder victims." Now he was flipping through the charts. "Each victim was under thirty years of age when killed."

"So they were," Priscilla said. "What are you getting at?"

"Think about it," he said. "One victim under thirty would not have significance. Two would be a coincidence. Three, a stronger coincidence. But five—six, counting Ben Mann—that defies any law of averages. All adults under thirty. All in their twenties."

"There does seem to be a pattern there." Priscilla said. "But what does it all add up to?"

"What, indeed? I'll tell you. You were absolutely right, Priscilla, my dear, when you assumed a genealogical motive. But I think you were wrong when you said it was inheritance."

"If not inheritance, then what?"

"Genetics!"

"I don't follow. What does genetics have to do with all this?"

To tell the truth, Mort was not perfectly sure himself. His brain was still adding up the facts. The Glenfiddich. Ben's disappearance. The first attempt to poison Dudley. Del Delano's being clubbed to death instead of poisoned. The answers were trying to break through to him, but he did not have a full grasp on them yet. He clutched at Priscilla's arm. "Can you get Bumpus to send his police boat over tonight to pick up my bottle of Scotch and have it analyzed?"

"Mort, are you sure you know what you're asking? If I could tell the lieutenant that it was a matter of life and death, or that it would solve this case, of course I could. But do you know what he might do to me if it turned out to be a false alarm?"

But Mort was beyond false alarms. The genealogist-hunter, like

a pit bull terrier, had his teeth into something, and he was not going
to let go. "Call him!"

Priscilla went up to her room to make the telephone call while
Mort went to his for the bottle. A few minutes later he knocked on
her door, carrying the bottle under his arm in a plastic shopping sack.

"He's sending the boat," she said. "He said it would be my ankle
if this turns out to be something that could have waited."

Mort laughed. "Did he say 'ankle'?"

"Not exactly." She took his hand. "Now tell me what it means,
Mort. This is no time to play guessing games. What do you mean,
'genetics'?"

"Let us go over these charts again," he said. "If I am right, some
of the victims might have been dead soon anyway. Let me try to give
you a quick and dirty idea, then we can go into more detail later."
They sat at her table, reexamining some of the charts and genealogical data he had prepared. Then he gave her his general conclusions.

"It sounds good," she said, "but how does it help us discover
the murderer?"

"I think I know who it is, but I am still not sure. We will know
much more once this bottle is analyzed."

They heard the put-put of the police inboard-outboard from
Priscilla's window and ran over to the dock to meet it. There were
two men in it, one uniformed and one in plain clothes.

The plainclothesman leapt out of the boat to take the bottle. "The
lieutenant says for you to go to the constable's office and wait for his
call."

"Will he definitely be calling tonight?"

"Yes. One way or another."

Mort and Priscilla headed toward the feed store. The rain had
stopped and the sky was clearing. They could see the Gorges mansion silhouetted above them like a huge sentry watching over the
town. Lights were on in various parts of the mansion, and Mort
wondered what effect, if any, his discoveries of this night might have
on the inhabitants of that house.

♦ ♦ ♦

Within the Gorges mansion, the inhabitants were pursuing their respective activities. The Senator was in his library reading Boethius. Martha Gorges was reclining in a chaise longue in her bedroom, contentedly rummaging through a box nestled in her lap that contained old pieces of a little girl's baby clothing. Lettice was changing clothes, getting ready to go out. Giffard was watching a British comedy on television in his room, feeling a pang of homesickness. Mrs. Beeton was in the kitchen preparing pastries; the kitchen telephone rang, and she murmured a mild curse as she wiped flour from her hands on her apron.

"Belinda, it's for you," she yelled toward the back bedroom. When she was sure Belinda had picked up the extension she put down her own, wondering who was calling. She had not recognized the voice, and in fact would not have been able to say if it were male or female. It sounded muffled, as if the person had a cold and could speak only in a hoarse whisper.

Belinda, who had been translating from a book of poems by Sor Juana Ines de la Cruz, was not happy at the interruption. Her overall mood, though, was sunny, for Mrs. Gorges had told her only this morning that the Senator had agreed to pay for the operation on her foot. Mrs. Beeton would not even have to contribute any of her own hard-earned savings.

Belinda had not yet been told that Martha Gorges was her real mother, and she was full of gratitude toward her supposed mother for never giving up hope. She would be eternally grateful to her, as well as to Martha Gorges and Dr. Delano for all their efforts on her behalf. When she was especially happy, she liked to read poetry and tonight she had picked up works of the poetess known in Mexico as the Tenth Muse. She decided to translate *Hombres Necios;* reading, "*¿Quién es peor, la que peca por la paga, o él que paga por la peca?*" she wrote, "Which is worse, she who sins for pay or he who pays for sin?" It was at this point that the telephone call came.

"You did . . . ? How nice of you . . . Yes, I guess I can." Belinda had instantly recognized the voice, which was no longer muffled.

"Not tell her . . . ? Of course. I understand . . . . All right. Thanks."

     She put on her Footjoys and took her parka from its wall hook. As she reached the back door, she heard her mother calling to her from the kitchen. "Are you going out in this weather, Belinda?" Belinda yelled back, "I won't be gone long." The door slammed shut behind her.

Twenty

"**K**NOW WHAT I THINK?" PRISCILLA asked, when she and Mort reached the feed store, "I think it looks as if my ankle's going to be in a sling after all. Bumpus is already against me for holding you here so long. And don't say it's your fault, it's mine. I deliberately kept you here and even had you accompany me in the investigation when you could have been completing your work. No one will blame me for it if we're successful, but if we're not, they're going to throw the book at me."

They walked into the constable's office and sat down. "The more I think about it," she said, "the more it seems that you've only got a theory. We need evidence, Mort."

"The evidence can be found. It's in the genes. Once we can be sure of the motive, your police technicians can help us catch the killer."

"I took chemistry in college, but not zoology. Explain to me in simple terms how this autosome-cum-sex chromosome works."

"If you were going to take just a single science," he said, "you should have taken zoology. It is the one that helps you relate the most to life."

"Thanks," she said. "If you'd told me that ten years ago it might have been helpful. Coming now, it smacks of a lecture on how superior you are."

"I'm sorry," he said. "I didn't mean it that way."

"Well, go ahead with your lecture on genetics, doctor. It sounds wild."

"At least it will help pass the time until we hear from Bumpus," Mort said. He began his explanation by reminding her that the human body is made up of cells, each cell normally having forty-six chromosomes, arranged in twenty-three pairs. Twenty-three chromosomes are inherited from the father and paired with twenty-three from the mother. Each chromosome consists of the many genes—also paired, with one each coming from each parent—that are responsible for all genetic traits, from the color of eyes and hair to the blood type and the predisposition toward coming down with certain diseases.

"That much I already know," Priscilla said. "I remember a little from high school biology."

"Sorry, I had to begin somewhere. You probably also know then about dominant and recessive genes." The strain was showing on them both, and Mort, knowing the pressure Priscilla was under, resolved to be as understanding as possible.

"I know that for some sets of paired genes, one is dominant and one is recessive," she said. Thus the child may inherit a particular trait from either the father's side or the mother's side."

"All right. First, we are vastly oversimplifying. I am speaking in generalities, and not giving all the exceptions. For a given trait, call the dominant gene big A and the recessive gene small a. If, say the father is Aa and the mother is aa, there will be on the average for every four children two Aa's and two aa's. That is because the father's A has the opportunity of uniting with both of the mother's a's, producing two Aa's. And the father's a might also unite with either of the mother's a's, producing two aa's."

"I'm with you," she said.

"It is important to know that genes have amazing resistance to change. A gene that happens to be passed through many generations will be the same for the last generation as for the first, even though centuries may have gone by. The only exception is mutation. Now, mutations are not as rare as might be expected. On the average one gene in a million might be mutated, and in some genes a mutation might occur in one of out every eighty thousand. When you consider that there are roughly 100,000 genes in every human, and 5 billion humans on earth, you can see that mutations are occurring all the time. Though not common, mutations are not a once-a-millennium event either. When a mutation occurs in one person, that mutated gene can—but not necessarily will—be passed on to the next generation, and to the next, and so on. Many mutations are not passed on since they are harmful to the organism, such as a fetus with severe brain or sensory damage. That can be caused by a mutated gene, but the mutation will not be passed on because ordinarily the fetus will not survive to have children.

"In some cases, though, a mutated gene might have a neutral effect in a person's early years and then become deadly in later years. An example is Huntington's disease, the cause of Woodie Guthrie's death. We can also see in hemophilia and sickle cell anemia, which must have started out once as mutated genes, diseases that allow the possessor to reach adulthood and have offspring. Such mutations do not keep the possessor from passing on the defective gene to at least some of the descendants. Now, what I'm hypothesizing here is that someone in the history of this island had a defective gene and was able to pass it on. Whether it causes a rarely known, but scientifically recognized, disease or is actually the very first manifestation of a new disease will probably take a great deal of scientific analysis. But let's start with somebody in the past on this island having a defective dominant gene that allowed the possessor to grow to adulthood, but then invariably caused the person to die before reaching the age of thirty. Such a bad gene could be passed on to other generations because the afflicted people could have children before the defect killed them."

"But isn't there some kind of self-corrective mechanism?" Priscilla asked. "Wouldn't there be a tendency for the majority of this type of people to die before having children? And wouldn't new genes coming from unafflicted spouses tend to drive out the defective gene in time?"

"Not exactly. Normally you could expect the afflicted descendants of a person having a defective gene to decrease as a percentage

of the total descendants, thus becoming a smaller percentage of the
total population. But on an island you would not expect to find the
normal situation, for island populations almost invariably become
highly inbred, not necessarily bad in itself, but quite serious when a
family has a defective gene. Take the example I just mentioned in
which an Aa father unites with an aa mother to produce two Aa and
two aa children. Suppose the two Aa children of the second generation each marry someone who is aa. This gives us the identical situation we just had—the two afflicted siblings on the average will each
have two Aa and two aa children. But as we go into the third generation, we now have the possibility of cousins marrying. When an Aa
marries an Aa, the average distribution of four children will be one
AA, two Aa's, and one aa. Since the defective gene, A, is also the
dominant gene, now instead of half the children being afflicted with
the disease, we have three out of four."

"And for the first time," Priscilla said, "one child will have a
double dose, so to speak, of the defective gene,—the AA person."

"Exactly. For when an AA person marries an aa person, all the
children will be afflicted. Four out of four, since every child must get
one of the two A's from the afflicted parent. And if there are a lot of
cousins marrying cousins in succeeding generations, we get a high
concentration of the defect in a small population."

"Okay. Now that I understand the mechanics of this hypotheti-
cal disease, tell me how it helps us discover the killer."

"Take a look at these charts again. It's not just Ferdinand, Cobber, Esther, Del Delano, Ben Mann, and Dudley Gorges dying in their
twenties. Look at all the people in the past who died before they were
thirty: Timothy Mann, Richard Mann, Elisha Mann, Charles Mann,
Obadiah Delano, Abijah Samson, Samuel Samson, Thomas Penrose . . ."

"They're all men."

"There is one woman, about what we would expect. What we
have here is called a 'sex-influenced' disease, not sex-linked or sex-
limited, but sex-influenced."

"Mort, I appreciate all you're doing to try to help, but it's not so
obvious to me as it is to you."

"All right," he said. "Now listen carefully. Some diseases are transmitted through a defective gene, but in order to be really dominant they must have something else present from other genes, such as the genes in the male sex chromosome. To make a long story short, some genetic diseases will occur ordinarily only in the male, even though they're not transmitted in the sex chromosomes. The females can also be carriers, usually without being afflicted themselves. So-called male-pattern baldness is one example. It's caused by a gene that can be carried by both men and women but usually affects only men, hence the term "male-pattern." But sometimes a woman gets what we were discussing before, a double dose of the defective gene, the AA. It happens only when both her parents are carriers, and then it's by chance—because if her parents are both Aa, she may be AA, Aa, or aa. In order to be afflicted, the male can be either AA or Aa, but the female would be afflicted in this rare type of genetic disorder only if she is AA. You see the same thing in sheep horns. The male sheep will have horns if either AA or Aa, but the female sheep will have horns only if AA. So essentially we are dealing with a disease which normally affects only the male, but can be transmitted by either the male or female, and on unusual occasions can also afflict the female."

"But how do you know this is true in this case?"

"Because when such a rare case affecting a female occurs, we expect to see it in a daughter of two afflicted cousins who marry and have children, just as we see in this case. Charity Mann must be the exception which proves the rule. Look here—where would you expect to find the original family carrying the defective gene on this island?"

Priscilla let her eyes wander quickly over the various charts. "Well, if we're going by men who died in their twenties, it seems to appear first in the Mann family."

"Good. Now, Charity Mann died at the age of twenty-six. That might be a coincidence. She might have died from any number of other causes. But as a hypothesis, let's say she died of our genetic disorder. What does that tell us?"

Priscilla paused to think—and then, looking proud of herself, said, "That she had to have a double dose. She was AA."

"And what does that mean?"

"Both her parents had to be carriers?"

"Right. And note that her father died at age twenty-eight. But equally important, what do you see that her parents had in common?"

"They were first cousins. Not only first cousins, but they both had a Mann father and a Cooper mother."

"There you have it. Neither Mann father died young, which strongly suggests that the Mann fathers did not carry the disease. The Cooper mothers were probably sisters, although they could have been cousins and it would not change the picture. The significant thing is that they both must have been carriers. The Cooper sisters must have brought the disease to the island—that's the only way we can explain all the facts.

"Their children, Timothy Mann and Sarah Mann, were cousins. Timothy Mann died in his twenties. Of the five children of Timothy and Sarah Mann, only one was a male, and he died in his twenties. Of the four daughters, one, Charity, died in her twenties. She got a double dose. All or most of the other daughters were carriers, not afflicted themselves. Keep in mind that when both parents are Aa, one child out of four on the average will be aa and not carry the disease. Timothy and Sarah Mann had two grandsons and a granddaughter. One grandson died in his twenties, and one enjoyed a long life—evidently Frederick Mann got the aa pair of genes. Even the granddaughter, Lucy Green, must have been a carrier, for her grandson Thomas Penrose died at the age of twenty-five. Does it make sense to you now, Priscilla?"

The gradual dawn not only of comprehension but of the possibility for salvation came over Priscilla's face. "I suddenly hear a hundred violins and a score of brass. *Allegro con brio, maestro! Molte vivace! Maestoso!*" She paused. "I mean, you're beginning to give me hope. You must be right! But let's check. If your theory is valid, then all six of the current victims—including Ben Mann as a victim—must go back to Timothy and Sarah Mann."

"Not necessarily. Must go back to one or the other of the Cooper sisters. Remember, both sisters had to be carriers, and Ann Cooper passed it on to her daughter Sarah Mann. But Ann Cooper also had two other children, Richard Mann and Eliza Mann, and one or both of these could also have received the dominant defective gene. Your idea is right, but you have to include descent from either Cooper sister as qualifying."

"Well, let's see. First, I note a virtual absence of early deaths in the Gorges family, but four of the victims come through the Gorges."

"Right. But notice that no one potentially carrying the defective gene came into the Gorges family until recent generations. But Atherton Gorges's wife, Martha, was a Mann by birth, and she goes right back to both Cooper sisters. The mother of Esther and Dudley Gorges, Myra Samson, goes back to Eliza Mann, a daughter of Ann Cooper. And Cobber Palgrave's grandmother, Dorothy Delano, was a daughter of the Sarah Mann who was a granddaughter of Charity Cooper. That takes care of the four Gorges victims. Delano Delano was the son of Hope Mann, who went back to Timothy and Sarah Mann, and thus descended from both Cooper carriers.

"When it comes to Benjamin Mann, note that his father, grandfather, and great-grandfather were all much older than thirty when they died, and thus they must have carried the aa pair of genes, which means their side of the family would be free of the disease. But Ben's mother was Myra Mann, and Myra went back to Charity Cooper. Myra's father, grandfather, great-grandfather, and great-great-grandfather all died in their twenties, and if that doesn't complete the picture then nothing ever will. But just for good measure, keep in mind that Ben Mann's brother, Percival, also died in his twenties."

"Then you think Ben is dead?"

"I'm not only convinced Ben is dead, I think he was already showing signs of being afflicted by the disease and that's why his body was hidden. An autopsy today might disclose more details about the disease than one would have years ago, details that could have been awkward for the murderer, and so Ben had to disappear. I doubt if his body will ever be found."

"What you say has to be true. But why? Why is someone killing off people who've inherited a disease that is going to kill them at an early age anyway?"

"That's what we've got to find out . . . ." Mort trailed off as he heard a loud knocking on the store's outer door. They both jumped up from their chairs, and Mort unlocked and opened the door. It had started raining again, and in front of them stood Lieutenant Nathaniel Bumpus with his head dripping water.

Bumpus pushed past Mort to get in out of the rain. Priscilla expected to find him angry, but as soon as he spoke she realized that he was more excited than anything else.

"All right," he said, "you're on to something, Sinclair. Your bottle of fancy Scotch contained enough cyanide to kill an entire football team. So how come you turned out to be psychic?"

Mort explained.

"Okay," Bumpus said. "So who do we arrest?"

"We don't know for sure yet," Mort said, "but we know the motive for the murders, or at least part of it."

"Start talking."

Mort turned to Priscilla. "You want to do it?"

"I don't know if I could." Then to Bumpus, "It has to do with genetics, Lieutenant, and it's scientific and quite complicated. But Mort did a good job of breaking it down in simple terms for me, and he can do the same for you."

Bumpus sat in a chair, put his feet on the desk, and waited.

Mort began to explain. He quickly covered the role of genes in determining many human characteristics, their existence in pairs, with one gene of each pair coming from the father and one coming from the mother. He described dominant and recessive genes, mutations, genetic diseases, and how such a disease might be distributed through the descendants of an afflicted individual, with particular emphasis on what could happen when afflicted cousins married. Then he spread out his five most important charts in front of Bumpus, who cooperated to the extent of taking his feet down so he could follow Mort's explanation with the charts. Mort pointed to the two Cooper sisters on the Mann chart and showed how a son of one sister married the daughter of the other, then he demonstrated the extraordinary frequency of male descendants from the marriage dying in their twenties.

"Only one female apparently was afflicted with the disease, Charity Mann, and, as I explained, under rare circumstances females could get the disease if they inherited a double dose of the defective gene. Are you still with me?"

"All the way," said Bumpus. "But knock off that baby talk about a 'double dose,' will you? Next thing you'll be asking permission to go tinkle. You mean Charity Mann inherited homozygous genes, while her siblings were probably heterozygous for these alleles. The mutant gene is autosomal but influenced by the sex chromosome."

"Precisely," Mort said in a weak voice, cursing himself for making the mistake of underestimating a Harvard-educated cop.

"But couldn't it be sex-linked, instead of influenced?" Bumpus said.

"Not with the pattern we have here," Mort said, with just the hint of a smile breaking through. "That would skip generations, you know."

"Oh, er, yeah, you're right," Bumpus said. "Well, so where does that leave us? How many more potential victims are still alive on this island? Where does the murderer strike next?"

"Lettice Gorges?" said Priscilla.

Mort smiled, touched her arm gently, then withdrew his hand as he saw Bumpus observing them with interest. "You're right, Sergeant Booth—Lettice would certainly seem to be a potential carrier. But have you observed something else? In all the murder cases, the victim was either getting married or expecting a child, or in a position to do so. Ferdinand was about to leave the island and get married. Presumably he would have had children. Cobber Palgrave, after a childless marriage with his first wife, had just married Lucy shortly before he died and of course might be expected to have children. Esther, though unmarried, we know was pregnant, and her child died with her. Del Delano was about to remarry his divorced wife Tina, and according to island gossip Tina more than anything else wanted a child. Ben Mann was asking you to marry him. Even if he became convinced that you wouldn't, he most likely would have gone on to marry someone else. Dudley was about to leave the island for Australia, where at the age of twenty-two he might sooner or later have gotten married and had children."

"And that's the motivation!" Priscilla said. "To prevent the genetic disorder from being perpetuated. Lettice has said she will never marry and never have children. So presumably she's safe."

"You two are making sense," Bumpus said, his eyes still darting from chart to chart. "And according to your reasoning Deborah Samson and Martha Gorges, even though they might be carriers, are in no danger because they're beyond the age of childbearing. I think you've got this whole thing just about wrapped up. But in that case, is there any other potential victim? I don't see any on the charts. It looks like the murderer has already made a clean sweep."

"What is it, Mort?" Priscilla said.

Mort had stood up and was looking down at them, his face drained of color. "Oh, my God," he said. "I was fooled by my own charts. I made them according to the official records, but there is one person who is a potential carrier and potentially marriageable—and shown on the charts in the wrong biological family."

"Belinda Beeton!" said Priscilla. "And her real mother is Martha Mann. You mean she's at risk?"

Bumpus jumped up. "Can you get in touch with this girl, Booth?"

"Call up and tell her to stay with her mother until we can get there," Mort said.

Priscilla grabbed the telephone. "Hello, Mrs. Beeton? This is Sergeant Booth. May I speak to Belinda?" She paused to listen to the response. "She what . . . ? But where? When did she leave? Was anyone with her . . . ? No . . . no message."

She put the receiver down and stared in horror at Mort and Bumpus. "Belinda went out more than half an hour ago, right after receiving a mysterious telephone call. Mrs. Beeton has no idea where she went."

Twenty-one

Lieutenant Bumpus slammed his open palm down on the desk. "I'll bring over a massive force and make a house-by-house search for her. I'll scour the island." Then silence.

Priscilla asked, "What's wrong?"

"Damn it, you know what I'm limited to. I don't have a massive force. You think the other commanders, already understaffed, are going to tell their men to do a double shift? All because of a hunch by a contract consultant? In Homicide, what've I got? Fourteen men."

"Eleven men and three women, sir."

"Eleven goddamned men and three goddamned women, and some of them on leave or sick. Some on assignment where they can't be taken off. What can I get tonight? Four or five men, maybe? Maybe four men and one Sergeant Booth."

"What'll we do, sir?"

"Suppose you tell me."

"Well, how about telephoning every person who knows Belinda? Find out who her friends are. See if any of them have any idea of where she might be."

"Not bad, Booth. Not good, either, but it's better than doing nothing."

Mort stared outside the window, nervously watching the rain.

He knew, possibly better than the others, how much Belinda was at risk, but he was not thinking directly about Belinda now. He was turning over in his mind all the many facts that seemed to bear on the problem, some of which stood out more than others. There was one house he wanted to go to—but if he were wrong, the visit would just cost them time, and they did not have time with which to gamble.

Spinning around, he tossed a question to Priscilla. "The attempted poisoning of Dudley in the library—could Nehemiah Gorges have had access to that glass before it was sealed?"

"Nehemiah? No, I don't think so. Let's see. Nehemiah wasn't on duty at the time. He was off that day and went shopping in Bay City. No he couldn't have. Why, Mort?"

"I am thinking of my bottle of Glenfiddich. Who knew that I would be asking for that remaining bottle? Not even the bartenders, for Ben Mann got the first bottle for me. I told Ben of my preference for it, and two others were present at the time. Nehemiah might have had the opportunity of killing all the actual victims, but he could not have put the poison in Dudley's glass at the library. The murderer has to be someone who was in the library at the time. One person, and one person only, was in the library then, and present when I told Ben Mann I preferred to drink Glenfiddich."

"I think I know," said Priscilla. "Let's go."

Bumpus said, "You can explain while we're on our way. I'm not going to hold you up asking questions."

"Fortunately it's not far," Mort said as they hurried through the light rain. "Just a short block, and I only hope we are not too late."

As they approached the house, Mort said, "Good, the car is still there."

Priscilla said, "Yes, but it could still be too late. She could have gone and come back."

"That we'll have to find out," Mort said. "We have lost enough time for anyone to murder Belinda five times over. But let us not give up hope."

The three of them rushed up the front walk to the veranda of the house and rang the doorbell. If no one answered, Mort was ready to suggest that they break in. But they could hear steps.

Apparently the door was not even locked, for it opened

noiselessly. Margaret Mann looked from one face to another and said, "Well, this is quite a delegation. To what do I owe the honor?" She seemed calm enough, but Mort thought he could detect an inner nervousness, a peevishness at the interruption.

Mort deferred to Lieutenant Bumpus, who in turn nudged him, as if to say, you keep carrying the ball, you're still the quarterback.

"Is Belinda Beeton here?" Mort said. There was no politeness in his voice, nor did try to disguise the fact that he was there in an official role.

"Why, yes, she is. She's having a cup of tea. Won't you join us?" She ushered them into the large kitchen, where Belinda and Tina Samson were seated at a round table. Margaret took two light chairs from an adjoining wall and placed them in a circle with the other four at the table. "Please sit down," she said. "We can always make room for one more. Or three."

Mort looked at Priscilla's face and saw that she was relieved beyond measure to find the imagined victim safe, comfortable, and even apparently enjoying herself. Priscilla took a seat next to Belinda and said, "How long have you been here?"

"Oh, at least half an hour," she said. "I should have gone home before this, but Margaret wanted to talk."

"How long have you been here?" Mort asked Tina.

"Belinda and I got here at the same time. She was ringing the doorbell when I arrived."

Mort looked first at Priscilla, then at Bumpus. They, he saw, had not missed the significance of Tina's timing—Margaret could not have done anything while Tina was still there. If, that is, Mort was right and Margaret had plans for Belinda. Of course, if Margaret had been expecting Tina, it might indicate that she had not really intended any harm to Belinda.

Priscilla turned to Tina, "I thought you'd been staying with some friends at night," she said.

"Well . . . er, yes, I sort of had been staying with a 'friend' temporarily."

"But not tonight?"

"Well, no. That is, I thought I'd be staying with my friend, but something came up at the last minute."

"Ah. Then you weren't really expected here tonight? Your coming home must have been a surprise for Margaret."

"I just assume every night that Tina may or may not come home." Margaret's voice came from behind them. She was at the counter pouring hot water into the tea pot, and she stopped to face them. "After all, she's a grown woman and doesn't have to answer to me."

"I'm not accusing Tina of anything," Priscilla said. She touched Mort's shoulder, then his tea cup, and shook her head. Mort nodded almost imperceptibly. Priscilla then addressed Tina and Belinda, "Did we interrupt something?"

"Oh, no," Tina said. "If you hadn't come when you did, I'd be in bed now. I was just about to go to my room."

Belinda said, "I'd only planned to be a few minutes, but Margaret insisted I stay until Tina went to bed, then she's going to drive me home." She smiled shyly. "It's only a block, and the weather's not that bad. I can walk more than a block with this foot—and anyway, I'm going to have an operation!"

Priscilla told her how glad she was for her sake, then asked, "What brought you out on a night like this anyway?"

Belinda laughed again. "Oh, Margaret called to tell me she had gotten a book for me." She held up a used book entitled *The Beeton Family of England and America*. "I'm going to give it to my mother for her birthday. Margaret saw it when she was in Bay City and offered to buy it for me."

"That was certainly considerate of you, Margaret," Priscilla said.

"Well, Alice Beeton has a tremendous interest in her late husband's family." Mort noted that her words were being uttered through almost closed teeth. By now Margaret had readied the teapot and brought it snug in its cozy to the table to let it steep.

Tina yawned and said, "Look, I've got to go to bed now."

"Just a few more minutes, Tina," Mort said. "There is something we need to clear up."

Tina looked apprehensive; Bumpus looked nervous. "Well, now," Bumpus said, "I think at this point we'd better . . . ."

"Now wait a minute," Margaret said. "What's going on here? You come barging in my house in the middle of the night, and now you're going to return our hospitality with cross-examinations? What are you after? Let's stop the cat-and-mouse game. Out with it!"

Bumpus turned to face her. "Now you look, Mrs. Mann. I'm representing the police in an official investigation into six murders on this island, and we're going to ask some questions. You can either answer them here or come over to Bay City with us. Dr. Sinclair is a part of the official team, and I would advise you to answer his questions."

Margaret said, "Six murders! Who's the sixth?"

Bumpus said, "Ben Mann."

"Is one of us under suspicion?" Tina wanted to know.

Mort turned to Tina. "When you made a statement to the police following the murder of Del Delano, you left out a lot. Nowhere did you mention that you and he planned to get married again. Why?"

Tina's hands were shaking, and she clasped them together tightly in an attempt to stop. She looked at Mort, then at Margaret, then back at Mort again. "I was only doing what Margaret told me to do. She said I shouldn't mention the coming marriage because it might point suspicion at me."

"That's a lie!" Margaret roared. "I never told you anything of the kind!"

"Margaret," Mort said, "a bottle of Scotch whiskey I was going to drink was poisoned at the hotel. It is an unusual brand. Only you, Nehemiah Gorges, and Ben Mann knew my preference in brands, and Ben is dead now."

"How do you know Ben's dead?"

"Never mind that, let's get back to the whiskey. We know that Nehemiah could not have done it. Only you, Margaret, could have put cyanide in my whiskey. I don't have the genetic disorder, Margaret—so why were you trying to eliminate me?"

His words were spoken very softly, but the effect they had on Margaret Mann was dramatic. The phrase "genetic disorder," in particular, seemed to hit her like a wet fish slapped across the face. Her eyes opened wide; her neck muscles flexed to contort the lines around her mouth. "I don't know what you're talking about!"

"Do you want us to believe that you know nothing about genetics? What did you major in at college? Where did you work before you came back to the island and married Percival Mann? Wasn't it a genetics laboratory in the Boston suburbs?" He knew from old newspapers that she had taken a job with some high-tech industry, and now he was guessing that it was a genetics laboratory.

Margaret stood and glared at him, her face stamped with rage and fear.

"You wanted to stop the cat-and-mouse game, Margaret. Can we stop it now? No? Then let's go further. Dudley Gorges borrowed money the night before he left for Bay City. The next night he came back loaded with money from his uncle. He called his cousin, Lettice, and paid her back three hundred dollars. And he told her he was expecting someone else at the hotel to whom he owed three hundred fifty dollars. Margaret, he called you from his hotel, told you he was going to Australia, and asked you to come over so he could pay you the three hundred fifty dollars he owed you. You didn't make many mistakes, Margaret, but a few were inevitable. It was a mistake to use the keys you had taken from Ben Mann and come up the back stairs without anyone seeing you and then to lock Dudley's door after. Had you come up openly like Lettice, it would have been more difficult to prove that you had come to murder Dudley. But coming surreptitiously, as you did, you cannot explain your way out of it."

"Difficult to prove?" Margaret said. "Impossible to prove! You have absolutely nothing to show that I lent Dudley money, that I visited him, that he paid me back, or that I murdered him. You're guessing, that's all you're doing."

"All right, I am just guessing. I am guessing that when we go to your bank tomorrow morning, the records will show a withdrawal of three hundred fifty dollars in cash, on the day Dudley was trying to borrow as much money as he could."

Mort almost felt sorry for Margaret, for he was giving her blow after blow. The last one hit her hard again, like a medicine ball caught in the stomach; she groped for the back of her chair, and Mort stood up to help her back into it. Then he too sat again.

"You knew this was coming," he said. "Surely you had prepared yourself for it. You just can't commit six willful murders and get away without leaving any clues."

Margaret's face softened as tears came to her eyes. Mort decided he was probably right that she had always known some moment like this was coming, but it was something no one could prepare for completely.

"It was the loss of Percival, wasn't it?" Mort said. "You saw him in horrible misery with his life draining away, and with him dead you felt yourself ruined. You knew he was afflicted with something rare, but you didn't know what it was, and so at that time you didn't do anything. It was only after you started working at the library and learned something about genealogy that you realized what must have happened. And even that was possible only because you majored in zoology and worked for a few years in a genetics laboratory. You were the only person on the island capable of adding genetics and genealogy together and coming up with the right answer. And you were also the most embittered person on the island because of what genetics and genealogy had taken away from you."

Margaret took a small handkerchief from her sweater pocket and gently blew her nose in it. Her sobs were spaced further apart, and she looked very tired and weak.

At this point, Bumpus stood up and said, "Mrs. Mann, before we go any further, I'm going to read you your rights." He intoned the words from his Miranda card.

Mort knew Bumpus was now concerned in the opposite direction, wondering if he had let the interrogation proceed too far before advising Margaret of her rights. But Margaret had not broken yet. She could stop talking right now and she would have made no confession. Although the others could testify to her guilty reactions, a good defense attorney could make it all look like the normal behavior of an innocent woman being bullied with outrageous accusations.

"I understand, Lieutenant," Margaret said. "It's over now. I've done what I had to do, and . . ." She turned to look at Belinda, "perhaps this girl doesn't carry the poison seed, anyway. If so, then I've wiped it out, singlehandedly. I'll probably go to prison, perhaps execution, and the world will little realize what I've done to save it." Then, more quietly, "I'm sorry, Belinda, I didn't want to hurt you. It would have been over quickly."

Belinda, understandably bewildered, looked from one face to another.

"Could we clear up some of the details?" Priscilla said, as she took her note pad out of her purse. "What happened at Ferdinand's reception?"

Margaret laughed. "It was so easy. I watched to see what he was drinking and had the same thing, put poison in mine, and then waited until he put his glass on a table. He always was such a gesturer. When he was a boy we used to say he couldn't talk if you tied his hands behind him. So I knew he'd put his glass down sooner or later. I put my glass beside his, then picked up his glass and walked away. Bingo!"

"Bingo?" asked Priscilla.

"I won the game," Margaret said patiently. "Cobber was pathetically easy. I brought him a bottle of gin when I knew he would be alone. We had a drink together, and when he went to the bathroom, I put cyanide in the remainder of his drink. I stayed around until he drank it, because I wanted to see firsthand how it worked—I was on the other side of the room when poor Ferdie got his, and I missed seeing his reaction. Don't think I'm ghoulish or anything. I was just interested in the technical part, filing it away for future reference in case of need. Cobber came out of the bathroom and the first thing he did was reach for his drink. It was over in a matter of seconds. Bingo!"

"Bingo!" Priscilla echoed, still scribbling on her pad. Mort and Bumpus threw her dirty looks.

"And Esther?" Mort said. "That one took some doing."

"Wasn't it clever, though? Can you imagine, Esther had been all over the world, and had gone after every thrill imaginable, but she'd never tasted absinthe. She and I used to be good friends when she was a girl, coming into the library all the time. Later I ingratiated myself with her by acting as her messenger when it was inconvenient for her to go to Bay City and buy drugs. I never touched them myself, but I would buy them for Estie. I got to know quite a few of the drug dealers, and they treated me just like one of the boys, or girls, whatever. Well, I told Estie all about absinthe and Hemingway and the Lost Generation, and got her so excited about trying some that she was ready to fly to Europe just to get it. Of course, that wouldn't do, but I had a bottle at home from my last trip to Denmark—I bought it with something like this in mind, you know. I always like to think ahead. Well, I didn't want to be seen around the Gorges mansion when Estie took the stuff, so I had her come to my house. We each sampled the absinthe, and then I took it out to the kitchen—right here—to put cyanide in, wipe my prints off, and put the bottle in a bag. I knew she would never mention it to anyone. She took it home, and bingo!"

Priscilla looked at Bumpus and then Mort, but she did not say "bingo."

Mort said, "You did not plan to kill Del Delano, did you?"

"Not at the time. But I had him on my short list. The actual way I killed him was sheer opportunism. Tina came home and told me about the fight with Dr. Delano. I waited until she went to sleep, then hurried over to Del's place. He was sitting at his table, and I pretended to sympathize with him—even got him a drink at the bar. I could have put cyanide in it, but it occurred to me that it would be better to make it to look as if Dr. Delano had killed Del in anger. Del wasn't paying any attention to what I was doing, so I just picked up the stool and bashed him one. That's all it took. Bingo! I was pleased at the thought that I could improvise so readily, and at the idea of how confused the stupid police would be by a non-poison murder—sorry, no offence, Priscilla. Anyway, I turned out all the lights, went home, and came back in the morning to 'discover' the body. I thought that was a nice touch."

Mort asked, "Was the attempted poisoning of Dudley a matter of opportunity also?"

"Sort of. Actually, I sort of goofed there, but no one knew it. I had planned to poison both glasses, Ben Mann's and Dudley's, so I could get two for one. But I had to be careful since I was putting the cyanide in the glass virtually in plain sight of everyone in the library. I was putting away books in the free-standing stack closest to the trustees' table when the trustees got up to see some books. So I slipped over to the table and put some cyanide in one of the glasses. I intended to get the other one, too, but Sylvia Mann started coming around the alcove, so I just went over to the bookshelves behind the table and pretended to be reshelving more books. Then when Sylvia went out the door, probably to go to the toilet, I went back to the table and I thought I was putting the cyanide in the second glass, but I guess I got confused and put more in the glass that was already poisoned. The laboratory analysis probably showed a strong dose."

Lieutenant Bumpus nodded in agreement.

Priscilla stopped her note-taking long enough to say, "I don't see how you could possibly put poison not just once, but twice, in a glass with people all over the place. It wasn't like Ferdinand's reception, where you could just poison your own drink and then switch it with Ferdie's."

"It was easy. You see I was invisible."

"Invisible!" Priscilla said, giving Margaret a most peculiar look.

"Of course," Margaret said with a sneer. "Who is more invisible than a middle-aged widow? Your husband dies, and all of a sudden you're not invited out any more. People see right through you as you walk down the street. You're a fixture in the library, they notice you about as much as they notice a wall decoration or a chair—unless they happen to have some immediate need for you."

Her voice choked, and she wiped a tear from her eye. "Actually Ben and Dudley were both on my list, but Ben was by far the most important. You see, I could tell that Ben was already coming down with the disease. If he died from it, there might have been an autopsy, and I was afraid of what an autopsy might discover."

Priscilla and Mort exchanged looks.

"Ben was going the same way Percival went, so I knew more or less how he would be. I called him late at night and gave him the opportunity of telling me how bad he felt. I offered to come over and drive him to Dr. Delano's clinic. Ben stumbled out of the hotel when I drove up, and I helped him into the seat. When he started getting suspicious, because the drive was taking too long, I stopped and gave him some cyanide to put him out of his misery. I was really doing him a favor—he wouldn't have lasted a month, and he would have been in so much pain. I always liked Ben."

"How did you dispose of the body?" Bumpus asked.

"I drove to the high point above Meerstead Cove. I had to be careful because it's a favorite parking place for teenage couples, but I was in luck, no one else was there. That was the best place—the road goes right up to the edge, the point juts out over the cove, and the water is deep there and meets the open sea. I pulled Ben out of the car, got the keys from his pocket, tied some metal weights to him all over, in case some of them slipped off, and rolled him over the point. Bingo! And the body still hasn't been found."

"We know about Dudley," Mort said.

"Of course, Dr. Sinclair. You had it all figured out. You're just too clever for words. I laid the groundwork long ago, lending him a little money every now and then. One thing about Dudley, he always paid his debts. It was the only honor he knew. He was not a high priority on my list, for he probably wouldn't have gotten married for a long time. As long as he stayed on the island or in Bay City I could feel comfortable. Even in Bay City, I knew he would keep in touch with me, and lending him the money before he left was one way to guarantee it. But Australia! The Senator didn't know it, but he sealed Dudley's death warrant. Not that Atherton would have minded, I'm sure. If I'd been a greedy woman, I could probably have worked a deal to have Atherton pay me for disposing of Dudley for him. But I didn't do this for dirty motives, you understand? I've wiped out a horrible disease." she said. "That is, if Belinda doesn't perpetuate it." She stopped abruptly, as if some new and horrible thought had just come over her, and turned to Belinda. "Promise me, Belinda, that you'll never marry. You'll never have children. You don't want to have sons and grandsons and see them die a horrible death before they reach thirty. Promise me, Belinda!"

"What is this?" said Belinda, who finally seemed to be catching on. "You were planning to kill me? Just like you say you murdered all the others?" Her face looked as if she were in physical pain, and she was shaking violently.

Priscilla put her arm around her shoulder. "You're safe now, and I'll explain it all later."

Bumpus reached over for the note pad, and continued the note-taking as Priscilla tried to calm Belinda.

"So you went to Dudley's room," Mort continued.

"Oh, yes, you're right. That was a mistake, too, using the keys to come in the hotel back door and then locking Dudley's door after. He paid me the money, and I dropped a little cyanide in his glass. Again it was easy. He was too concerned about counting out the precise amount. I stood between him and his glass, with my back to him—invisible again, for all practical purposes. I waited until he took his next drink, and bingo! I may have cheated him out of five or seven years, but his life wasn't worth much. You don't save a person's life just because he has the one good quality of always repaying his debts."

"But surely," Mort said, "you couldn't have known whether any of the people you killed, other than Ben, were actually carrying the defective gene. Some of them must have been free of it."

"I couldn't take any chances. Do you think I like to go around killing people? Too much was at stake; I had to play the game to win. Can't you see that?" And then she said, "But I do feel sorry for poor Ferdinand. You see, it was only recently that I learned that Martha was Belinda's mother, but not Ferdinand's. Ferdinand didn't really have to die."

Belinda reacted as if she had been hit. "Martha my mother? What on earth are you talking about?"

Priscilla said, "We have a lot of explaining to do, Belinda, but, please believe me, this is not the time for it. Try to be patient, and we'll explain the whole story as soon as we can."

Bumpus stood up. "I've got a man with a boat at the dock. I'm arresting you, Mrs. Mann, and taking you to the Bay City jail tonight. Priscilla, I'll want you to come with us."

Priscilla jumped at hearing the lieutenant call her by her first name. "Whatever you say, Natty." Then, turning to Mort, she asked if he would take Belinda home and explain everything on the way.

They all walked together to the bottom of the driveway at the Gorges estate, Mort and Belinda turning up to the mansion, Bumpus and Priscilla and their prisoner continuing toward the dock.

Twenty-two

AFTER A LEISURELY BREAKFAST THE NEXT MORNING, Mort checked out of the Mann Hotel, walked across the street, and left his suitcase at the ferry building. The sun was shining brightly, and it was one of those beautiful winter days on the New England coast when the air is delightfully crisp and dry and no one can tell how cold it is without looking at a thermometer. Mort felt the sense of relief that always came with the completion of an important piece of work, and as he strolled up Sea Drive on the water side, he whistled to himself Elgar's *Pomp and Circumstance*. In the distance he could see the ferry coming in, but he knew he would not be on it for the return trip. He could catch a later ferry. It was important to pay a final visit to FIGS and Deborah Samson.

No one else was in the library. Deborah sat behind the librarian's desk in solitary majesty, looking a bit like Queen Victoria after the death of Albert. "Well," she said, "I suppose I will have to go through all the trouble of interviewing for a new assistant again, and where will I ever find a half-decent one? And after I go through all that bother, then the real ordeal begins—do you have any idea of how much time and effort it takes to train a new assistant, Dr. Sinclair?"

Mort had to confess that he did not. "I just came to say good-bye, Deborah. I will stop at the police office in Bay City, and then

Priscilla is driving me to Boston to catch my plane to Salt Lake City. But I am grateful to you for giving me the clue that solved the case." He explained the significance of her remark about the prime of life, then said, "Had you observed the pattern of so many men dying so young?"

"Oh, yes," Deborah said matter-of-factly. "But I didn't know what to make of it. You see, I've never studied genetics." She gave him an apologetic smile. "I'm sorry to see you go, Dr. Sinclair. Tell me, is the genealogical library in Salt Lake City as good as they say?"

"Better. There is a new book out called *The Library,* I'll send you a copy of it. It's devoted to just the one library—now called the Family History Library—and it will tell you everything you could want to know about it."

"I'd love to visit it sometime," Deborah said wistfully. "I've never been off the island, you know, and probably never will be." Her fingers played idly with a pencil. "Certainly I won't have a chance to do anything if I have to spend all my time looking for and training new assistants. I suppose you didn't give any thought to that when you were making your brilliant deductions and solving the case."

"If I had, I could hardly have let it influence the outcome," Mort said with a wry smile.

"I suppose not. But no one ever thinks of me."

"You are too hard on yourself, Deborah. Everyone around here appreciates you. You are recognized as the most knowledgeable person on Fogge Island. In fact," he said, hoping this was the right moment to bring it up, "that is why I came to see you during my last hour or so on the island."

"Is it?" she said. "Well, I do feel that it is my duty as the executive secretary of the only permanent eleemosynary institution on the island to be of service to people. You know, people use us as a regular public library in addition to a genealogical library, as an information service, as a social center, and even as a news exchange."

"You certainly have a handle on the news," he said. "To be frank, Deborah, there is just one loose end I would like to tie up before I go home."

"What is it?"

Mort lowered his voice. "Esther was pregnant when she was

killed. Would you have any idea of the father?"

"Ha!" she said. "So there is actually something I know about this island that you don't know!"

"I am entirely at your mercy."

"All right, I'll tell you. It was Senator Atherton Gorges, of course—just like Dudley was trying to tell everyone. And if you're wondering how I know, Esther told me herself. We were good friends before Martha swung her away from genealogy, and we still enjoyed an occasional cup of tea and a little talk." She bent over her desk, as close to Mort as she could get. "Atherton would go to any length to have an heir. And I'll tell you something else. It's a good thing for Martha that he believes Belinda is his child."

Somehow Mort was not surprised that she even knew about that.

"He is paying for Belinda's operation," Deborah said, "and with her looks, intelligence—and now, money—she will have no trouble making a good marriage. I imagine Atherton will settle several million on any man who marries her, provided he changes his surname to Gorges so that both the line and the name can be perpetuated. But if Atherton ever suspected what you and I know to be true, Dr. Sinclair, he would divorce Martha in a minute and go out and marry the first twenty-three-old girl to come along, just to get a true biological heir to carry on his line."

"Of course," Mort said, "Belinda may be carrying the gene, but I do not think that is as serious a matter as Margaret wanted to believe. First, there is better than a fifty-fifty chance that Belinda does not have it, since we do not even know if her mother, Martha, is a carrier or not. Even if Belinda should turn out to be a carrier herself, any children she bears most likely will not get married or be in danger of coming down with the disease until they are in their twenties. When you consider the discoveries made in genetics during the past twenty years, you can see that the Fogge Island Syndrome—as the newspapers will undoubtedly be calling it—may well be curable before it takes any toll of Belinda's offspring."

"You'd think that might have occurred to Margaret."

"Haven't you found, Deborah, most people look for altruistic motives to camouflage selfish acts? Margaret was certainly motivated every bit as much by hatred and bitterness as she was by wanting to save humanity. The island had taken away her husband, her position, her comfort, and she was determined to get revenge. She was just looking for an excuse, and her combined knowledge of genetics and genealogy provided her with one."

"You know I never suspected Margaret," Deborah said with sadness in her voice. "My mother taught me everything she knew, but she had never studied genetics."

Mort, tacitly accepting her excuse for not having solved the murders, changed the subject. "Have you considered Belinda as a possibility for your new assistant? She's intelligent, and she shares your love for books. And working at FIGS would give her a good opportunity of meeting people with mutual interests."

"The thought has crossed my mind," she said. Her smile was an immensely self-satisfied one, as if to say: There's nothing you can think of that I can't think of first, provided you don't take unfair advantage and bring in things like genetics. "It probably would be a good thing for her, but no one ever thinks of me. I could spend all my time training her, only to have her get married just when she was ready to carry her weight. Then I'd have the trouble of going through all those interviews and training all over again."

"Just a suggestion," Mort said.

Again there was a pause. "Well, it is true that there are not many qualified people on the island, and certainly no one is going to commute on the ferry from the mainland every day for a job that pays as little as this does." Another pause. "Well, as a point of fact, I've asked Belinda to come in this afternoon for a cup of tea and a little talk."

Mort got up from his chair. "It's been a pleasure, Deborah, and if we ever meet again, I promise I will never, ever underestimate you."

"I'm sure you won't, Dr. Sinclair." She gave him an emphatic nod, smiled, and rose slowly to show her agreement that the audience was over.

"One more thing, Deborah. Margaret said you told her that Sylvester Mann was on Atherton Gorges's payroll at the time he sold Gorges her husband's most profitable division for much less than its value. How did you find out about that?"

"Oh, that Margaret—she never could get anything straight! I told her that I would not put it past Sylvester and Atherton to do a thing like that. But it was just speculation, nothing more. I suspect Margaret told you a number of things to make herself seem a less likely suspect, and you believed her. Which, frankly, astonishes me, Dr. Sinclair. Any person who murders six people might also tell lies."

"But we didn't know Margaret was the murderer then."

"Well, now, that was your problem, wasn't it? Don't expect me to solve everything for you." Again she smiled, this time sweetly. Mort thought he would be unlikely ever to forget that sweet smile.

◆　　　　　◆　　　　　◆

The trip across the sound on the ferry was uneventful. The sea, a deep purplish green, was as smooth as oil, and Mort spent part of the voyage on the rear deck looking back as Fogge Island gently receded and blurred.

As requested, he stopped by the police department to see Lieutenant Bumpus. This time there was no waiting—the receptionist told him to go right in. Priscilla was already there, her cup of coffee resting on Bumpus's desk. Bumpus was in uniform, his large but neat frame impressive in a Sam Browne-belted navy blue tunic and starched-collar white shirt, single gold lozenges on his shoulder straps denoting his rank.

"Well, Sinclair," Bumpus said, "it just goes to show that all kinds of consultants have their uses. You made Booth look good, Booth made me look good. That's what I like—all winners." Then, to Priscilla, "I have to hand it to you, Booth. You didn't besmirch this one." Mort, noting that the lieutenant was back on a last-name basis with Priscilla, wondered if she was still calling him "Natty."

"How about Margaret?" Priscilla said. "I wonder what will happen to her."

"She'll get her fair trial," said Bumpus. "Her attorney will probably use an insanity plea—they almost always do in mass killings. It's easy to plead that no sane person would do anything like that."

"Do you think she's insane?"

"Hell, no. No more insane than children are when they get angry and yell spiteful things. Only Margaret wasn't a child, and she used her spite in a far deadlier way. Now, that doesn't mean that she might not get off on an insanity plea. You know how the courts are these days . . . . What bothers me," Bumpus said with honest puzzlement in his voice as he turned to Mort, "is Esther's pregnancy. That has never been explained."

Mort raised an assuring hand and said, "Oh, the father was Senator Atherton Gorges, just as Dudley kept trying to tell everyone."

"How do you know?"

"Oh, I have my sources," Mort said smugly, and then suddenly frowned as he caught himself and realized what person he was sounding like. Changing his tone, he said, "Well, it seems she told Deborah Samson, and Deborah told me."

"And to think that Atherton Gorges's maid turned out to be his real daughter," Bumpus said.

Mort and Priscilla looked at each other, smiled, and started to speak simultaneously.

"He lost a son and gained a daughter," said Mort.

"Stranger than fiction," said Priscilla.

Bumpus said, "Now I understand that Sergeant Booth is taking the rest of the day off and driving you to Boston. Well, I guess we can call it comp-time—we certainly don't have money to pay for all that overtime you put in, Booth." He stood up and shook Mort's hand. "If we ever need a genealogist again, we'll call you."

◆   ◆   ◆

"I think he likes you," Priscilla said to Mort, as they walked down the outside steps.

"I think he's a pompous ass."

"You're right, he is," she said, as she buttoned her blue tweed topcoat and led him to her powder blue Ford Thunderbird.

They did not talk much during the drive to Boston. Priscilla turned on her forty-watt stereo system, and told Mort he could find a sack of tapes in back. He reached for the sack as if it held gold, and his eyes glistened as he sorted over the contents. "What are you in the mood for?" he asked.

"Something joyful. Not sad. Not ponderous. Not even stately. Something bright and cheerful. I might play Beethoven and Brahms going back. I might want something stately and profound then. But right now I think I'd like Mendelssohn or Schumann."

They agreed on a pair of fourth symphonies, Mendelssohn's to start, with Schumann's following. Most of the time they listened without speaking, except between tapes.

Once during the music Priscilla asked, "What will you do when you get home?"

"First a little writing. I have some articles I owe. Then to Oxford, England, where I've been asked to give a series of lectures."

"That sounds wonderful."

Between tapes they discussed the Genealogical Jubilee Conference which would be held in Salt Lake City in May.

"You'll be speaking, of course?" Priscilla asked.

"I've been invited to. But I also have the opportunity of going on an important archeological dig during the spring. Think you'll be attending the Jubilee?"

"I received the brochure in the mail, but I wasn't sure, because with the little leave I get I have to pick conferences carefully. But," she took her eyes off her driving and smiled at him, "I think I'll make a decision right now. I can time my vacation just so I can go to that one. I've never been to Salt Lake City—it will be nice."

"Watch the road!" he yelled, as a truck swerved to miss them.

The approach to Logan Airport was crowded as usual, and, once they arrived, it was impossible to find parking. Priscilla let Mort off at the curb in front of his terminal, and they said goodbye.

"Promise you'll write," she said.

"Of course. Promise you will come to Salt Lake City."

"But you might go on your dig."

"Well, maybe I will forget about the dig."

"And you'll be in Salt Lake for the Jubilee?"

"Oh, probably," he said in a casual tone.

"You be there, or else!"

"Or else what, Sergeant Booth?"

"Or else, Dr. Sinclair . . . ," she said laughing as she reluctantly released her foot from the brake, and the car slowly coasted forward, "or else, bingo!"

CROSBY CHART

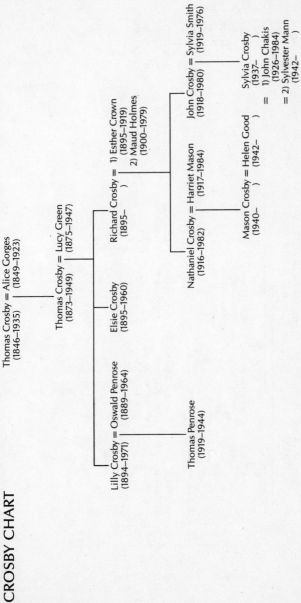

Thomas Crosby = Alice Gorges
(1846–1935)   (1849–1923)

Thomas Crosby = Lucy Green
(1873–1949)   (1875–1947)

Lilly Crosby = Oswald Penrose
(1894–1971)   (1889–1964)

Elsie Crosby
(1895–1960)

Richard Crosby = 1) Esther Crown
(1895–   )   (1895–1919)
                 2) Maud Holmes
                    (1900–1979)

Thomas Penrose
(1919–1944)

Nathaniel Crosby = Harriet Mason
(1916–1982)   (1917–1984)

John Crosby = Sylvia Smith
(1918–1980)   (1919–1976)

Mason Crosby = Helen Good
(1940–   )   (1942–   )

Sylvia Crosby
(1937–   )
    = 1) John Chakis
          (1926–1984)
    = 2) Sylvester Mann
          (1942–   )

DELANO CHART

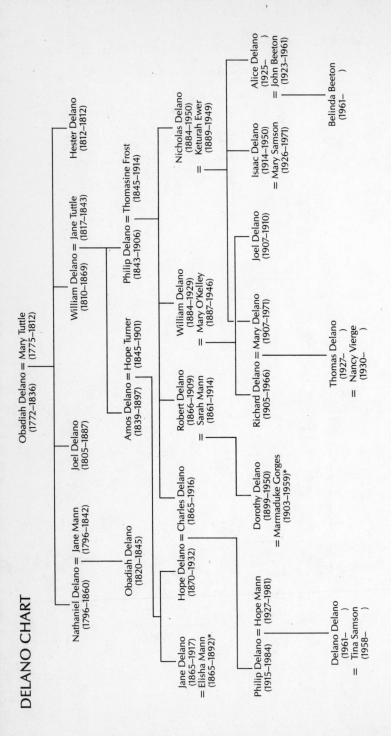

*Indicates that the children will be found under the spouse's entry.

GORGES CHART

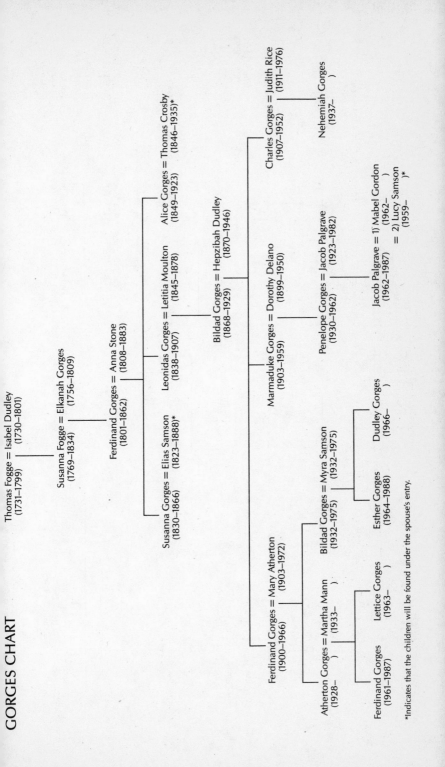

*Indicates that the children will be found under the spouse's entry.

MANN CHART

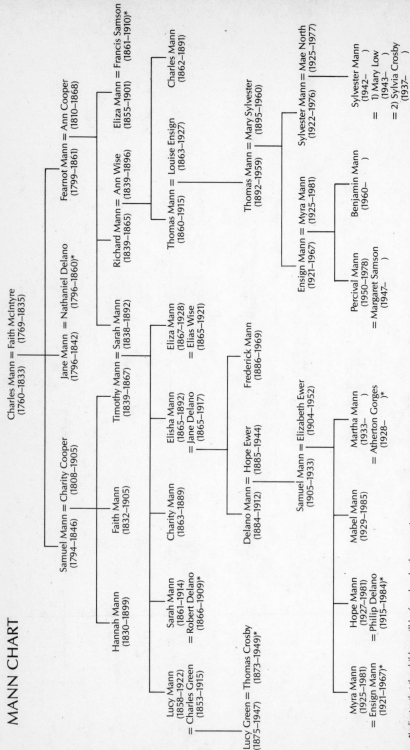

*Indicates that the children will be found under the spouse's entry.

SAMSON CHART

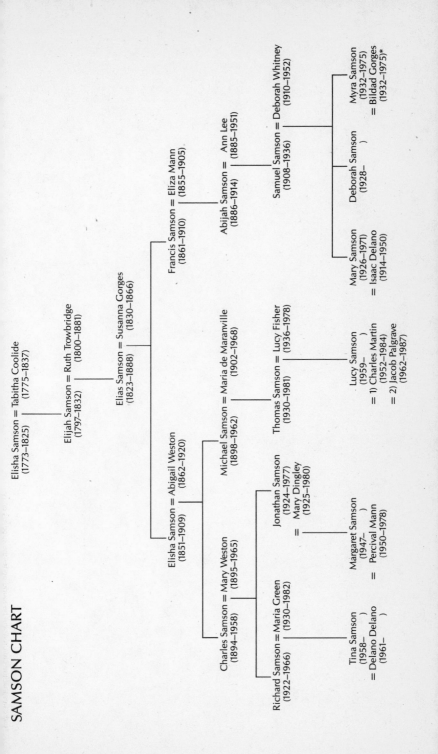